Marooned!

"The Sargasso Sea is two thousand miles long and a thousand miles wide," said Tabor. "Most of it is just sea. But here near the center of it is our little island of derelicts. The current moves in a circle, you see, and carries everything that has no power of its own to the center."

"But—how do you get back to land?" said Peter.

"There's no way back," said Tabor.

"But surely there will be rescue parties?"

"No one knows we're here," said Tabor.

He stared at Tabor and then at the island of boats, trying to digest what he had heard. "You can't mean that we're trapped here for the rest of our lives," he said finally.

We will send you a free catalog on request. Any titles not in your local book store can be purchased by mail. Send the price of the book plus 50¢ shipping charge to Leisure Books, Two Park Avenue, New York, New York 10016. Attention: Premium Sales Department.

Titles currently in print are available for industrial and sales promotion at reduced rates. Address inquiries to Nordon Publications, Inc., Two Park Avenue, New York, New York 10016, Attention: Premium Sales Department.

THE DRIFT

Lloyd Kropp

LEISURE BOOKS • NEW YORK CITY

A LEISURE BOOK

Published by

Nordon Publications, Inc.
Two Park Avenue
New York, N.Y. 10016

Copyright © MCMLXIX by Lloyd Kropp

All rights reserved
Printed in the United States

Published by special arrangement with Doubleday and Company, Inc.

CONTENTS

1	Drifting North	7
2	Tabor	21
3	Pao	43
4	The Outlanders	54
5	The Seafields and The Mary Strattford	65
6	The Caravel	79
7	Images	93
8	Shadowgames	101
9	Rose	111
10	The Scarfaced Man	119
11	Driftsend	129
12	The Dance of The Nine Islands	141
13	A Marriage and a History Lesson	157
14	The Shark	171
15	Nightsongs	181
16	Raven	189
17	Echoes and Loomings	201
18	The Hatchmaker	221
19	White Flowers in a Bowl	235
20	The Dream	241

Chapter One

DRIFTING NORTH

There is a great sea within a sea, two thousand miles long and a thousand miles at midpoint, that lies near the center of The Atlantic Ocean. Until the nineteen twenties it was still considered by some to be a hazard to boats because of the weeds and vast quantities of debris that gathered there, a consequent of the calm water trapped within a circle of giant trade winds and currents. Old sailors sometimes say that if one drops a cork anywhere in The Pacific or Atlantic Ocean, it will eventually find its way to the center of The Sargasso Sea.

A type of fish lives there that lives nowhere else in the world. Through hundreds, perhaps thousands of years of evolution, it has learned to crawl across the mats of weeds and bits of flotsam that circle endlessly in the slow-moving water. Its shape is curious. It is festooned with long spines or quills and wormlike fingers that obliterate its outline and make it difficult to see as it half crawls, half swims across the swampy patches of vegetation where other fish cannot see it or reach it. It lives on smaller fish and on other life forms that make their home among the gulfweeds on The Sargasso Sea. It has no natural enemies except when it ventures away from its swampy home and swims in the open water.

Some people who have seen them think that Sargasso Fish are very beautiful. Their coloration is brilliant and varied. Their shape is exotic and unearthly. One might say that their beauty springs from the fact that they have given up the natural habitat of fishes and have become denizens of a strange world where they themselves have become strangely beautiful.

After six days of sailing, Peter Sutherland began to drift north toward The Sargasso Sea. He could never have known then what lay ahead, nor could he have understood that the events before him were an extension of his own drifting, an extension of something that was already happening inside him. In his own understanding of things it all began when the old man standing on the deck of the schooner shouted a single word into the morning wind.

"Storm," said the old man.

Peter raised his hand against the sun and squinted along the angle of the long sail that pointed into the sky. Stratus and cirrus clouds drifted in long strands and wisps thousands of feet above him. He closed his eyes. The boards of the old ship felt hard and substantial beneath his back. They creaked when the boat rolled from side to side. Miles away he heard the cry of an ocean bird.

It had been a long time since he had known peace, so long that he could not really remember when there had not been a feeling of being hunted, of being pursued by a world he did not really understand. He smiled now as he thought of how bored he had been and how foolish it had all seemed the first day of the voyage. He could not think why he had come or what he was doing in the middle of an ocean. And then very slowly The Caribbean began to hypnotize him. The clouds hovered and moved in an enormous drama of silence, and his past life with its pains and humiliations seemed remote and unreal. On some days he would fish. On others he would simply watch the sky and the water. Occasionally a ship would pass at the horizon and he would peer at it through his binoculars for a half hour or so until it disappeared.

Never in his life had things been so simple, so easy. He wanted only to be at peace and listen to the water and let his mind wander in circles. Slowly he was beginning to feel young again. His senses seemed more open and receptive, his mind aware of everything and yet thinking of nothing. It was as if he were waiting at the edge of some profound but unimaginable event, something in the drift of the ocean that would show itself in good time.

"Storm," said the old man.

Storm? Peter glanced at the fourteen-foot aluminum dinghy that was lashed with ropes near the stern of the ship. He had meant to have it stowed with emergency rations and a flare gun and a sail. Perhaps tomorrow he would get around to that.

The aluminum dinghy, he remembered, was Miriam's idea. Out here on the ocean it was his one concession to the civilized world. Miriam had always been vaguely afraid of storms at sea and had insisted that he buy a metal lifeboat with airtanks. Even then she had been apprehensive. The schooner was too big for three men, she had said, and too old. And Puerto Rican deckhands? Why not hire a boat in Miami where he knew people? And why an old sailboat? Why not a nice new cabin cruiser with outriggers and an auxiliary engine? In short, why not something sensible? But of course that was the whole point. He was thirty-six years old now, a teacher in a small but respectable New England college, a sensible and practical sort of man who had worked hard for everything. Aside from Miriam, this trip was the first real indulgence he had ever permitted himself.

He glanced again at the dinghy. In a way it reminded him of Miriam. It was very shiny and very sleek and unsinkable.

Miriam of course had become a kind of symbol for all his failures in that cloudy world that was now two thousand miles away. His marriage had ended in boredom and divorce, his career in routine and drudgery, his friendships in cool acquaintances. But it was the divorce that had made him wonder for the first time in years what he was doing with his life. His youth was gone now, not traded for something valuable, but given away for a song. For a while the thought of all his losses, both real and imaginary, had been paralyzing, a kind of avalanche that tumbled across his mind and made it impossible to move on blindly as it seemed he had been moving for so many years.

It was ironic, perhaps, that Miriam had taught him to love boats and to love the water. It was the only thing she had given him, the only thing he had taken from her when they had parted six days earlier, still good friends, and he had sailed out of The Condado Lagoon, away from the island of Puerto Rico, through The Windward Passage, and finally into the open sea.

"Storm," said the old man. "Bad storm." He waved his white sombero above his head, gathering hatfuls of air. Suddenly the sail began to flap. The two Puerto Ricans, the old man and his young helper, lowered the jib, one loosening the jib sheet while the other stood on the bow of the ship gathering and folding the sail in his brown arms. Peter sat up and looked around him. The sun was still bright and there were still no storm clouds anywhere in the sky. It had been that way for six days. He could not imagine that the sky or the huge, formless world of the sea could ever change from what it was at that moment.

An hour later it was raining. Two hours later the boat rocked and heaved as heavy waves broke across the bow, sending white sheets of water seething across the length of the deck. He watched the mast tilting back and forth, once or twice almost touching the high crest of a wave. For a while he tried to go below, but the rolling of the boat made him seasick and he returned to the deck where the spray of water and the waves and the desperate necessity of holding onto something made sickness impossible. The young man was shouting now; the old man was silent and baleful as he stared out into the stormdark water.

Suddenly the wind rose to a howling shriek and the mast tilted until it touched the white edge of an enormous wave that rolled toward the boat. Very calmly and with a profound sense of detached curiosity, he watched the boat turn farther into the water. It was as if everything moved in slow motion. For a moment it seemed that nothing at all would happen, that time was gradually coming to a stop at the edge of that giant wave.

Then the world was a chaos of green water and hissing foam. The deck of the boat disappeared somewhere beneath him or above him. He struggled for a moment against that disorientation, that sense of nowhere being up or down, and then surrendered to the water that roared in his ears and turned him over and over. Something struck him on the back of the head. The water went dark and he could no longer feel or hear the storm that raged above him.

A few moments later he felt the deck of the boat come up beneath him. Suddenly he was coughing violently and clutching the guardrail. For a long time it was all he could do to breathe and cough the water out of his lungs and hold on when the waves smashed against the side of the boat.

Finally the storm settled into a heavy rain, and for a while he lay on the deck unable to move. He had a vague awareness now that the schooner was sinking, sliding down into the water. He crawled to the stern and after a great deal of fumbling managed to unlash the aluminum dinghy. Five minutes later the stern was awash and the waves quickly carried him out into the open sea. Dimly he wondered about the two Puerto Rican sailors. Had they escaped in another boat or had they gone down in the storm? Then he thought of Miriam and his comfortable, monotonous life at the university. His thoughts began to disintegrate into fragmented images, flashes of memory and desire, until finally he was aware of nothing but an immense loneliness, a sense of helpless isolation that made him tremble. He closed his eyes and listened to the sound of the rain.

When he awoke, the sky was very dark and very silent. He could not tell if it was morning or evening, and he had no idea how long he had lain there. He sat up and blinked at the water, wondering what to do. Then he remembered the emergency box clipped to the underside of the rear seat. He reached under and tugged at it for a moment until it came free. Inside was a quart canteen of drinking water, some bandages and sunburn ointment, a small vial of antiseptic, and a compass. The water, he thought, was at least something. It would be enough to keep him alive for two or three days. He hitched the canteen to his belt, emptied the remaining contents into his shirt, and began to bail, using the emergency box as a scoop. In an hour he had emptied about a third of the water. After another twenty minutes he fell back against the aluminum slats and almost immediately fell asleep.

When he awoke again it was sunrise. Had a whole day passed or had it been near morning when he fell asleep? The water everywhere in the east had turned yellow and red, and the shifting colors were reflected in the giant cumulus clouds that hung motionless near the horizon. It was a beautiful sight, he thought dimly. He drank three swallows of water and then set to bailing out the rest of the boat.

For the first time since the storm, he began to take

stock of things: there was a bruise on his left shoulder and a bump on his head, but aside from that he seemed to have no real injuries. There was nothing to eat, but the ocean was full of fish and and perhaps he could contrive some sort of net out of his shirt and pants. In the meantime there was at least the drinking water, and with a little luck, he now thought, he might survive for a week or more. There was even a chance that he would drift into a trade lane and be picked up. But then, he reflected, he had never in his life been lucky in anything. More probably he would be dead in four days. It was, he thought bitterly, a rather stiff price to pay for a few days of peace in his noisy, meaningless life.

But his head was clear now. He began to look at things more carefully. The sea was fairly calm and the waves rolled in long, gentle swells. An hour later a light wind began to follow them, occasionally roughening the surface with skittering patches of shadow. He felt the slow drifting of the boat and sensed again the vastness of everything around him. He was moving northeast, somewhere in the blue streams of The North Equatorial Current.

Occasionally he saw small greenish minnows skittering a foot or two below the surface of the water. How far down, he wondered, could he actually see? The water seemed very clear, but there was no way of judging the limits of his vision in that emptiness. He leaned over the edge of his boat, dipped his face into the water, and opened his eyes. For a few moments he saw nothing, and then, quite suddenly, half obscured in the shifting deeps, there appeared the pale form of an enormous gray fish, a shark or perhaps a dolphin, nosing back and forth perhaps a hundred or two hundred feet below him. The sudden perspective was very alarming. There was nothing between him and all that infinite depth of water with all its shadowy carnivores, nothing but the thin aluminum hull of his dinghy. Suddenly he was very much afraid of death.

He brushed the seawater off his face, leaned back against the slats of the boat, and closed his eyes. He felt very tired now, and as the hours passed, the breadth and the sound of the ocean began to grow in his mind and ears like a chorus of voices. Voices in an enormous room. A ballroom where Miriam was dancing with Harry Ranton at The Connecticut Inn. Her back and shoulders were brown from hours of tennis and swimming and boating at her father's country club, and with her arms lifted and her body turning there on the dance floor, she was a dark star amid the blaze of white lights.

"Peter?" she was saying. "Of course I remember Peter. I adored him and thought the world of him, but unfortunately we nearly bored each other to death. Our divorce came just as I was going into Cheyne-Stokes."

Harry Ranton laughed pleasantly.

"I don't think he ever talks to anyone," she continued. "That's his real problem. At parties he's like a clam."

"A simple bivalve," said Harry Ranton. "That's Peter all over."

"Did you know that no one knows him even in his own department? They all call him Mr. Sutherland. Of course," she added, "he is kind of distinguished looking —so dark and athletic looking and quiet. I used to think he was kind of mysterious."

"Yes," said Harry Ranton. "He's a fascinating man to know slightly."

"You never liked him, did you?"

"No. But then I never like college professors, and besides, he was married to you and I found that rather inconvenient," he said, smiling.

"Poor Peter," she said. "He's always been so helpless. He never knows what to do about anything. What do you suppose he'll do now that his boat's sunk?"

"He'll drown," said Harry Ranton. "And he'll do that badly."

And then it seemed that all the dancers were floating

in green water and Peter found himself floating among them in his aluminum dinghy.

"Look!" said Miriam. "There's Peter! Peter! We're over here!"

"He's come back," said Harry Ranton dismally.

"Over this way, Peter!" cried Miriam.

Now his boat was bearing down on them. Vaguely he wondered if his aluminum prow was sharp enough to split Harry Ranton in two.

Suddenly he awoke. The images and whispers of the dream were dark and strange against the sound of the water lapping at his boat. He opened his eyes. It was morning again. Apparently he had slept another eight or nine hours. He was very hungry now and his head felt light and unreal. He drank another three swallows from the canteen and then sat up. Water had washed into the boat again and for a few minutes he made a desultory attempt to sweep it over the side with his hands and arms. It was a painful effort, for his head ached and his back was stiff from hours of lying in the bottom of the boat.

He was very hungry now, but the idea of making a net no longer seemed very practical. He would never catch anything that way unless he ran into a school of small fish and could simply scoop them out with his shirt. For a while he tried chewing on the occasional pieces of seaweed and kelp that passed by the boat, but finally spit them out in disgust. Perhaps, he thought, seaweed would taste better when he got hungrier.

He wondered why he was not frightened. Fear had come only for a single moment, like a flash of light in his brain, when he had seen the shark swimming below him. He felt instead a sense of peace, a kind of certainty about things. Perhaps, he thought, this was simply the mind's defense against the near certainty of death, but he did feel as if he were going somewhere, drifting north to some new world he had never seen, a world that lay just beyond the horizon of water. Then it occurred to him that all this might very well be the first step toward hallucination. Today it was only a sense of anticipation. Tomorrow when there was no more drinking water it would be green islands, mermaids, and treasure ships.

For a long time he simply watched the movement of the water around him, sometimes looking for fish, sometimes dreaming into space. Dimly he wondered why there was so much vegetation. Every few minutes he saw a patch of something floating in the water. It didn't seem reasonable that he could be anywhere near land. The equatorial current, he knew, was taking him slowly toward the United States, but that would still be nearly a thousand miles away. There were of course many small islands to the south in The Caribbean, but every hour carried him farther away from them. He seemed to be floating in the midst of an oceanic wasteland, a broad sweep of current in which he would drift for weeks. And then in his mind he saw a map of The Atlantic Ocean and tried to visualize just where he might be. A black speck on the blue map paper, somewhere northeast of The Bahamas and perhaps a thousand miles southeast of Cape Cod. Perhaps he was somewhere near Bermuda. Perhaps eventually someone would pick him up. But no, he reminded himself, that kind of luck would for him be atypical, even unthinkable.

And then he saw the currents of The Atlantic, broad yellow lines superimposed upon the gridded blue. Suddenly he thought again of the clumps of vegetation. Of course! He was somewhere in The Sargasso Sea.

The Sargasso! That great circle of water that superstitious fishermen had feared for hundreds of years. There were so many stories about The Sargasso Sea. The old men who hung around the docks in Puerto Rico had told him that it was haunted by the ghosts of dead sailors and by the ghosts of their ships, and when he was little he had read dozens of sea stories and listened to the Sargasso Tales that sailors would tell in the summertime on calm days when the sea off the New Jersey coast was like glass: tales of sea monsters, a whirlpool that led to the bottom of the ocean, a great island of Sargasso Weeds that went down thirty feet and extended as far as the eye could see, a swampy graveyard for derelict ships.

Of course he had known all along that he was moving near its edge, but somehow the thought of it had not intruded, had not seemed relevant to his situation. Now he realized that part of his sense of expectancy, his sense of peace, was connected with The Sargasso Sea. There was a subtle change in the air. It was as if—but he could not form the thought of it in his mind. Perhaps it was only the possibility of finding food. He had once read (apart from the myths and sea stories) that crabs and eels and strange crawling fish lived amid the large mats of weeds that drifted near the center of The Sargasso. He felt an unreasonable good cheer. It was almost as if he were approaching something familiar, something that would take care of him. Perhaps, he thought ruefully this was indeed the beginning of hallucination and madness.

The next day he ran out of water, and by that afternoon hunger and thirst had dulled his senses. Only dimly did he notice that the seascape around him was beginning to change. Small patches of gulfweed floated everywhere in the water, sometimes in strange whirling eddies of current. For an hour or so he sat in a kind of stupor, half awake, thinking of his wasted life and his pointless death—a life wasted with a beautiful woman who had been kind to him in her way, and a death consummated in a mindless ocean that was neither kind nor unkind, an ocean that brought nothing and took nothing away. He closed his eyes.

"But try to get back as soon as possible," Dr. Ratcliffe, his department chairman, was saying. "We understand your problem of course, and we do sympathize.

But the university must go on and we do need your services at registration this September."

Dr. Ratcliffe was perched on the edge of the dinghy, one foot resting on an aluminum slat, the other dangling in the air. He looked distinctly uncomfortable.

"I'll try to get back as quickly as I can," said Peter, "but you see my boat sank and just now I'm drifting here in the middle of The Atlantic Ocean."

"I understand perfectly, Peter. Sometimes these things just can't be helped. But do try to wrap this up quickly." Trying to look congenial, Dr. Ratcliffe pinched his face into a painful smile that narrowed his eyes to slits and knotted the skin at his cheekbones.

"It's very good of you to be so patient," said Peter. "You see there was a storm—"

"So I understand. The weather has been rather dry back home. Not a cloud in the sky all week long."

"I'm sorry to hear that, sir."

"Yes. Well, the flowers do wilt so quickly toward the end of the summer when there's no rain." Dr. Ratcliffe stared out across the water and for a moment seemed lost in contemplation.

"That's a shame, sir," said Peter.

"Yes. Well, give my best to your wife."

There was an awkward silence.

"Oh, I'm sorry, Peter. I'd forgotten."

"That's all right, sir. Everyone forgets."

"The truth is I've seen too little of you this year. We must get together sometime very soon."

"That would be very nice."

"In the meantime I'd be happy to see your face at faculty meetings with a little more regularity."

"Yes, sir. I'm sorry about that. But you see—"

And then for a few minutes he awoke. He had a vague memory of Dr. Ratcliffe falling off the boat and being carried away by the current. He looked apprehensive, but Peter could see that Dr. Ratcliffe was the kind of man who never lost his dignity, not even when wet.

Now everywhere around him the ocean was mottled with green masses of fernlike plants that lay in long chains that rose and fell with the undulations of the water, and rich brown Sargasso Plants festooned with golden pods and flecks of ivory color. Soon even the clear places were clouded over with plankton and algae and long strands of seaweed. Perhaps, like the sailors in the old salt tales, he would be caught in the swamps of The Sargasso and his bones would lie there in the middle of the ocean until the earth ran dry.

He realized now that his strength was gone. There was an odd shimmer in the air and a roaring in his ears. The drift of green weeds and brown Sargasso Plants became a blur, a smear of color without sharpness or definition. He closed his eyes and leaned against the side of the boat. It would be a bitter thing, he thought, to die as he had lived: to die alone here as he had lived alone in the noisy world of Harrington University. To drift here as he had drifted in his own life, without friends and with that curious inward silence that followed him everywhere.

"I hearby leave my thirteen cases of note cards to Dr. Ratcliffe and to the History Department," he said out loud. "To do with as he or it sees fit," he added after a moment. He tried to laugh, but the sound of it was horrible, like the turning of a crank.

An hour later he lifted his head just once more. A heavy mist had settled on the water. It swirled in large circles all about him, obscuring the sun and blinding him. For a moment he imagined that he had reached the edge of the earth and was just at the point of falling off. Then somewhere ahead of him he saw a brown shape, something very large resting in the water. He could not imagine what it was. His eyes would not focus, but he could see that the thing was moving toward him now. Suddenly he was afraid. He tried to cry out, but his throat was closed, swollen with thirst. He tried to sit up, and then quite abruptly everything seemed to dissolve and pass away into a vortex of sounds and colors and then into a cool darkness, a damp cave of sleep where he lay, it seemed, for an endless space of time.

Chapter Two

TABOR

"Hello. My name is Tabor."

The voice came out of the darkness, out of the labyrinth of his delirium. He opened his eyes.

"How do you feel?" said the voice. It belonged to a tall bearded figure in a black seaman's cap who spoke with a faint European accent, perhaps German or Norwegian. The man was bending over him, and in the background he saw a blur of other shapes bent forward, to peer at him.

"What's your name?" said the man named Tabor.

"Peter Sutherland," he answered. "Where am I?"

"You're in The Sargasso Sea."

"Sargasso Sea," he repeated.

"You look a little better," said Tabor. "You took some soup a half hour ago. Do you remember that?"

"Took some soup," said Peter. He blinked several times, trying to focus his eyes. "No, I don't remember. But what ship is this? Where are we going?"

Tabor smiled and shook his head. "This ship no longer has a name," he said, "and it's not going anywhere."

Peter stared into the dark eyes of the man, trying to read the meaning in his words.

"Do you think you can stand up for a moment?" said Tabor. "The only way you'll really know where you are is to stand up and look around."

He could see them all now. Two shirtless old men stood behind Tabor. One was very tall and thin and sharp-boned, with a narrow white beard. The other was shorter and rounder. Behind them stood a young girl dressed in a man's white shirt and black shorts.

"I can stand," he said. "But why isn't the ship going anywhere?" He hardly dared ask the question. The possibilities were too strange, too much a part of the dark world from which he had just emerged.

The two old men helped him to his feet.

"Now look around you," said Tabor.

For a long moment Peter could not understand or believe what he was seeing. It was as if he had never awakened at all. It was as if somehow this awakening were only an extension of his sleep, a kind of gentle nightmare. How many times would he awake, he wondered, before he awoke into the real world?

He stood on the edge of a sloping cliff, a cliff of many broken ships floating together in the open water, that extended as far as he could see to the east and west. To the south, the ships went for several hundred yards down to a strange shoreline of kelp and seaweed. The boats were of many different types—East India trading ships, frigates, corvettes, bilanders, flutes, an enormous Chinese junk, a seventeenth-century Spanish galleon, clipper ships and New Bedford whalers, and many smaller twentieth-century yachts, schooners, and motor launches of American and British design.

Some of the ships listed at steep angles; others lay on their sides, apparently suspended by thick growths of Sargasso Weeds. Some were nailed together, and some had walkways that connected them with others. Some rested across or on top of other ships that had almost completely submerged in thick growths of strange sea flowers and exotic green plants that Peter had never seen before. In some places there were pools of decaying wood where ships had rotted away. Again, the weeds had apparently not allowed them to sink. In other places, parts of ships had decayed and fallen together with parts of other ships to form a weird progeny of shapes in which it was impossible to tell where one ended and another began. Beyond the shore of the cliff he saw the ghostly outlines of ships sunk just a few inches under the water. And beyond that, a broad extension of water where clouds of fog moved slowly along the surface, clouds that rose high enough to obscure the sun and turn the air gray.

Aside from the four people who stood around him there seemed to be no one else in any of the boats. Everywhere there was silence except for the creaking of wood and the lapping and gurgling of the green water. It was like an enormous elephant's graveyard set in the middle of a barren ocean.

"The Sargasso Sea is two thousand miles long and a thousand miles wide," said Tabor. "Most of it is just sea. But here near the center of it is our little island of derelicts. The current moves in a circle, you see, and carries everything that has no power of its own to the center."

"But—how do you get back to land?" said Peter.

"There's no way back," said Tabor.

"But surely there will be rescue parties?"

"No one knows we're here," said Tabor.

He stared at Tabor and then at the island of boats, trying to digest what he had heard. "You can't mean that we're trapped here for the rest of our lives," he said finally.

Tabor began to answer him and then apparently thought better of it. "I don't think we can answer all your questions just now," he said. "You need to rest for a while. After you've had some sleep and something to eat we can talk again."

Tabor nodded to the two old men, who with a strength that belied their age, lifted Peter in their arms and carried him across several old wrecks and then down eight steps into the cabin of a large American schooner. The room was clean and it smelled of varnish. In the forward section stood an instrument panel, the wheel, and a series of cabinets for instruments and supplies. Through a large steering port above the wheel he saw the boat adjacent to his, and beyond that, a curve of blue water. On the opposite side of the room stood an antique fourposter bed and a circular wooden table with two hurricane lamps and a brass bowl filled with water. The sight of these things was somehow enormously reassuring, and for the first time since the storm something inside him let go, like a cold fist around his heart opening suddenly, releasing him.

The two old men set him down on the bed, nodded rather formally, and left. There were a hundred questions in his mind, but when he tried to form them into words they dissolved into pieces and he could not even speak; it was then he realized that he was too tired to get up, to follow them, to find out in a clearer way just where in the world he was. In an agony of fatigue and pain he undressed and then lay back on the bed. The clean sheets and the firm mattress were an almost unbearable luxury to his exhausted and bruised body. The sound of the water and the creaking boards faded away. He slept very deeply and without dreams until the next morning. When he awoke, a young girl was standing near the foot of the bed, looking at him with great curiosity. Long black hair fell past her shoulders. Her eyes were lustrous and dark, like black pearls.

"Good morning, Sutherland," she said. She held a wooden tray with two steaming wooden bowls and an earthenware pitcher and cup. For a moment he couldn't remember where he was.

"I see the sharks have eaten your tongue," she said. "Perhaps it will grow back after you've had breakfast."

She set the tray on the edge of his bed. In one bowl steam was rising from a kind of porridge made from something that looked suspiciously like seaweed, and a yellowish meal that he did not recognize. In the other bowl there were pieces of boiled fish.

"It looks delicious," he lied. "Thank you very much."

But when he began to eat he discovered that it really was delicious. And the taste of food awakened his hunger, a hunger that for days had been dulled by monotony and then by sickness.

"You mustn't eat too quickly," she said. "You'll get sick."

He looked up at her. She wore a man's shirt and black shorts. Suddenly he recognized her as the girl he had seen on deck the previous day. Then everything came back to him: Tabor, the two old men, the strange island of derelict ships.

"I see you are beginning to remember," she said.

"Yes. The ships. All the hundreds of broken ships."

"It must have given you a strange feeling. I mean, seeing it for the first time."

"I still don't quite understand. Just where are we?"

"On The Drift. All the boats together are called The Drift."

"And where is The Drift? At the center of The Sargasso Sea?"

"We're at the center of the current, which is a little east of the center of the sea. No one knows exactly where in latitude and longitude."

"How many people live here?"

"Over a hundred. We live all over The Drift in different clans. Ours is the smallest. It's called The Mary Strattford. The Madrids are up toward Northside on the west side of The Cliff. The Bluewaters go from the southwest side up to The Bridge."

Peter stared at her and tried very hard to listen, but the words would not register, would not make sense. "How long has The Drift been here?" he said.

"No one knows. Tabor says the first people here were called Carthaginians. He says there's a piece of one of their ships in our museum at The Bridge. I can take you there someday if you like."

The girl was smiling as if she enjoyed his questions. She could not have been more than nineteen or twenty.

"Tabor said no one ever gets off The Drift. Is that true?"

"Sometimes new people come, as you did, but yes, it's true that no one ever leaves. But there is one story about how once thirty years ago a man got permission from The Hatchmaker to go back home."

"Who's The Hatchmaker?"

"He's something that lives at Driftsend—that's the stern of The Drift. He gave this man a white boat with an immortal golden sail and the next morning he went back to Philadelphia."

"Philadelphia?"

"It's only two day's ride by boat. It's out there just beyond where the sun comes from, on an island called Pennsylvania."

"An island called Pennsylvania?"

"The name means 'Penn's Woods.' Tabor told me that."

"Did Tabor also tell you that Pennsylvania was an island?"

"Oh no," she said. "Everyone knows that."

"I see. Well, tell me about the man who got away in the boat with the golden sail."

"There isn't really anything else to tell," she said. "No one knows how he persuaded The Hatchmaker to let him go, and no one knows what happened to him when he got to Pennsylvania."

Peter finished his breakfast, got out of bed, stretched his arms, and walked out onto the deck of his boat. It was a strange, impossible world, unchanged since yesterday. The long slender deck of his ruined schooner ran to a sword's point at the bow, and beyond it, ships lay everywhere locked against each other in bizarre, tilted patterns. To the south patches of mist blurred the horizon.

Surely, he thought, it was all a weird game of some sort. Or a hallucination. He was sure that such a thing as The Drift was not scientifically possible. But at any rate, he had been saved from death at sea. The question was, what had he been saved for? How would he live here? How would he escape back to his own life? He stood with the young girl near the rail of his schooner and looked out at the vague mist.

His own life. He tried to think back to what that might have been. A few weeks before, he had been a history instructor at Harrington University in Connecticut. Generally it had been a dismal life filled with students, committe meetings, and his wife's country club friends who found, even after the divorce, that it was fashionable to have a college professor in their circle who could play a decent game of tennis. He had hoped that a week of fishing in The Caribbean would give him time to think, time to sort things out. He smiled. Certainly now he would have that time. Weeks or months or perhaps even the rest of his life if one took the girl and Tabor at their word.

His life in Connecticut seemed now like a comfortable misery, a familiar desperation that he had learned to live with, when he compared it to the prospect of lifelong solitude on an island of wrecked ships. At least in his old world there was hope that he would eventually discover some continuity in his life, something beyond the small pyrrhic victories and redundancies of the teaching profession and the casual amusements he shared with Miriam's friends, things that stood out like small glacial boulders in a vast desert. It was true that his life had always been a series of isolated events, but at least the hope, possibly only the dream of things changing, was something to hang on to.

During his lonely years with Miriam he had imagined that love would change everything. But love never came. Miriam, he knew, had always found him cold and unspontaneous; she had never known that in his heart he was desperately romantic. At a distance he had loved many women, both real and imaginary, but he had never found a way to express love without seeming terribly foolish. Once, on a sudden whim, he had visited an ex-student, a lovely young girl named Elizabeth Greer, who had called him from time to time and had made it very clear that she had an enduring crush on him. They had talked for several hours in her apartment. Several times that week they agreed to meet, but each time she had made some excuse out of fear and uncertainty, until finally he had completely frightened her away by his insistences of love and his sudden offer one evening on the telephone to divorce his wife and marry her. It had been an altogether miserable experience, a clear indication of his inability to deal with people, his essential remoteness, his failure to communicate, his isolation from everyone and everything.

But Connecticut was still a real world where struggle and change were at least possible. It was a theatre of operations that he understood. Here on The Drift he was completely at a loss. Who in his right mind could ever cope with such a place? His muscles began to itch. How pleasant it would be to play a hard set of tennis or to climb in The Adirondacks until the sweat darkened the back of his shirt and tickled his eyes. There would have been so many pleasant things to do during the summer months if only he had stayed home—violent physical things to release the floodgates inside him and, for a time, wash away all the poisons of his bitter and lonely life.

Suddenly he noticed that the girl in the white shirt was watching him very closely. It was as if she were listening to his thoughts. "I have to go now," she said after a moment.

She turned and climbed across the precarious catwalk that joined his ship with the next, and her departure gave him a sudden, foolish sense of loss.

"Wait! I'm afraid—that is, I was wondering if there was someone who could show me around."

"Oh, I forgot," she said, calling back to him. "Tabor is waiting for you on The Cliff. That's up on Northside. He's going to take you all around The Drift this morning. I'll see you at dinner."

He was about to ask for more specific directions, but saw that she was already three boats away, disappearing now amid the forest of spars and masts and torn sails.

Slowly he made his way upward toward what he guessed was The Cliff. At first he noticed clear places between the ships where he could see the greenish swamps below, but as he neared the top, the high hulls of boats rising over each other left the narrow riverways in deep shadow. He had the distinct impression that he was on an island, and that the sea was some distance away.

Tabor was waiting for him on the deck of an old Howker, a round tub of a ship with its two bare masts pointing into the sky. He wore the same hat, a kind of mate's cap with a black visor, and a gray turtleneck sweater. When he saw Peter he smiled and waved.

"Hello," he shouted. "I've been waiting for you."

"Good morning," said Peter. "How do I get over there?"

"You jump."

"Isn't that a little dangerous?" He surveyed the five-foot gap between the boat he stood on and Tabor's boat.

"Only if you don't jump far enough. Otherwise it's perfectly safe."

Peter smiled. So the captain had a sense of humor. Well, that was something. He walked to the far edge of the boat, gave himself a running start, and cleared the edge of The Howker with nearly a foot to spare.

"That took courage," said Tabor. "We need courageous men on The Drift."

"An ounce or two of physical courage is one thing," said Peter. "The courage to live the rest of my life here is another."

Tabor looked at him very closely, still smiling. "You need courage for that only at the beginning," he said. "Later on it takes no courage at all."

"I don't understand."

"I think you will after a time. But this morning I thought I'd show you around The Drift. By the way, have you had breakfast?"

"Yes. A girl came into my room this morning and brought me something. Who is she?"

"A young girl? That must have been Pao. She's one of our clan. Lovely, isn't she? But don't be fooled by all that enchanting long hair and those black eyes. Pao is very quick, and very wise in some ways, and she has many talents. The first thing I learned about her is that she has a mind of her own."

"Really?" He was curious about Pao, but he hesitated to ask pointed questions. It would be better, he thought, to wait until he knew Tabor a little better and until he understood more about his own status among the people who lived here.

Together they walked to the north rail of the old Howker and looked out into The Sargasso Sea. A large island of gulfweed turned in a slow circle a hundred feet or so beyond the edge of The Cliff.

"Everything here seems so improbable," said Peter after a moment. "Like something out of a dream."

"That's the way everyone feels when they first come here," said Tabor. "But actually The Drift was inevitable. Perhaps it's always been here."

"But what makes it all happen? I can't believe that the old salt stories about The Sargasso Sea are really true. It's too fantastic."

Tabor smiled. "In many of the old stories there's a

giant whirlpool that draws everything together, but actually The Sargasso Sea is rather shallow and rather poorly defined. Currents are never quite the same from season to season, and the inward motion is very generalized and inconsistent. The Gulf Stream and The West Wind Drift move north and east above us, and The Canary Current and The North Equatorial Current move south and west below us, and that does make for a relatively calm circle that rises a little in the center, a sort of lens-shaped sea of warm water that floats on top of the deep layers of The Atlantic. And so the currents drift inward and deposit things—driftwood, weeds, and the like. But that's about all it amounts to. The small islands of weeds and the animal life that lives on them are fascinating of course, but beyond that—"

Peter waved his hand impatiently. "I understand about The Sargasso Sea," he said. "But what about The Drift? I would think that everything would simply move around in an aimless way over a large area. Why has all this collected in one place?"

"If you drop petals in a large washbasin and then move your hand around the edge, all the petals will eventually gravitate toward each other as the current moves them in the same direction," said Tabor. "With an inward-moving current they collect near the center. I think that's part of the answer. And of course there may be other factors we know nothing about. For example, I sometimes suspect that there's a local eddy, a vortex of some kind that no one has ever discovered. I don't know what would cause such a thing. Perhaps a high mountain ridge on the ocean floor that affects the deep currents."

"That's a little hard to believe," said Peter.

"Many things here are hard to believe," said Tabor. "All the stories about The Sargasso Sea have an aura of the fantastic. They all suggest that strange powers operate here. The Carthaginians and the Greeks told stories about a sea of spiked grass near the western edge of the world that was inhabited by monsters. Later there was a tale about how The Lost City of Atlantis lies at the bottom of The Sargasso Sea. Some of the elders still talk about Atlantis. They say that people still live down under the sea, that they exert some sort of influence over us and that the vortex is their doing. But of course that's only superstition. All we really know is that derelicts and weeds and other lost things are moved by the currents and eventually find their way here."

"I see," said Peter. But he was disturbed by the expansive, imprecise nature of Tabor's explanation. Petals in a washbasin. Unexplained currents. Lost cities. Tabor's words had increased rather than diminished the feeling that nothing here was real or even plausible.

"At any rate," said Tabor, "The Drift is a fact. I've lived here for over twenty years now."

Twenty years. That in itself was implausible, unacceptable. His mind rebelled against the possibility of living twenty years in a graveyard of antique ships. He looked up and saw that Tabor was still smiling a little, as if something were vaguely amusing.

"But why is it that no one knows about you? Why haven't you been rescued in all these years?"

Tabor hoisted himself up on the wooden railing of the ship, which creaked under his weight, and lit his pipe. "There are several reasons for that," he said. "First of all, we take up very little room in the middle of The Atlantic Ocean. Except for some outlying wrecks, The Drift forms a sort of ellipse that's less than a mile long and only about six or seven hundred yards wide at its midpoint. It seems enormous from our vantage point, but it's hardly the sort of thing that anyone is likely to discover in all these thousands and thousands of miles of water. The nearest air and shipping lines are hundreds of miles away. Perhaps it's never occurred to you, but there are still vast areas of the ocean's surface that no one has ever seen, simply because no one has had any reason or occasion to go there.

"Of course there have been a number of scientific expeditions to this part of The Atlantic—in fact I have some recent books on oceanography from a small expedition ship that drifted in about two years ago—but even so we have to remember that The Sargasso Sea is in itself about two thousand miles long. The Drift is still only a pinprick on the map."

"But surely in all these years someone must have discovered this place!" said Peter. "It just isn't reasonable to think that no one has rescued you because you're off the trading lanes. Too much time has passed. People have been exploring and crossing The Atlantic for hundreds of years."

Tabor sucked on the end of his pipe and let the smoke drift out into the blue air, watching until it dissolved into nothing. "It's true that people sometimes stumble across us," he said. "Once in a great while we see a plane flying overhead. But I don't imagine they really see what's here. One sees what one is prepared to see, I suppose. And no one is prepared to see a myth. Perhaps from a distance we look like an island, especially with all the vegetation floating around us. Ships, that is, ships under their own power, are much less frequent. The last time was about three years ago. Three American fishing vessels sailed by, sloops I think. Something like the schooner where you've been quartered. They never got close enough for us to signal or call out, so we never knew quite what they saw or what they thought about what they saw. We waited for months, but no one ever came back. If they did see us clearly I suppose they finally decided we were some sort of hallucination, or perhaps a figment of the devil's imagination. Or perhaps they did tell people about us and were simply laughed at. No one believes the tales of a sailor. Not even other sailors."

Peter smiled tolerantly. All of Tabor's explanations seemed to be diversions, clever words that only skirted with the truth. It was annoying. The man seemed to be playing with him. "I still don't understand," he said after a moment. "So far you've attributed everything to chance and human error. It seems impossible that with hundreds of thousands of people crossing the oceans every year in ships and planes, no one has found you. Surely in the last hundred years—"

Tabor nodded in agreement. "You're right, of course," he said. "There are other factors. But I was hoping to avoid the more scientific explanation."

"Why?"

"Because it makes everything seem so final. I think it's better for a newcomer on The Drift to feel for a while that life here is some kind of elaborate hoax and that he will be back on firm ground soon enough."

"Never mind that. What's the real reason you haven't been rescued in all this time?"

Tabor looked down over the edge of the boat into the water, and in an absent way he began to scratch his beard. "The scientific reasons," he corrected. "The other reasons are real enough too."

"The scientific reasons, then," said Peter.

"Well, first of all, there's something very strange about temperature conditions just outside The Drift. The water seems to be unusually cool and the air unusually warm by comparison. Perhaps there is a deep current that surfaces out there somewhere; perhaps there is an eddy of warm air. I don't pretend to know what might cause all this, but that's not important. What's important is that it constitutes a temperature inversion, a reversal of the normal continuum of warm to cool as one moves from sea level up to the stratosphere."

"I don't understand what that has to do with the fact that no one has ever discovered this place," said Peter.

"Temperature inversions affect visibility," said Tabor. "First of all, there is a continual condensation of mist where the warm air meets the cool water, and so the air is hazy much of the time. This in itself makes

The Drift difficult to see from any position. But there are other problems as far as visibility is concerned. Temperature inversions also mean abnormal refractions —queer bending of light rays that trick the eye in a number of ways. This is especially true, for example, in antarctic regions where there is often a marked difference between water and air temperature. Sometimes things loom above the water, flatten out, sink into invisibility; sometimes there is a blurring or streaking that destroys the outline of what you're looking at."

Peter crossed his arms and tried to look unconvinced. "I never heard of that," he said flatly. Then he looked up and saw that Tabor was smiling at him again. Suddenly he had an image of himself as a petulant child who would not believe anything that anyone told him. "But of course I'm not a scientist," he added.

"Neither am I," said Tabor. "But I know the ocean, and the ocean is full of optical tricks. I remember once back in nineteen-thirty I was sailing on the *Mauritania*. I was only a boy then, but I remember it very clearly. My father and I were on the deck one morning and suddenly we noticed that a ship was sinking about a half mile off. It disappeared completely under the water, and I remember some woman cried, 'My God, she's gone,' or something like that. But then the boat reappeared again a few minutes later. Then it seemed to bulge in an odd way and break in two pieces. Everyone was mystified, but my father smiled and said that the ocean air was full of poltergeists and that he had learned that well enough sailing clipper ships out of London Harbor in the old days."

He laughed. "I don't think he ever told me a sea story I didn't believe after that," he said.

"Interesting," said Peter.

"There are some even stranger things that are attributed to temperature inversions," said Tabor. "Have you ever heard of Deception Island?"

"No."

"It's one of The South Shetlands. Apparently it changes shape, position, and even becomes invisible a good bit of the time because of temperature inversions that seem to be a consistent part of the climate in that part of the world. A friend of mine was a member of a scientific expedition to The Shetlands about thirty years ago, just before the war. He said they searched for a whole day, moving in circles at the map coordinates where the island was supposed to be. They had no luck at all until all of a sudden there was a shimmering in the air and two pinnacles of stone appeared before them out of nowhere, guarding the entrance to the bay of the island. It was like a dream."

"It sounds more like a miracle," said Peter.

"Perhaps so. But then, the ocean is full of miracles," said Tabor.

Peter looked out beyond The Drift to where wisps and feathers of mist seemed to be rising and rolling above the surface of the water. He could not see the horizon. "It must clear up sometime," he said dismally.

"Sometimes the air seems quite clear," said Tabor. "But air is always an uncertain medium, especially above water. It's filled with inconsistencies of temperature and density that are like little mirrors and lenses, some only an inch, others nearly a foot long, always changing, shifting. Over any reasonable distance it's very difficult to see clearly if there are abnormal atmospheric conditions. When I was a sailor it was not uncommon for ships to pass within a space of two hundred yards without ever seeing each other."

Peter smiled. He remembered Tabor's little joke about the leap that was not at all dangerous if only one jumped far enough. It was like his whole specious explanation of this impossible place: the inductive leap was reasonable enough if one was capable of making it, and that seemed to him a matter of faith. He thought about the illusion of the sinking ship and the disappearing island, and he looked around him at the huge wasteland of ships floating in a caged sea. Nothing seemed to make sense.

He shook his head. "Well, as you say, The Drift is a fact. I suppose I'm bound to accept that. But I still don't understand about all the ships. Most of them are so ancient. Why haven't they just rotted away in all this time?"

"Everything that comes here decomposes eventually," said Tabor. "But it does take longer than it would in harbor or in the open sea. I don't know why exactly. There are so many things about The Drift in particular and The Sargasso Sea in general that I may never understand. The salinity of The Sargasso Sea is higher than in any other ocean. Recently someone discovered that between the five- and eight-hundred-meter mark there's an unusually high percentage of strontium. And then perhaps you've noticed that the water here has a subtly different smell. I don't know what all these things mean. Perhaps they're part of the reason why the boats disintegrate so slowly. Perhaps not. We do some repairing and caulking and painting, but of course our resources are very limited, so that could only be a part of the answer."

"How about the number of old ships as compared to the number of new ones?" said Peter. "Or is that another mystery of the sea that no one can explain?"

"That's no mystery at all," said Tabor. "Ocean liners and warships are generally larger and much stronger than wooden ships. They don't flounder as easily in storms and they don't get blown hundreds of miles off course. And most of them have long-range radios and radar and sometimes even their own foundries for damage repair. Then too, the loss of a large modern ship is a national event. Within hours there are planes and ships answering distress signals. And so there are far fewer modern derelicts. Most of the ships on The Drift are between sixty and three hundred years old. The only newer ones are small fishing boats and cabin cruisers.

This means of course that The Drift will slowly get smaller and perhaps even disappear unless the world plunges into a dark age and people forget their steel technology and atomic power plants, and begin to build wooden ships again."

Peter nodded. He had the vague feeling now that if he could get a firm grasp on just one impossibility, if he could defy Tabor and The Drift with one articulate, absolute, unanswerable question, then the whole world of The Sargasso Sea would disintegrate in the storm of his rhetoric and he would find himself back in his office at Harrington University, the victim of a dyspeptic daydream.

"But what happens when there's a storm?" he asked. "I should think a really good storm would break everything apart. These old wrecks could never hold up in a heavy wind and a rough sea."

"There are no storms here," said Tabor. His voice was calm, reassuring, as if storms occurred only on other worlds or in legends. "In the first place, there is relatively little wind or rain anywhere in The Sargasso Sea. But for some reason it's especially calm on The Drift. Sometimes the winds whirl around us a mile or so away; sometimes we see large waves breaking in the distance. But we are always at the eye of the wind and current. Nothing ever touches us here."

"Nothing at all?"

"Occasionally we do get gusts of wind or a light breeze. Sometimes it rains. But often the rainbarrels get so low we have to depend on fishjuice and even seawater in very small amounts. No, there's never been a real storm here." Then his eyes lost their focus and he seemed to be thinking of something far away. "At least not for three hundred years," he said finally.

"I see. Then actually we're quite safe."

Tabor laughed. "Much safer than on land," he answered. "But of course you have to be careful about the condemned ships. Only about two hundred and fifty are still safe. The other four or five hundred are broken up or half submerged."

"That's a lot of ships," said Peter.

"Yes. And that's not counting the ones underneath."

"Underneath?"

"Here on the eastern part of Northside the boats sit on top of other boats in a sort of artificial cliff that The Madrids and Bluewaters have been working on for almost a hundred years. Our divers have found many boats that are entirely submerged now. Apparently the weeds go down a hundred feet or more in some places, and it seems they can hold a boat suspended even after it's completely waterlogged. There may be hundreds of ships down there that none of us have ever seen."

Peter tried to imagine a hundred boats lurking under the weeds, dark and enormous, like sleeping whales. It was one more odd possibility in a world of extravagantly odd things. Then he glanced up and saw that Tabor was looking at him very closely, smiling a little, his head cocked to one side as he perched on the edge of the rail and smoked his pipe.

"It's not so bad after a few days," said Tabor. "The first thing that will happen to you when you begin to adjust to life here is that you will get used to all these mysteries, and many more. They become a part of you. The sea has always been filled with mysteries, and men who live by the sea have the power to accept them, to live with them as they live with their own shadows. No one knows why the deep scattering layer reflects sonar long before it reaches the bottom. No one really knows where the deep currents come from or where they go or how they affect the surface currents. No one knows why monsters swim in Loch Ness."

"There are no such things as monsters," said Peter. He was growing very weary now of Tabor. The man seemed friendly enough, but he was clearly in love with his own words and he was full of misinformation.

"I have photos of the Loch Ness Monster in a magazine I got from that expedition ship I mentioned a while back. I'll show them to you someday, if you're interested."

Peter did not answer. There was no point in arguing the matter, he thought. He was in Tabor's world now and it would be best not to argue too openly with anyone. Tabor seemed to him a strange man, given to odd analogies and a curious sort of erudition based on a miscellany of scattered information. He had a predilection for the mysterious. He seemed in a gentle way to enjoy Peter's confusion, and the tone of his conversation was too openly expansive, too romantic. Peter could not quite put it all together, but it seemed to him that Tabor was initiating him into a spirit world, and Peter had never believed in spirits, not even as a child.

As they talked, Tabor motioned him toward a narrow gangplank that led to another ship, opposite the point which he had jumped. They began walking from boat to boat along the edge of The Northside Cliff. Toward the western end of The Drift it sank to a depth of only two ships, and here The Drift narrowed so he could see water on both sides. A group of sloops and small yachts extended in parallel rows for another hundred yards. They rose and fell very gently in a long rolling chain above the gentle undulations of the green water.

"This narrow channel of boats just before The Drift comes to an end is called The Bridge. Once there was a story about how the people who lived here two hundred years ago were trying to extend it all the way to The New World, but that's probably just superstition."

"It does look like a bridge," said Peter.

"The children sometimes play here in the morning," said Tabor. "They have some sort of shadowgame about The Bridge leading somewhere underwater. Perhaps they'll tell you about it after they get to know you."

It had taken them less than fifteen minutes to walk

from the center of The Northside Cliff to The Bridge, but the tour of The Southern Edge, as Tabor called it, took nearly an hour. It did not move in a more or less straight line as did Northside, but described a curve that swung outward and then inward so that The Drift was not strictly an ellipse as Tabor had suggested, but more of a bow shape. At first they came to long ribbons of seaweed and garlands of yellow and red vegetables growing like vine fruit for dozens of yards out into the water. It was like an enormous pool of sunset colors shimmering in the morning light. Narrow pontoon docks extended out into the water at different angles, occasionally turning and joining so as to cut the area into odd-shaped fields of color.

"These are called The Seafields," said Tabor. "They take up about a third of The Southern Edge. Most of our food comes from here. Reuben and Javitt will show you how we farm here in a day or so."

Halfway down The Southern Edge, The Seafields disappeared, and there was no longer any sharp line of demarcation between The Drift and the open swamps that bordered on The Sargasso Sea. Here there were many places where pieces of wood and wrecks of small ships had spread out into the water for nearly a hundred yards. Occasionally he saw spots where moss or Sargassum had bound boats together into green islands. In other places, pieces of wood had been nailed together to make a series of bridges and walkways out into the water, connecting the separate ships beyond The Southern Edge.

"Out there is a kind of no man's land," said Tabor. "I suppose you've noticed that here on The Drift many of the old ships have been caulked and varnished recently. And we spend a good deal of time scraping barnacles and keeping the weeds out of the ship's hulls. sometimes we even try to move ships around when a new one comes in or when one of the big ones threatens to float free or topple over. But out there it's very untidy and we make no attempt to keep it up. We call it The Outland. It's a good place to stay away from."

"You mean it's dangerous?"

Tabor nodded. "Many of the boats are on the point of sinking or capsizing, and the walkways between them are too long and usually very unstable. And besides, there are people who live out there."

"Out there? You mean by their own choice?"

"More or less. Well no, not exactly. They're what you might call exiles. I don't think they would want to live with us here, but the fact is they're not permitted on The Drift. They're all people who can't get along with the rest of us for one reason or another, so they've been sent out on the water to live by themselves. There are only about eight or nine of them now, and we very seldom see them during the day. But they're very hostile to anyone who goes out into their world."

"Has there been no attempt to—well, to rehabilitate them?"

"It's better to leave them alone," said Tabor. "The Outlanders are all right if you leave them alone. They prowl around The Southern Edge at night, but if you stay inside your cabin they won't bother you."

A few minutes later they reached the eastern end of The Drift, marked by three large nineteenth-century clipper ships.

"This is called Driftsend," he said, pointing to the three ships. "It's another place we generally avoid. Pao sometimes calls it 'The Stern,' and the children have picked that up and insist that there are little men who live inside the last three ships who always frown and have very 'stern' looks. Driftsend is harmless enough, but still it's the custom to stay away."

"Then no one really lives in the last three ships?" said Peter.

"No. Well, no one that we really know of." He shrugged his shoulders and smiled in an embarrassed way. "Only The Hatchmaker," he said finally.

Chapter Three

PAO

That evening in his room after Pao had brought him dinner and he was alone near the lighted circle of his oil lamp, he thought about the mysteries of The Drift. There were certainly many of them: the nature of the inward-turning currents that had brought all these derelicts hundreds and thousands of miles to this place over so many centuries; the fact that so many old ships had managed to survive, or at least partly survive, for so long; and the incredible fact that The Drift had never been discovered—incredible even with all of Tabors explanations of temperature inversions and seasonal mists and what not. Had no one ever tried to leave? Had no one ever repaired one of the ships and returned to land to tell the story of this impossible world? And finally, The Hatchmaker. Who in the world was The Hatchmaker?

Peter had always thought of himself as a speculative, thoughtful kind of person, and yet he had never really speculated very far or thought very much about anything. He was a victim of his first impressions, and in his own quiet way he was at the mercy of his feelings, of fleeting images, of a quixotic intuition that had nearly always led him astray, and he realized now how inadequate, how utterly incapable he was of evaluating what had happened to him in the last two days. He could not imagine how people lived here, castaways from the world. He could not imagine what they thought or what they did with their time. He could not imagine himself living here for more than a few more days. Escape was the only idea his mind seemed able to hold onto, the only thing that seemed really important. He would have to ask questions—careful questions. He would have to make plans.

Suddenly his thoughts were interrupted by an odd sound. At first it seemed to be an echo in his imagination, something from the dream world in which he had spent so much time while lost at sea. It reminded him of a water organ, or perhaps a weird harp played by the random fingers of the wind. Its vague rhythmical recurrences suggested some order, some form that he could not quite grasp. He got up, went to the window, and stared out into the night. For a moment the sound seemed to come from the white moon that dipped near the horizon, silvering the water. Then it faded beyond the moon and disappeared. He rubbed his eyes and lay back on the bed. It was too late and he was too tired to contemplate yet another mystery. The music played on in the darkness of his imagination until finally everything faded in the oblivion of sleep.

When he awoke the next morning Pao was again standing at the foot of his bed and again she had brought breakfast.

"You sleep very badly," she said. "You have bad dreams."

He could not think of an answer. He rolled over.

"It's nine o'clock," she said. "Time to get up."

"Nine o'clock is no time at all to get up," he mumbled. He opened his eyes and scratched his head. "You and breakfast both look very good this morning," he said.

"You also look very lovely, Sutherland," she answered.

"Don't kid me. I look like a tree full of owls."

She laughed. "What are owls?" she asked.

"Owls are funny birds. They look like this." He turned his head slowly from side to side and made a face like an owl. Pao laughed so hard she finally had to sit down on the bed, nearly upsetting his breakfast.

"No bird ever looked like that," she said.

He was very pleased. No one he had ever known had ever found him amusing before. Especially no woman. But then, he thought, Pao was not exactly a woman. She was only a girl.

"Tell me," he said after her laughter subsided, "what's your name? Tabor calls you Pao. Is that short for something?"

"No. That's my real name."

"What's your last name?"

"I have only one name," she answered. "No one on The Drift has more than one name. My father's name was Paolozzi. He gave me an Italian name that no one could remember, so finally The Madrids began to call me Pao. Pao is my real name now."

"Is your father alive?"

"He died a few weeks after we came here. My mother was lost in a storm after an ocean liner sank. I was only four then. I really don't remember much about it."

"Do you remember what it was like to live on land?"

She smiled distantly. "Not exactly. I remember being in different rooms, and I remember blue wallpaper with silver birds. I had a very large bedroom window and when I got up in the morning there were all sorts of colored things outside, but I can't ever think what they were. I can't remember anything about the outdoors except that my mother warned me never to go there alone.

Tabor says that land gives you a different feeling about things. He says you never feel the land moving. Is that true?"

Peter shook his head in a kind of baffled amusement. "Yes," he said. "The land never moves."

"How far down does it go?"

He looked at her for a long moment before answering. "All the way to the bottom," he said finally.

"The bottom of the ocean?" And then it was her turn to be silent as she looked beyond him into her own imaginings. "I used to dive sometimes with Tabor," she said after a while. "Sometimes we got down nearly a hundred feet, but we never saw anything but more water. It seems to go down forever."

"It seems to, but it doesn't. Everything has a bottom, an ending. At least everything on earth."

"Everything on earth?" Again she was silent for a moment. "I wish," she said, "there were more books to read. I would like to read about everything."

"Who taught you to read? Are there schools here?"

"Someone in each clan is responsible for teaching the children."

"Who's the teacher in your clan?"

"When I was little, Rose taught all the Mary Strattford children. From her I learned music and dancing and shadowgames and mathematics. But Rose is too old to teach now. She goes on The Long Journey almost every week and no one can really speak to her. So Tabor is the teacher now for The Mary Strattfords. He taught me English and Spanish and German and marine biology and poetry."

He paused in the middle of his seaweed and scallops to look at her again very carefully. Tabor was right. She was full of surprises. And what a shame to throw away all her beauty and intelligence in this wasteland.

When he had finished eating, they went out onto the deck of his schooner. He looked around him. Today things seemed much more familiar. His ship was about seventy-five yards below Northside and about as far from the three forbidden ships to the east at Driftsend. Tabor's boat was somewhere above him on The Cliff, and all the other boats in his clan were apparently gathered in the same area.

He looked down at the lovely young girl named Pao and shook his head very slowly. "Well," he said, "I'm shipwrecked in The Sargasso Sea. It's morning and I've just had a delicious breakfast. What now?"

Pao smiled up at him and took his arm. "You'll see how things are here very quickly. Then you won't feel so strange."

The mists of the last two days had dissipated and the air was bright and clear. He took a deep breath.

"Follow me," she said to him. "I want to show you something."

As they talked, she led him from boat to boat across the center of The Drift. "Over here," she said. She pointed to a place where two large French brigantines had been tied together. The deck sidings had been removed, and a rough, continuous deck had been built where the boats normally would have curved away from each other. At the south end he saw something that looked like a slide. It went down over the stern of the first ship and disappeared in the shadows.

"This is called Twoboats," said Pao. "It's where all the meetings and dances are held. Anything that involves all the clans together."

Suddenly he remembered the strange music he had heard the previous night. "Was there music here last night?" he asked.

"I don't think so. Why?"

"I heard something very strange last night just before I fell asleep."

"There are many strange sounds on The Drift," she said. "You will get used to them after a while."

"Perhaps I was dreaming." He looked across the long

empty deck of the two ships. "What were you saying about this place? About the music . . .?"

"This is our place for dancing and music. And once every two months we do The Dance of The Nine Islands. You'll see it next week."

"The Dance of The Nine Islands?"

"It's a celebration. Something I made up."

"Something you made up?" Again he was surprised. "You mean people come to see your dance?"

"Everyone comes. It's a tradition now. Sometimes I change the story a little, but people are offended if I leave out anything important. It's been almost the same now for two years."

"Pao, how old are you?"

"Eighteen."

"Eighteen. Hmmm. Well, Tabor warned me about you."

Pao smiled and looked up at him. "What did he warn you about?"

"He said you were full of surprises."

She laughed. "Everyone is full of surprises," she said. "Even you."

"No. I'm not full of surprises at all. I'm the most unsurprising person you've ever met."

She laughed again her easy, spontaneous laugh and then took his hand and together they walked up toward Northside. Soon Pao was telling him more about life on The Drift.

"Things here are really very simple," she was saying. "The men work on the boats during the day. They pump water out of the old ships and caulk up the hulls and scrape off the seaweed and barnacles and do carpenter work in some of the rooms to make them more pleasant. And every day in the morning two men from each clan go down to The Seafields to gather vegetables and weeds and hunt for fish and prawns. The women stay in their boats and cook meals and tend to the children. Sometimes in the evenings after dinner people go out on The Bridge and play Nightsongs until the moon sets. Sometimes there's a new song that someone has written and then everyone goes to listen. Children are very happy on The Drift. They go weedwalking and they play shadowgames and they learn from the teachers."

"What are shadowgames?"

She looked very surprised. "Don't you have shadowgames on land?" She moved her fingers and turned her wrist in a little circle, as if looking for words in the air. "There are different kinds of shadowgames," she said. "In one kind you make up a form and then everyone improvises on it until someone can put all the variations together in his mind. Then he goes into The Moon's Circle and gets to make up the next form."

"I still don't understand. What's a form? What's The Moon's Circle?"

Pao gave him another curious look. "Don't you play games on land?"

"I guess we play different kind of games. Tell me about the ones you play."

And so for a while they wandered together in the bright sunlit morning while Pao talked about the children's games. Her explanation seemed to Peter very obscure, and soon he found that he was listening only to the syllables and the intonation of her voice.

Occasionally he noticed people working together in small groups. Once he saw three women boiling an enormous pot of sea crabs and combing seaweed in long shallow pans to remove bits of wood and kelp. They were singing an old English carol that he had heard somewhere before. The beauty and tranquillity of the scene were vaguely disturbing to him. Did they never think of the world beyond The Drift? Had they forgotten that they were castaways, condemned forever to float in a lost corner of the ocean, a thousand miles from land?

"Pao, are there any sailboats or motorboats here that anyone uses?"

"No. We never use boats for sailing."

"Why not?"

"I don't know. Perhaps it's never occurred to anyone."

"Doesn't that seem a bit odd to you? I mean considering that boats were built to be sailed?"

"Perhaps." She looked down at her hands.

"Well, tell me this: are there any small boats that could be used for sailing that you know of?"

"I suppose many are seaworthy. But most of the sails have been removed. We use sailcloth for clothing. And the engines in the motorboats are all rusted. And besides, there's no gasoline. Reuben and Javitt have a raft they use for farming The Seafields, but that's the only boat I know of that anyone uses, at least on this side of The Drift."

"Where's the boat I came in?"

"The little metal boat? The Outlanders have it. I forgot about them—they do use boats sometimes. They took your boat and left you on one of the outlying wrecks. That's where Reuben and Javitt found you." Suddenly she turned and stared at him. "You would have died in another few hours if we hadn't saved you," she added. Somehow she made it an accusation.

"I realize that and I'm very grateful," he said quickly.

"Then why do you want to leave us?"

"I want to go back to Connecticut. My work, my whole life is back there."

"No one has ever left The Drift," she said. "If you try to leave he'll kill you."

"Who'll kill me?"

"The Hatchmaker. So you mustn't try to leave. No one can leave The Drift."

"Pao, you must understand—"

"Never mind," she said quietly, turning away from him. "I'm hungry now. I'm going to eat with some friends. I'll see you at *The Mary Strattford*." And a moment later she was gone.

He sighed. It was very flattering to have a girl not much more than half his age so concerned about the possibility of his departure, but on the other hand, her attitude could make things difficult. He wondered if Pao reflected any general sentiment about the idea of leaving The Drift. He had assumed at first that people here considered themselves stranded and simply made out as best they could under the circumstances. But now he was not so sure. He wondered again why no one ever tried to leave. Surely the obstacles could not be that great, not with all these people and all this raw material. But perhaps it would be better if he kept his sentiments to himself, at least for a while. He smiled. That was something he had been reminding himself to do all his life. Somehow it had always seemed to be the best policy.

But first he needed a plan. Some way of finding the things he would need to sail back to America. He could not stay here for the rest of his life. There was a whole world beyond The Sargasso Sea, and the idea of never seeing it again was absurd, unthinkable.

That evening Pao and Tabor knocked on his door and then entered before he had a chance to answer.

"The Madrids and Bluewaters are playing Nightsongs in a few minutes over on The Bridge," said Pao. "Come along with us and listen."

"No thanks," said Peter. "I like to get to bed early. I feel better in the morning."

"But the music is so lovely," said Pao. "And everyone brings torches, and sometimes we dance."

"No thanks. I have a headache anyway. I need some rest."

"Just come for a little while then," she said.

"Not tonight. I don't feel much like dancing and singing just at this point. I have some reading to do and then I'm going to turn in."

"I think Sutherland wants to be alone for a while," said Tabor. "There'll be Nightsongs again next week. We can all go then."

"Yes," said Peter. "That would be nice. But just now I'm tired." He tried to smile. "Dancing and singing just wouldn't be my cup of tea."

"What are you going to read?" asked Pao.

"Read?"

"You said you had some reading to do."

"Oh, yes. Well, it's just a book I found yesterday on one of the boats nearby."

Tabor smiled and put his hand on Pao's shoulder. "Come on," he said. "We'll be late. We'll see you in the morning, Sutherland."

When they had gone he closed the door behind them and then closed the wooden latch. God, how he missed the privacy of his old life. Here everything and everybody was everyone else's business. It reminded him of a small town in Ohio where he had once taught, a town where all the children smiled and said hello and everyone on the street tipped his hat and the old men at the tavern where he drank on Friday evenings to get away from students and colleagues and examination papers would drape an arm around his shoulder and talk into his face about crops and politics and the birds of central Ohio and the hunting season. That sort of thing had always made him uncomfortable.

He lay down on his bed and folded his hands behind his head and sighed deeply. Singing and dancing and torches in the moonlight, he thought. The clichés of a romantic, pagan world. But the broken ships and the Outlanders and boiled fish and vegetables growing in the water and beautiful young girls chasing after strangers? It was a strange place built upon strange necessities, an uncivilized nightmare that he felt he could never understand.

On an impulse, he left his cabin and wandered over to the schooner adjacent to his own. The sun touched the horizon now and the higher ships cast long shadows across the parts of The Drift that he could see. There was no one in sight. Everyone, he thought ruefully, had gone to the fertility rituals with his torch.

On the deck in front of him lay the crumpled remains of sails that had been cut up for clothing, and some coils of rope. Underneath one of the pieces of sail, someone had left a canvas bag with four tennis balls and two rackets, the old-fashioned kind with oval heads and hexagonal handles. He fondled the old rackets in his hand and stretched his fingers to feel the tenseness of the strings.

In less than a minute he was back on the deck of his own boat, tennis racket and ball in one hand, the other three balls lying at his feet. He stared at the wooden wall of the fore side of his cabin. Anything below the porthole is in the net, he thought. Then he reached into the air, released the ball and bent back to swing all in one long, familiar motion. A split second later the white ball struck the wooden boards an inch above the porthole and the whole cabin seemed to reverberate. But the ball returned too quickly, leaping back from the wall and shooting past him before he had time to bring his racket around for a backhand swing. My reaction time, he thought. He felt terribly slow and the deck of the schooner seemed terribly small. He picked up the second ball, this time serving very slowly and cautiously. The ball bounced back to him, and with a smooth forehand swing he sent it spinning back toward the boards. Soon the long-familiar practice rhythm moved him first a step to the left, then a step to the right. Strikehitbounce, strikehitbounce, the white ball sailing through the air, the instant servant of his will. Then a backhand shot hit the wall at an angle, and the second of the four balls bounced wide over the rail of the schooner and into the water. He picked up the third ball.

He played on into the sunset, on into the darkness, his eyes slowly adjusting in a marginal way to the loss of light. He played in the bright moonlight, and the last of the four tennis balls was now almost beyond the limits of his vision, a puff of smoke in the dark air. Suddenly it was gone. It had flown past him somewhere in the darkness, and he had no idea where it was or even what direction it had taken. The spell in his mind and the rhythm of his muscles ended together. For a moment he felt paralyzed.

"What are you doing?" said a voice behind him. "What kind of game is that?" It was Pao.

He turned around and looked at her, and then he looked at the jagged, irregular silhouette of The Drift that surrounded him on all sides like a jungle outlined in the moonlight. He thought of the four tennis balls lost somewhere in the water below him.

"What's that in your hand?" said Pao.

He looked down at his hand. The racket hung loosely in his fingers. The sound of the thudding tennis balls reverberated in his mind, but outside in the dark world around him, the world from which Pao stood looking at him, there was only stillness and the broken ships and the murmur of lapping water.

"It's a tennis racket for playing tennis," he said. His voice sounded unnaturally loud. "Tennis is a game for two or four people played on a large court on sunny days. I've always been an exceptionally good tennis player. I played on the varsity team in college."

His words were like ghosts. He felt the silent ships looming around him, and he began to tremble.

Chapter Four

THE OUTLANDERS

The next morning Peter awoke early, made his way to Northside, to The Bridge, and then, satisfied at last that his sense of direction was reliable, walked down to the part of The Southern Edge that bordered on The Outland. Shading his eyes against the bright sunlight that glanced off the water, he spent several minutes looking for his aluminum dinghy.

Later on, Pao brought him lunch which they ate together on the forecastle of an ancient barque whose spars and foremast, looming in a broken canopy of lines above them, had been shattered in some nameless storm of long ago. When they finished eating, Peter excused himself on the pretext of a headache and went back to his own cabin. When he opened the door, he saw lying across his bed a heavy white shirt and a pair of knee-length white shorts made out of sailcloth. They looked very handsome in a rough sort of way, and very durable.

When he turned, Tabor was standing in the doorway.

"I thought you could use some new clothes," he said.

"I certainly can. Thanks."

"Thank Pao. She was up all night making them."

Peter turned red. "She shouldn't have done that," he said.

"I think she wanted to," said Tabor.

"Pao needs more supervision," said Peter. It struck him as a rather stupid remark, and now he was doubly embarrassed.

"I told her she needed her sleep more than you needed new clothes, but she quietly threw me out of her cabin and bolted the door. Pao has a mind of her own."

"I've noticed that," said Peter.

"Did you two have a nice walk yesterday?"

"Very nice. She took me to a place she calls Twoboats and told me about the festival next week. She claims she's composed a dance of some sort."

"The Dance of The Nine Islands," said Tabor. "She does it every other month, and by popular demand, I might add."

"Where did she learn to dance?"

"From Rose. Have you met Rose?"

"No."

"You'll meet everyone in our clan tonight at *The Mary Strattford*. That's our main ship. We have all our meals there and all our meetings." Tabor leaned against the doorway, and withdrew a pipe from the pocket of his leather jacket.

"Frankly," he said after a long pause, "I'm rather anxious to know you better. It's been a long time since I've talked to an educated man."

Peter did not know what to say. There was always something vaguely disconcerting about the prospect of someone knowing him better. Perhaps, he thought, it was only that he had always secretly bored himself and was afraid of boring others.

"I'm not really an educated man," he said. He looked about in his mind for some way to answer Tabor's invitation. "I'm a history teacher, but I'm hardly what anyone would ever call a scholar. I've spent most of my time lecturing at students and playing tennis and trying to avoid people," he said with a self-conscious laugh.

Tabor laughed easily and clapped Peter on the shoulder. "Perhaps so. But everything changes here on The Drift."

"For some people, nothing ever changes. Not even their address."

Tabor laughed again. "Well at least that's not true in your case. About your address, I mean."

"I'm not sure that it matters," said Peter. "I wasn't expecting any important mail this summer. Or any visitors, for that matter."

"Here you'll have many visitors," said Tabor. "No one is ever alone on The Drift."

They talked until Tabor finished his pipe. Then he waved and disappeared from the doorway, and Peter heard his black boots against the wooden deck of his schooner. It occurred to him that he had said a rather strange thing to Tabor, strange at least for him. Not that it was a very revealing statement or an admission of something not obvious to anyone who had ever known him. It was only that he seldom talked about himself to anyone and almost never joked, no matter how feebly, at his own expense. There was something about Tabor that caught him off guard, something that led him into saying things he wouldn't ordinarily say. He was an appealing sort of person, Peter decided. He seemed independent and self-assured, and yet in some way that Peter could not define or locate, he also seemed wistful, perhaps even lonely.

It was nearly three in the afternoon before he left his room. Slowly he made his way back down toward The Southern Edge. Soon he stood where the boats no longer formed a solid pattern, but spread out unevenly across the water. Somewhere here in The Outland, somewhere in this swamp of decaying hulls, one of The

Outlanders had his aluminum dinghy. He had reason now to believe that it might be the only dependable boat on his half of The Drift, and he meant to find it before nightfall.

Of course it would be dangerous. The Outlanders might very well be guarding the dinghy. And even if he did recapture it there would still be the problem of finding a good sail, a good motor, and gasoline. Of course it would be more than a little foolhardy to sail out into the open sea in a small dinghy. But still, he had to do something. He had to begin somewhere.

He walked across the catwalk that led to the first ship. Now, suddenly, he felt more comfortable. He was moving, doing something. Whether he would succeed or fail did not, for the moment, seem so important as the fact that he was now on more familiar ground. He would use his eyes, his ears, his muscles, toward a specific end that was clearly attainable. It was a game called Get The Dinghy, and Peter had always been very good at games. Especially outdoor games. Games, no matter how complicated, were simpler than life. He smiled a kind of rueful inner smile. At least in games there was an objective that anyone could understand.

He noticed that all of the boats here were smaller and in very poor repair. Often there were large stretches of open water between them, but weeds filled in much of that empty space, and only occasionally did he see clear water. In some places the weeds had entirely overgrown the boats, turning them into drifting green islands.

Between the boats there were crude pontoon bridges —flat boards with floating crosspieces nailed to their undersides like railroad ties. For the most part they were simply set on thick patches of Sargasso Weeds so that as he walked he sank several inches into the water, soaking his feet and ankles.

A silence fell all around him. The Outland was without most of the small noises of The Drift: no distant footsteps, no creaking decks, no shouting children.

After a while he found himself listening to even the tiniest sounds: the squish of his own sneakers, the scuttle of prawns across the weeds.

After a few minutes he came to a small sailboat that was isolated from the boats beyond it. There seemed to be no way of going any farther without retracing his steps several hundred feet across precarious bridges to another line of boats.

The boat was perhaps thirty feet long, a single-masted runabout. No rowboat floated nearby, and there was nothing anywhere on the deck except a single oar lying near the stern. He glanced down into a stern hatch. A foot or two of water glistened darkly inside the hull.

Then he had an idea. Perhaps he could cut the boat loose from the wooden bridge and row it through the weeds to the next ship. He found that two of the cords holding the boat to the bridge could easily be untied. The third he cut with his pocketknife. Then by rowing first on one side and then on the other, he made slow progress toward the next ship, about a hundred feet away. Suddenly his boat came upon a large pool of water where the shifting current had left a gap in the maze of weeds. Slowly the boat began to take in water. In a minute it was listing very badly to the port side, and he had trouble keeping his balance and rowing at the same time. The boat moved very slowly now in spite of his frantic rowing, and in a few more seconds the hull was half filled with water. It was clear that he was sinking. The next ship was still twenty feet away. All around his own boat the weeds had returned, whispering, pressing against the sinking ship. Perhaps he could swim the few feet that remained. But he had never tried to swim through weeds. Would they hold him up or would they choke him, drag him down into the water? He looked around. There was no one, no help anywhere. In another moment his boat would slip beneath the surface. Suddenly he remembered the oar. Perhaps . . .

He walked to the stern of the boat, carefully judging

the distance. Holding the oar in both hands, he ran the length of the boat, fixed the oar in the ridged point of the bow, and vaulted into the air. The bow sank under his weight, and for one terrible moment he was suspended over the water, the oar sinking slowly in the green weeds. But the momentum of his leap had carried him over. He dropped the oar and reached out toward the rail of the boat he was falling toward. He felt his body strike the wooden hull; a terrible pain shot through his leg, and for a second he clung to the iron rail at the edge of the deck. Then very slowly he pulled himself over the side. There was a very large bruise on his right shin, but aside from that he seemed to be all right. He was at the point of congratulating himself on his quick thinking when he remembered how stupid he had been in the first place to row a swamped boat out of its resting place in the thick weeds. He looked behind him. For just an instant he could see the outline of the boat underwater, crossed by a pattern of Gulfweed and white seaflowers. And then it was gone, dragging large patches of vegetation with it, leaving behind a circle of dark water. Somewhere below he knew the boat was still going down. The Sargasso Sea was very deep.

All at once he realized that his efforts were getting him nowhere. He had been so busy balancing on precarious bridges and walkways and then saving himself from disaster that he had forgotten to look around for his dinghy. It gave him a start to realize that he had lost sight of his objective so easily. Beyond the boat on which he now stood there were two more walkways, one leading back in the direction of The Drift, the other out toward what looked like an old houseboat. In dim resignation, he decided to go on and explore the houseboat before turning back.

As he approached, he saw that it was indeed a houseboat, a square barge with a large square cabin set in the middle that allowed an even distribution of deck on all four sides. The houseboat was attached to long walkways extending out into the water to form a rectangle. About forty yards away, on one of the long sides of that rectangle, the structure was supported by an old lugger with broken decks and a shattered mast. The other two sides were held up with rowboats. The total effect was of a sort of square pier elevated two or three feet above the water. At several points he saw small boats tied to it, including three rafts with large sails.

Until that moment Peter had seen no real evidence of life in The Outland, but here someone had obviously gone to a great deal of trouble. Very quietly he made his way across the last few feet of walkway and then jumped onto the pier and listened. Somewhere in one of the rowboats crabs scuttled and clicked. Beyond that he could hear nothing.

As he walked around the pier he saw his aluminum dinghy tied to one of the supporting rowboats on the opposite side. His elation at the sight of it was pierced by an equally sudden thrill of fear. The Outlanders lived here, and Tabor had said they were very dangerous on their own ground. He began to feel extremely vulnerable. He was still a fairly young man, quick and strong from years of hill climbing and tennis and golf, but he was alone now and he had no weapon but his pocketknife.

Soundlessly he made his way across the old lugger and then onto the other side of the pier. The dinghy was moored just a few feet away. Just then he happened to glance up at the houseboat on the opposite side. There was a man standing in the shadow of the cabin.

Peter could not see what he looked like, and he had no idea that the man was thinking or what he would do. Perhaps he could get to his boat and push off before the shadowy figure could do anything.

His boat was tied with a thick rope and a bowline knot around one of the aluminum slats. On his hands and knees he tried to saw through it with his pocketknife, bending over the pier. He looked up. The man had left the shadows of the houseboat's cabin and was walking toward him. He was very tall, and his shoulders and arms looked enormous.

Suddenly Peter realized he would need an oar. He remembered there were several lying on the deck of the lugger. He ran back to fetch one, but by the time he returned, the man was standing in front of the dinghy. In his right hand he held a long-handled gaff with a curved iron hook. He smiled very broadly. His left eye was missing, and a horrible scar, a blotch of purple, covered that side of his face. He wore nothing above his waist except a blue handkerchief tied around his neck.

"I came for my boat," said Peter. He pointed to his dinghy. "The metal boat. It belongs to me."

The man with the scar did not answer. Just then another figure appeared about a hundred yards behind him on one of the walkways leading to the pier, a small man who was shouting and laughing in a high-pitched voice that ended in a kind of delicious squeal. He waved a long knife back and forth above his head.

The man with the scar began moving toward Peter. He was still smiling, and his smile stretched across large yellow teeth. Suddenly he lashed out with the gaff. Peter jumped back and the hook missed his head by an inch.

For a minute the two men fenced back and forth on the pier. Peter's oar was longer than the Outlander's hook, and by jabbing with it he kept the larger man at a distance. But the hook was more of a weapon. The Outlander used it to strike at the oar, cracking the wood and sending chunks of it flying into the air. Soon it would break or be whittled down to nothing.

Twice the Outlander ducked and lunged, trying to end the battle quickly by slipping under Peter's guard, but each tme Peter stepped back just as the gaff hook slashed through the air. He could see now that he would have to change his tactics. The oar was a clumsy weapon. He could jab with it, but a powerful lunge would mean rushing forward, which would be fatal if he missed, or swinging it over his head, which would leave him open to attack as he raised it.

As he began to tire from the weight of the oar, he wondered how much it would shorten his reach to hold it in the center with both hands. Suddenly he realized that he was using it as a spear or a lance when it would be much more effective as a cudgel. That way he could make short, powerful strokes to either side without leaving himself open.

The little man had reached the houseboat. Peter guessed that he intended to go around the pier and come up behind him. He would have to make his move quickly.

Shifting his hands toward the center of the oar, he swung it sharply to the right. The big Outlander avoided the swing by jumping back, but it caught him off balance. As he raised his arm to strike a counterblow, Peter took a step forward and swung to the left. His oar struck the Outlander on the shoulder. A third swing struck the big man in the neck. With a dreadful moan, he staggered backward, his legs collapsing under him. With arms flailing at the air, he fell sideways into the water. Peter whirled around to find the little man creeping up behind him with his knife. But as he turned, the man squealed and ran back to the lugger, from which he shouted curses in Spanish.

Peter finished cutting the mooring rope and then jumped into the boat. The little man was still shouting at him. The big man with the scar cried out in pain and clutched at the edge of the pier.

After a few minutes, the complicated pattern of boats and walkways made it impossible to row any further, and he was forced to drag and carry his dinghy across the walkways and decks. Once, a piece of iron shot struck about a yard to his left and sprayed him with water. He turned just in time to see an old man with no teeth laugh and then duck behind the cabin of a boat forty feet away. Apparently The Outlanders were always cheerful. Perhaps, thought Peter, it was the clean outdoor living.

When he reached The Southern Edge, he hid his dinghy in the hull of an old bilander where no one lived, and made his way back to his own schooner. He felt very weary. The sun was near the horizon now. Already the clouds had turned orange and the waters below The Southern Edge were growing darker.

Chapter Five

THE SEAFIELDS
AND THE MARY STRATTFORD

"Where were you this afternoon?" said Tabor. "Pao said you had a headache."

"I got over my headache and I went exploring," he answered.

Tabor looked at him with interest. "By yourself?"

"Yes."

"Well, you're back just in time for dinner. Did I tell you you'll be eating with the rest of us from now on at *The Mary Strattford*? It's time you met everyone."

Peter waited for the next question, but it did not come. He looked up at Tabor, and then to his surprise he added, "I wasn't just exploring. I was looking for something."

Tabor smiled, but still he said nothing.

"I was looking for my boat. I thought it was time I began to make some effort toward getting back home."

"And did you find it?"

"Yes. I went down to The Outland. It was tied to a kind of square pier about two hundred yards out."

"You might have been killed. The Outlanders are

very unpleasant to people who wander into their districts."

"I nearly was. Two of them attacked me. I finally dumped one into the water and the other ran off."

Tabor was silent.

"I just can't wait around. I can't leave my whole life behind me simply because no one here thinks it's possible to get back to land. I have a good boat now. All I need is a sail and a motor and some provisions."

"I understand how you feel," said Tabor. "Perhaps we should let people live with us for a few weeks before we tell them there's no way back. Perhaps that way it wouldn't be such a blow."

"Has anyone ever tried to leave The Drift? Why are you so convinced that it's impossible?"

Tabor did not answer.

"I really don't understand. It's almost as if people here are against the idea of leaving. I said something to Pao about it this afternoon and I got the feeling she was upset. It was almost as if I had insulted her."

"You told Pao?"

"Sort of. Not in so many words."

"That was unfortunate," said Tabor.

"Why?"

"Pao expects to marry you."

"She what?!"

"She loves you. She expects to marry you."

"But that's absurd! She knows nothing about me! And besides, she's only eighteen years old!"

"She's nearly nineteen," said Tabor. "And she knows a great deal about you. More than you think."

For the rest of their walk to *The Mary Strattford*, Peter was very silent. It was upsetting to think that the girl was trying to involve him, to pull him into her world. Surely, he thought, there must be some boys around somewhere that were her own age. But secretly, he was rather pleased. Pao was a beautiful and enchanting woman, even at eighteen. There could be worse ways of spending one's life. But no, that was unthinkable. She was younger even than his students at Harrington University. He shuddered when he remembered the scandal over a professor in the Psychology Department who had dated one of his students. He remembered his own revulsion. It had seemed in such bad taste, and it reminded him of a trap he himself had almost fallen into. It made him think of—and the word "incest" came into his mind before he could suppress it.

Tabor led him to an old New Bedford whaler, a square-rigger over two hundred feet long that lay about seven or eight boats to the south of Tabor's own ship. On the bow he saw a greenish bronze plaque nailed into the wood, on which were engraved the words THE MARY STRATTFORD. In front of the mizzenmast a hatchway led down a flight of stairs into an oak-paneled room that flickered warmly in the plentiful torchlight. In the center of the room stood a long oak table filled with bowls of crabmeat, broiled fish, pitchers filled with juice, and different kinds of boiled vegetables in clay dishes. Around the table, the people of the clan sat on wooden benches.

Tabor led him to a place next to his own at the head of the table. Then, with an elaborate air of preoccupation, Pao took her place at Peter's other side.

Tabor crossed his arms over his breast and closed his eyes.

"No storms have come to The Drift for three hundred years," he said. "May God grant that no storms come for another three hundred. May we live in peace."

"Amen," said everyone.

Then he raised his hands to hold the silence. "We have a new man this evening at *The Mary Strattford* whom we hope will become one of us. His name is Sutherland."

Everyone turned to look at Peter while Tabor made the introductions. There were nine people in all: an ancient woman named Rose; the two old men, Reuben and Javitt; Tabor's two children, David and Michael; a very slender young man with a great shock of black hair named Raven; Pao; Tabor; and a plump, middle-aged woman named Bright.

"On behalf of everyone here," said Reuben in a high, reedy voice, "we deem it our pleasure to welcome you to our ship and to our circle of fellowship."

"My sentiments exactly," said Javitt.

"What they mean is, we're glad you're here," said Bright. "We want you to stay with us."

Peter smiled at everyone. "Thank you," he said.

The dinner hour was filled with conversation. Bright talked at great length about the antics of Tabor's children, whom she looked after during the day. They had been doing something called weedwalking and she called them both "little Jesus" because they had the power to walk on water. Reuben issued proclamations about the weather and about The Seafield harvesting, with which Javitt invariably agreed. Pao drew Tabor into a discussion of Spanish and English grammar as compared with German. Later she talked about *The Ballad of El Cid*, which she had just finished translating. They laughed together a great deal. Peter had the feeling that somehow their whole conversation was very largely for his benefit.

Peter said very little during dinner, and strangely enough no one asked him questions about his former life or his arrival at The Drift. Everyone looked and smiled at him from time to time, but no one really seemed very concerned that a new member was entering the clan. No one except the old woman named Rose, who stared at him all through the meal. He smiled at her, but she did not smile back.

Finally, when dinner was nearly over, she said, "You're the man from the sea, aren't you?" Everyone looked up at Rose, smiled tolerantly, and then went back to eating and talking. Everyone except the boy named Raven, who seemed oblivious to all that was said.

"You got your boat today, didn't you?" said Pao very quietly as Bright was taking away the dishes.

Peter looked up at Tabor in surprise and anger.

"I didn't tell her a thing," said Tabor.

"No one has to tell me things," she snapped.

Peter could see that she was furious. For some reason, her anger made him miserable. He could think of nothing to say.

Soon the dishes were cleared and everyone got up to leave. "Breakfast is at eight-thirty," said Bright. "Try not to be late. These wolves eat everything I bring to the table in ten minutes."

"Thank you," said Peter. "I'll remember."

"After you go hungry for three or four mornings you develop a sort of alarm clock in your head," said Tabor. "I haven't missed breakfast in nearly ten years now."

"We would be honored and flattered by your presence at The Seafields tomorrow," said Reuben. "Our experience and our knowledge will be at your disposal."

"I concur," said Javitt.

"But your afternoon belongs to me," said Pao. "We can go exploring together." She smiled. Suddenly, and for no reason he could discern, her mood had changed completely.

"That would be wonderful," he said. A sudden and unreasonable surge of happiness made him smile and press her hand. Eighteen years old, he thought. It was getting more and more difficult to remember that Pao was only eighteen.

As he walked back to his schooner he saw Rose standing like a marble frieze on the deck of *The Mary Strattford*. She was staring at the moon. Raven, who had said nothing to anyone during the whole meal, shuffled off toward his own boat, his hands in his pockets. Pao was talking to Tabor. He could not hear what she was saying, but she seemed to be pleading with him, and occasionally her voice would rise as if in sudden indignation. The two children were running from boat to boat like rabbits. They were playing some sort of signal game with their hands.

"You used the moon yesterday," said David. "You can't use the same form two days in a row."

"Let's try the moon's shadow then," said Michael in a shrill voice.

"Okay. But let's go find Blanca first," said David. "Blanca is good at moon things."

"She has a moon in her mind," said Michael, and they both laughed.

Peter shook his head and smiled. The casual conversations at the oak table had been an illusion. Nothing here on The Drift was really very normal, not even the children. It was a strange world that he still could not begin to understand.

He had spent five days now on The Drift, and he imagined that if it had not been for his adventure in The Outland he would have gone mad in that time. At least his encounter with The Outlanders had been a simple, brutal, competitive sort of thing that made some sense. But The Drift itself—the improbable, aimless life, the strange people—was something he could not cope with. Why had there been no interchange with the outside world, no rescues? What consolation was there in this dead place? Tabor was friendly enough, but he was a mystery. What in the world did he do with his life? And even Pao, in a subtle way, made him uncomfortable. For a young girl, she was too mature, too perceptive, in spite of her naïveté and her ignorance of the world beyond The Drift. It was troubling to be at the mercy of these people. He could not ignore them or escape from them; for once, those possibilities were not open. He had to talk with them and smile and be grateful and try to act if life here on The Drift had some purpose.

That evening before he slept, he heard the weird

music again. It was like a jangling harpsichord terribly out of tune. It seemed now to come from somewhere on the eastern side of The Drift. The sound of it was unsettling, as if somehow it were a metaphor of unreality, a token of this vast hallucination over which he had no control.

After breakfast, the next morning, Reuben and Javitt led him down to The Seafields on the western side of The Southern Edge. Apparently the two old men went everywhere together. Reuben, the older, taller, and skinnier of the two, kept patting him on the shoulder and smiling as he informed him, in his incredibly pompous diction, of his duties that morning. Javitt smiled and added every now and then a word of agreement, clicking to himself like an old hen. They were like two ancient mariners, smiling and ineffectual, giving their wisdom and experience to the young. Peter enjoyed their company in spite of himself.

On their way to The Seafields they passed along the edge of The Outland, and Peter thought about his adventure there the previous day. At the time, it had seemed only a bizarre contest, like grim children quarreling over a toy. But now as he gazed over the maze of ships and sinking walkways he felt the truth of what Tabor had said. The Outlanders had had every intention of killing him, and indeed had come very close to doing so.

But now at least he had taken the first step. The risk had been worth it. The next step was to find a good sail, a good mast, and an outboard motor with plenty of gasoline to get him out of the wind-dead center of The Sargasso Sea. There was a fair chance, he imagined, of getting into a trade lane before his food and water gave out, if only he could find enough gasoline and a decent outboard motor. Surely there must be an outboard motor somewhere on The Drift, one that worked.

Reuben nudged him with his elbow and pointed a

bony finger toward the edge of The Seafields. "Notice the golden weeds at the periphery," he droned. "A strange marginal world of enigmas and dark mysteries."

"Enigmas and mysteries," said Javitt, nodding his head.

"The snails bore tubes in the weeds," continued Reuben. "Tiny, spiny fish build nests. Worms hollow out stems and leaves. Millions of God's secret, blind creatures live there and copulate and bring forth new generations and never leave the weeds. The weeds are a world for tiny things," he concluded, making a gesture of infinite smallness with the thumb and third finger of his trembling hand.

Reuben and Javitt led him to the third walkway, a slender pontoon dock that extended out into The Seafields for nearly a hundred yards at an oblique angle. Reuben explained that everything within the sloping triangle made by this dock and the next one belonged to The Mary Strattfords. Beyond it were other fields, large triangles and rectangles of color that extended outward from The Southern Edge, that belonged to The Bluewaters, The Madrids, and The Conquistador Blancos.

From a distance the brilliant colors of The Seafields were only an undulating blur; up close he saw three distinct kinds of plant groups arranged in long, meandering rows. One was a series of interlacing yellow vines suspended by large green seed pods that acted as floats. Hanging down in the green water from these vines were globes of yellow, pear-shaped fruit. With these plants grew another vine, very similar to the first, except that its seed pods were bluish purple, and its fruit shone a brilliant red. Reuben explained that all these were indeed the same species, and that the blue and red plants would soon move into their yellow phase, while the yellow ones would move into their blue and red phase. The second plant group was composed of different kinds of seaweed and a brown rubbery vine with hundreds of seed pods that from a distance looked something like kelp. The third plant group consisted of lilies and sea hyacinths and a strange calyx plant that looked like floating skunk cabbage.

In contrast to these exotic plants were common scallions and carrots that grew in long wooden trays along the docks. The soil, Reuben informed him, was made from pulverized wood mixed with plants dried in the sun and then ground into a powder.

Together the three of them paddled up and down the narrow lanes of water between the rows on a large wooden raft that Reuben kept at the far end of the dock. They drew the vines over the raft to gather the vegetables into large basket, and snared the cabbages and lilies, which Reuben assured him were edible, with long-handled hooks. Later they paddled to a place near The Southern Edge where the vegetation was especially thick, and speared prawns and crabs and an odd-looking multicolored fish that crawled with its fins over the seaweed and vines. It blended so well with its environment that Peter never saw it until the raft was a yard or so away and Javitt, under his leader's careful instructions, caught him with the sharp end of his hook.

It was an altogether pleasant morning. Peter could not help but smile, and once he caught himself humming an aria from *The Marriage of Figaro*. Occasionally Reuben would look at him and puff and then smile approvingly, as if somehow they had all done a long day's work and had done it very well.

"Lived here all my life," said Reuben as they tied their raft to the pier and began unloading their vegetables and fish. "And all my life I've been a fisherman. When I was only seventeen I caught a whale with only a coat hanger and a rope."

"One coat hanger, one rope," affirmed Javitt.

"He was a veritable giant, a behemoth of his breed," said Reuben. His eyes glittered as he began to get the feel of his story. "I fought the beast for six days and six nights, and when the fight was over we had meat on The Drift for six years."

"It must have been a great fight," said Peter, who managed not to smile.

"On the morning of the seventh day he came to the surface and I got him in the brain with my last hundred-foot spear. He spouted blood a hundred boatlengths into the air and the whole Drift turned crimson red before he gave up his ghost! Arrgh! It was indeed a fierce and gruesome sight!" The old man shrieked with happiness, and Javitt listened to his master's words with a look of awe and adulation.

It was only after several moments of respectful silence that the little man had anything at all to add. "When I was young," he said rather quietly, "I could dance like anything."

At noon they began the long upward journey across dozens of ships back to *The Mary Strattford*. When he had gone about halfway he saw an odd thing that he did not understand: a long slide that curved back and forth between the ships, slowly descending toward The Southern Edge. He leaned over the rail of a large topsail schooner and stared down at it and tried to imagine himself sliding, curving back and forth down into the shadows. It was made of long sections of fluted wood that were supported by crosspieces rammed into portholes or suspended from deck rails by heavy ropes. He could not see where the slide began or where it ended. It moved very slightly from side to side when the ships moved in the water. Then he remembered the slide at Twoboats, the meeting place where Pao had taken him. Perhaps this was another part of it.

After lunch at *The Mary Strattford*, Bright called him into the galley, where she and Pao were scrubbing dishes in a large wooden tub.

"Reuben and Javitt approve of you," she said. "They told me you did a very good job today."

"But I hardly did anything."

"Never mind. You watched them. That's very important. The children used to watch them, but they lost interest after a few months. So they had nobody to watch until you came."

Peter smiled. "Well, that's very nice. But I really don't feel that I'm earning my keep."

Bright laughed. "You don't have to earn anything here," she said. "But wait until the men start fixing the ships. You'll only work for an hour or so a day, but you'll be sore all over."

"I'll welcome that," said Peter. "Hard physical work always makes me feel better."

Pao turned from his dishes and looked at him curiously. "Why?" she asked.

Immediately he was on the defensive. "Hard work is the only way to get anything done that's worth doing," he said. "If you lived on land you'd realize that." He smiled weakly. Even to him the words sounded foolish, inappropriate.

"Reuben and Javitt never work hard, but they always seem to be happy," said Bright. "Did they give you their little lecture about Sargasso Weeds this morning?"

"Sargasso Weeds? I'm not sure. They may have."

"It's really quite interesting. They have a little speech they learned from Rose about how there are two kinds of Sargasso Weeds. The first is rock-bound and always lives near land. It has holdfasts for clinging to rocks. Sometimes it gets torn away and drifts here, where it lives for a while and then dies."

"Why does it die?"

"It's not made for the open water," she said. "That's how it's different from Natan, the kind that has evolved here. Natan has floats instead of holdfasts and it has a much nicer color sometimes. Rose says that if it ever finds its way to land it gets dashed to pieces by storms. So it can't live near land, just as its cousin can't live in The Sargasso Sea."

She smiled and scrubbed away at the last of the wooden plates, while Pao rinsed them, shook them, and put them in a cabinet. "The Sargasso Weeds that grow here have no parts for reproduction. No males, no females. They just grow at the tips and waste away at the base. They grow, but never reproduce. Such simple plants, but so lovely to look at when you look closely. Rose said once they were all just a form of algae. No real leaves or stems, just a seaplant that branches out in all directions and grows pods for floating in the water."

Then she looked up from the dishes and began to dry her hands on her long skirt. "Now why is that such a pleasant thing?" she asked. "Why is there such pleasure in such simple things?"

Pao put the last dish away and then reached up and kissed Bright on her eyes. "Because you are the mother of us all," she said, laughing. "You gave birth to all the weeds and all the children and all the fishes."

"My goodness, child, I don't even have a husband! Now you take yourself and your sweet words and Sutherland and go someplace. I've got to start thinking about the next meal." And with that, she put her hands on Pao's cheeks and shook her very gently.

"Upstairs," she said.

A moment later Peter and Pao stood on the deck of *The Mary Strattford,* and from there they walked to a high boat that overlooked The Northside Cliff.

"I thought of something really wonderful we can do this afternoon," she said. "We can explore some of the old ships. I mean the really old ones. I haven't been inside them for months. And I fixed some seabread in a bag in case we get hungry later."

She smiled and looked up at him expectantly. Her long black hair flashed in the noon sunlight. "I can show you all sorts of things," she said. "But you'll have to do exactly as I say." She smiled her beautiful smile and squeezed her hand.

"That sounds wonderful," he said. "I'm yours to

command." And although a part of his old self seemed to hold back, thinking of the dinghy and his impending voyage on the open sea, he surrendered for the moment to an irrational burst of happiness, to the soft, still air, and to the ruined romantic silence of The Drift.

"Come on then," she said. And together they ran across the deck, squinting in the bright sunlight, and jumped to the next boat that pointed along the edge of The Northside Cliff.

Chapter Six

THE CARAVEL

As they walked together along Northside they saw the boy named Raven swinging from one of the lines of a large whaler ten boats below them.

"Have a great time," he shouted. "Just don't eat any of Pao's seabread unless you want to puke all over the boards."

Pao reddened. She was about to shout something back at him, but then finally thought better of it. "He's always been like that," she said quietly. "He doesn't get along with anybody."

"Why not?"

"He wants things that—things that he can't have," said Pao. "And he hates The Drift. Sometimes I think he hates everything. Rose told me once that he has the blindness, that he has no power in his mind to see anything that isn't there. He lives with Bright. She's the only one who can really make him behave. Peter and Michael say he was scratched once by The Hatchmaker and has been mean ever since."

Peter shrugged his shoulders. "Well, I guess I'm not

really interested in all that," he said after a moment. "But I do wish you'd explain about The Hatchmaker. Is he a real person or a superstition or what?"

"I only know what the others say. The Madrids say he lives at Driftsend and that sometimes at night people hear him walking around below decks."

"I still don't understand. Is he supposed to be an ordinary man or some sort of spirit? Everyone talks about him as if he weren't quite real."

"I don't know if he's real or not," said Pao. Her eyes narrowed, and she looked up toward the horizon. Peter had noticed many times that when she was thinking very deeply she looked at the horizon, the edge of the world where she had never gone except in her thoughts.

"Is it important to know whether things are real or unreal?" she said at last. "Perhaps everything that someone is thinking of is real. Or perhaps people like The Hatchmaker are just a different kind of real. The Madrids say he controls the lives of everyone on The Drift because he lives in another world and has powers no human beings have. They say he's good luck, and sometimes very bad luck too. Anyway, it's bad to go near Driftsend, especially at night."

"Has anyone ever seen him?"

"The Madrids say he's a very handsome man and that he dresses in coat and tails. But that's silly. Only fish and land animals have tails."

"They mean he dresses in an old-fashioned suit that's very long in the back. Do you know what a suit is?"

"There are suits in some of the old ships," she said. "But I don't know why anyone would want to wear them."

He smiled. "Yes. Well, never mind that. Tell me more about The Hatchmaker."

She tilted her head and made a helpless gesture with her open hands. "There isn't much more to tell. Rose says he's two thousand years old, but of course that's impossible." She looked out across the water and then up at Peter. "I think," she added.

Peter suppressed a laugh. "But why is he called the Hatchmaker?"

"I don't know. I guess no one knows. Peter and Michael say that when he was young he lived on an island off the island of Norway, where it was his job to make the hatches on boats. And now that he's here where there are no new boats being made, he crawls around at night, sawing new hatches in the bottom of old boats just to keep in practice. They say that when an old boat sinks, it's because The Hatchmaker has been sawing new hatches."

Peter smiled again, this time a little wearily. "Everybody here tells stories about questions they can't answer," he said.

"The children are very good at stories and shadowgames," said Pao, who seemed to have caught his words but not his judgment. "But I forgot. There is something else. Rose told me once she used to know The Hatchmaker years and years ago, long before I was born. She said his real name was Hatchetman."

"Hatchetman. That means hired killer in my country."

"A hired killer?"

"A man who—well—a man who kills for a living."

"Kills what?"

"Other people."

"I don't understand. Who would employ such a man?"

He could see now that he had made a mistake. "Evil or sick men who wish to destroy other men," he said finally.

She looked up at him very seriously. "Tabor says that many on land are like that," she said. "Is it because the land never moves?"

"Why should the land not moving make people evil?"

81

"I thought—I don't know. I thought perhaps with things so still, people might get sort of nervous."

Pao was startled by his laughter. It was the first time he had really laughed in a long time. "Perhaps that's it," he said. "It's as good an answer as any I've heard recently."

For a few minutes they walked together in a comfortable silence, hand in hand. Once, a flight of white gulls passed overhead like a cloud of snow. Later they saw the twisting wake of a large eel and heard the whispering of long fernlike formations of Gulfweed as the eel swam through the green water. The smell of salt and old wood and green water was very strong and very pleasant. Here, he thought, there were no hatchetmen. The world was at peace.

It was hard for him to remember amid these preoccupations that he had an ulterior motive. A specific purpose in exploring the ships with Pao. He thought of the supplies he would need for his dinghy. Perhaps today he would discover something.

"Would you like to know where we're going?" she said.

"Does it really matter where we're going?" he said.

"I thought we'd go see the caravel first."

"What's that?"

"It's one of the oldest ships that's still in one piece. No one has lived there for as long as I can remember. Rose says she used to play there when she was a little girl."

Caravel. The word began to emerge from his knowledge of The Renaissance and The Age of Exploration. Prince Henry's ships were all caravels, and they were the first to explore and round the coast of Africa. Columbus sailed on caravels. They were the great ships of exploration of the fifteenth and early sixteenth centuries, if he remembered correctly. But the ship before him now that Pao was pointing to seemed much too large, and it had a high, ornate stern that was characteristic of a later age.

It seemed to him a rather strange-looking ship. The quarter-deck was doubled, one level raised a few steps above the other, while the forecastle formed a small island in the front that towered a dozen feet or so above the bow. The foremast was square-rigged; it made a strange contrast to the lateen-rigged main and mizzenmasts with their spars fixed at an angle to form the sloping triangular sail pattern that made him think of *The Arabian Nights*. By some miracle the sails had survived the weather, time, and the shears of the women. They hung, yellow with age, like the ghosts of giant birds.

"This way," said Pao.

When they had climbed over the side he saw in another way how different the caravel was from the schooners and brigs where most of the people lived and worked. Here the wood itself seemed ancient, marked as it was with initials and diagrams carved by a thousand knives. In some places the deck had rotted away to show the hatchways and rooms beneath. Near the mainsail lay a cutlass, brown with rust, that someone had perhaps discarded hundreds of years earlier. Toward the bow lay a row of trunks with enormous brass hinges.

Everything now was cast in shadow from the sails and from the high sides of the boat that extended several feet above the level of the deck. The total effect was of a kind of shelter or enclosure. The sounds of the water, the birds, the women and children shouting to each other across the ships, all seemed miles away now, and the pale shadow of light that came through the yellow sails made everything brown and quiet. It reminded him of the attic of an old house, and for a moment he felt like a little boy listening to the closed-in silence, listening to the tiny buzzing sounds in the dust that seemed curiously loud when he would close his eyes and stop breathing and listen.

A few feet aft of the mainmast, a hatchway led down into the ship. The first two levels below were open gun decks, enormous uncompartmented areas stacked with barrels and cases and balls of shot. As they descended into the darkness of the third level, Pao leading the way, he was overwhelmed by a sudden odor: the sweet, musty smell of old wood and dust and rotting seaweed. When his eyes adjusted to the fainting light, he found that he was walking down a long corridor. Fastened into the walls on either side were iron braziers that had once provided illumination, and doors that led into other rooms and into other corridors.

"This way," said Pao. She disappeared around a corner.

He followed her, groping about in the semi-darkness. Then he saw her standing in the door of a large room illuminated by two large windows. The room was flanked with eight arched mirrors of a very baroque design with flutings and wreath and flower patterns set into the silver frames of each one. In one corner lay piles of rotting fabrics: faded silks, cottons, and an enormous bolt of green velvet. Scattered about the room lay dozens of trunks, some piled on top of each other, some open and lying on their sides, spilling their contents onto the floor: gray and blue capes, a doublet of gray camelot, a white fustian jerkin, stockings in gray and white, shirts of fine Holland lace that were yellowed now with age, a black cap of velvet, and, lying on a white frieze coat, a silver whistle on a long silver chain.

"I've never taken anything from this room," said Pao. "I don't think anyone knows all these things are here."

At first Peter could not speak. He stared at the exotic riches of another age long dead. He wondered where the ship had once been bound for, and what great lord had owned all these treasures.

He bent down and looked more closely at the silver whistle. The fluted blowpiece widened into a gargoyle face with an open mouth. What lips, he wondered, what lips long since turned to dust . . . ? Then Pao lifted the whistle to her mouth and blew very gently. It made a long hollow sound that trembled softly in the air, a sound that reminded him of woodpipes.

"Now," she said, "we have a secret together."

He knew that it was true, but he could not have said just then what the secret was. The secret of the whistle's sound that no one else had heard for hundreds of years? The secret of the room and its faded treasures? Or was it the secret of what these things meant in some larger way, an existence or mode of being that he could feel at that moment but not quite put into words?

For a moment he imagined that he was a ship captain who had discovered long ago that his journey was only an illusion, a trick of the wind and water, and that the islands he sought were as far away as the stars. But then one day while he was mourning those lost lands where he had planned to exchange his goods for an enormous profit, he wondered about the rigging of the sails, the cargo in his hold, and the interior rooms that he had never seen, or perhaps had forgotten. Yes, of course that was it. There was an outward journey across the sea, but also an inward journey from room to room, from corridor to corridor. One could be defined in the marketplace of the world where goods were bought and sold and admired; the other way was only a feeling, a way of looking at things. It seemed to him a very curious flight of fancy.

"What is the secret, Pao? Can you put it into words?"

But he knew that for the moment Pao would put nothing into words. She took his hand and led him back into the dark corridor and then into a room that held a gallery of portraits, mostly of Spanish noblemen. Across one wall hung a large tapestry of a country manor with several gabled houses, gardens, a stable and a faded yellow meadowland for horses and cows, and an intricately woven forest where the lord of the manor hunted deer with a crossbow. Another room was filled with trays of tarnished silver, faded linen, and a long velvet lounge.

"The rooms on the lower levels are all swamped with water and weeds," she said after a while. "But there is something else we still haven't seen. It's up this way."

He followed her up a wide turning staircase carved with figures of saints and medieval knights until they reached a long, narrow room, a library. Bookshelves filled one of the long walls all the way to the ceiling. There were hundreds of volumes, all bound in leather and in boards. On the opposite side, a series of casement windows looked out over The Drift. He realized now that he was standing in the ornate section of the caravel's stern, near the very top of the quarter-deck.

Most of the books in the library were in Spanish or French. Many were beautifully illuminated copies of romances and accounts of travel. Others were philosophical works, poetry, and geography. One incunabulum, bound in lacquered red leather with tooled and gilded lettering, told the history of The Middle Ages. It was printed in Spanish in what looked like a kind of Gothic type. At the beginning of many chapters, stylized maps showed the gods of the sea, their cheeks puffed, blowing ships toward the shell-scalloped edges of eternity or across the trade lanes of The Mediterranean, and dozens of woodcuts portrayed the lives of kings and knights. Peter knew only a few words in Spanish, enough to order meals and fishing supplies, but he could see that the book was a kind of grand, romantic distortion. One whole chapter was given over to El Cid's horse and armor. Another to the witchcraft of the Moors. For nearly a half hour he sat at one of the reading benches and slowly turned the stiff, ancient pages, hypnotized by the extravagance of the book. Pao sat next to him. Sometimes she would translate for him, reading and fingering the words over his shoulder. Finally he came to the end of the first volume. The colophon was a great bird clutching a book in his talons.

"This is incredible," he said in a half whisper. "This whole place is incredible. It's a museum. Back in The United States it would be worth a fortune."

Pao seemed very pleased. "I've read nearly all the ones in Spanish," she said. "Lots of times I just sit here all day and read."

She led him back into the dark corridor of the ship and then out again into the shadowy stillness of the deck. In another minute they were standing in the afternoon sunlight, squinting in the sudden brilliance and looking back at the giant caravel that had held their interest for nearly three hours.

"Where shall we go now?" he said.

Pao pointed to an old fishing ship, a barquentine, that lay several hundred feet down toward The Southern Edge. As he followed her from ship to ship he suddenly remembered his second reason for the day's exploring. He nearly laughed at the incongruity of it. Perhaps there had been an outboard motor hidden in the corner of that ancient library or behind the baroque mirrors. He sighed. At this rate he would never find anything he needed for his journey back to the world. The Drift was an enchantress, distracting him with her exotic wares until thoughts of home and the outside world seemed only a useless dream.

The barquentine was not nearly so old or large as the caravel. The foremast was square-rigged, but the main and mizzenmasts held large gaff sails that suggested the lines of a more modern schooner type. It was perhaps two thirds the size of the caravel and flat across the deck, with no sheer toward the quarter-deck or forecastle. Inside they found large stores of rope and line equipment and barrels of tar. Many of the rooms were littered with skeletons, some of them fully dressed. Peter could see that Pao took them very much for granted, but for him they were incredibly grotesque, especially the ones in dresses. Some had apparently died on deck of battle wounds and had then been stacked on the gun quarters below. Pao explained that no skeletons were allowed on deck anywhere.

"It simply doesn't look very nice," she said quite seriously.

Before they returned to *The Mary Strattford,* Pao showed him the newest addition to The Drift, a thirty-foot motor launch.

"How long ago did it come here?" he asked.

"Last year," she said. "The ribs and beams are all made of metal." She nudged the bow with her foot and looked up and down the hull in a doubtful way.

Peter climbed down The Cliff to where the boat was moored in the swampy water. The cabin, he soon found, was empty. The food locker had been ransacked. But in the sleeping quarters below he found an outboard motor and five gallons of gasoline in a metal jerrycan. Later that night, he decided, he would carry them down to The Southern Edge where he had hidden his dinghy. The gasoline, of course, would not be enough. But if there were five gallons here, there was bound to be more somewhere on The Drift.

Perhaps in a week or so he would have everything he needed for his journey. He felt sure now that he could get back into the stream of The Equatorial Current before he ran out of food and water. His dinghy was fourteen feet long and there would be room for supplies and perhaps thirty or forty gallons of fuel, if he could find that much. And his aluminum boat was unsinkable. There were really a number of things in his favor. Perhaps he really would make it after all.

But when he looked at Pao walking ahead of him, humming to herself, he had to remind himself that he really did want to leave. The alternative, of course, was to spend the rest of his life on The Drift. Better to risk death at sea, he thought, than to stay here and do nothing. He thought of the elegantly dressed corpses on the English barquentine—the bones of men and women who had simply waited here for death. No. He would leave as quickly as possible. His whole life was back in The United States and there was nothing for him here except a pretty girl who was eighteen years his junior and the romantic illusions of a decaying world that he suspected would soon lose its charm. Perhaps when the time came he could convince Pao and Tabor to come with him. There were other boats and other sails . . .

"What are you thinking about?" said Pao. She was looking out across the water again.

"What am I thinking about? I'm not thinking about much of anything," he lied. "What makes you ask?"

"You're thinking about going home," she said.

"What makes you say that?"

"No one has to tell me things," she said. "You're thinking about going home."

For a moment she seemed very sad. And then suddenly she smiled and took his hand and together they ran from boat to boat, leaping from one hull to the next, making their way across the wrecks toward *The Mary Strattford*. It reminded him of rock jumping, something he had done one summer when he was a boy, the summer his parents had sent him to a boy's camp in Massachusetts. And for that one month, a strange oasis in the middle of a barren childhood, he spent his days swimming and making sailboats out of napkins and bits of wood, hopping from rock to rock, pretending he could walk on water. For those few days he had been a different person, a child his parents would not have recognized. And now with Pao he was that child again. Leaping mindlessly from place to place and listening to the sounds of the ocean. And now again he had forgotten about his dinghy and the long journey that loomed ahead.

The sun touched the horizon. It sent long sheets of fire across the water.

"It's been a lovely afternoon," said Peter. "I've enjoyed everything."

Pao smiled. "We never got to eat our seabread," she said.

"I never got hungry. There were so many things to see I never thought about eating. Besides, Raven says your seabread isn't much good."

"Raven doesn't know anything," she answered. "He's only seventeen."

"Ah, that explains it. Seventeen. The age of ignorance."

"I'm nearly nineteen, you know," said Pao. She looked up at him very earnestly and then suddenly blushed and turned away.

When they reached the hatchway of *The Mary Strattford,* he paused for a moment before descending. Something strange had touched the edge of his awareness. Something that for a moment he could not find or identify.

"What is it?" said Pao.

He listened.

"Did you hear something?" she asked.

In the distance children's bare feet skittered across the deck of some creaking ship. Beyond that, the sound of a rare wind somewhere across the water. And beyond that—yes, he could hear it quite clearly now—the odd rhythmical sounds that he had heard before only at night, the jangling music of some mad musician.

"Do you hear that sound, Pao?"

"It's only the children running around on *The Conquistador Blanco.* They play there in the afternoons."

"I don't mean that. It's something farther away. Like weird music."

She listened.

Suddenly he felt very stupid. "You know," he said, "I think I'm beginning to lose my mind."

But Pao was not listening to him. Her ears were sorting out the distant sounds of The Drift, the creaks and groans and murmurings of the ships and the water. Then she smiled. "I hear it now," she said.

"You do?"

"I'm surprised you didn't hear it earlier today. He's been playing off and on for most of the afternoon."

"Who's been playing?"

"The Hatchmaker," she said.

Chapter Seven

IMAGES

After dinner that evening, Peter, Tabor, and Pao stood together for a few moments on the deck of *The Mary Strattford,* watching the moon rise like a great silver wheel throwing off sparks of silver light everywhere in the rivers of water between the boats. Occasionally the splash of a fish or the whirring of a nightbird marked the silent progress of the evening. Once there was a trace of wind against his cheek.

"Good night," said Pao. She kissed him on the temple and then turned and made her way to the deck of the next boat. "I'll see you very early tomorrow," she called back out of the darkness.

"Good night, Pao," he said.

Tabor smiled in the moonlight. "After you finish with Reuben and Javitt tomorrow, why don't you come up to The Cliff," he said after the sound of Pao's footfalls had disappeared. "We're caulking up one of the old schooners. You might find it interesting, and you can help if you like."

"I'd like that very much," said Peter.

"Fine. Well, good night then."
"Good night, Tabor."

Later that evening when he was alone in his room, he tried to think about the problems that faced him. In a way, things were looking up. Tonight when everyone was asleep he would carry the motor and the gas he had found that day down to the dinghy. Tomorrow perhaps he would find a sail somewhere that would not be too large. That was the external problem, and he had a certain tentative confidence now that everything would go well. But the internal problem, something he had only really been aware of for a matter of hours, that was something else again. He realized now that it was becoming very difficult to assess his own feelings. Was it possible that at the last moment he would not want to leave, not want to return to his own world? Was it possible that The Drift would hold him here with some power, some force that he could not combat? The issues were not very clear in his mind. There was a power in the old ships, in the peaceful life, and in Pao. But could such things hold him here for a lifetime as Tabor seemed to think? He could not believe it. How could anyone willingly spend his life in a marine museum? And yet Tabor had never tried to escape, and Tabor seemed to be a strong and intelligent man. How could such a person be content here? Would whatever had happened to Tabor happen to him as well? Perhaps it was only that Tabor had been deeply wounded in some way. Perhaps for him The Drift was a kind of refuge from some weakness or some profound guilt. Perhaps. Perhaps not. Part of the problem in assessing anything here was that The Drift still seemed improbable, dreamlike. He could not quite take it seriously.

An hour later when the motor and the five gallons of gasoline were safe in the hull of the old schooner where his dinghy was hidden, he returned to his cabin and fell into bed. He was very tired. Slowly his thoughts began to blur, to tumble over each other into the darkness of sleep. Vaguely now he could hear the music of The Hatchmaker drifting in from his window. He could not tell if the sound were real or merely a dream woven from the night noises of the boats and the sound of his own heart beating. He took a deep breath and then sank more deeply, hovering for a moment at the brink of sleep. Perhaps when he awoke he would be in Connecticut and it would be morning and the sun would be streaming in through his own bedroom window.

The next morning when he opened his eyes there was a yellow flower on his dresser. Pao. So that was what she meant when she said she would see him very early. He dressed and made his way up to *The Mary Strattford*. He wanted to thank her for the flower, but she did not appear for breakfast, and after a moment's thought he decided not to ask after her. When he had finished eating, he followed Reuben and Javitt down to The Seafields.

His senses, he noticed, were much sharper now than they had been the previous day. He could see the prawns and crabs and strange sucking fish that clung to the weeds from several feet away. Once in a while he even caught a glimpse of a Sargasso Fish, the strange filigreed monsters that crawled on their fins across the swamps, blending in with their environment so well that even at a yard or two they were hard to recognize. How beautiful, he thought, and how ugly.

"Where do those fish come from?" he asked. "The ones that crawl over the weeds."

"Of the particulars of their origin I have no knowledge," said Reuben, smiling his toothless smile. "But this much I know. A thousand years ago they swam like any other fish. Then they came to The Drift, and lo, a metamorphosis. They grew strange with many fins and spiny quills of many hues. A veritable plethora of rainbow hues. A feast of color."

"But can they swim like other fish?"

"They swim, but poorly. I have never seen them swim. Perhaps they don't swim at all. No, perhaps not."

"Probably not at all," added Javitt.

Peter's distant vision was also improving. That afternoon while working with Tabor and two men from Bluewater on the hull of an old schooner, he noticed that he could make out the rigging and sheer of ships two hundred yards distant in a way he could not have done before. It was a matter of selection. What seemed to be a forest of spars and masts became less confused as soon as he decided at what distance he wished to see. He could then mentally erase everything except the things at that distance, in much the same way that, as a child, he had once erased the irrelevant shapes in a puzzle maze in order to see the rabbit or the elf that was hidden there.

And the more he looked, the more there was to see: cannon with brass rings strewn over the deck of an old French bugalette; a small corvette nearly cut in two by the falling mast of a giant clipper; lanterns of beautiful designs hanging from the sterncastle of a Spanish brig; a dozen boys in black arm bands attacking a three-masted topsail schooner which a dozen in green arm bands defended with wooden swords and wooden shields and seamen's curses; three dark-skinned dark-haired musicians from The Madrid clan playing weird modal tunes on a lute, a mandolin, and a guitar; a school of porpoise, a flight of seabirds, a hundred things upon which to feed his senses.

He turned his attention to the large metal pot in which boiled a terrible-smelling liquid that would be used, Tabor had told him, to seal the leaking bow. Tabor watched with a critical eye and occasionally gave directions in Spanish to one of the Madrids, a very tall and lanky young man who hunched his shoulders together and cackled like a witch as he stirred the mixture with a large paddle. Tabor and Peter both laughed.

"The witch of Endor," said Peter.

"Quite right," said Tabor. "And his magic is very strong."

"How do you make your magic?" Peter pointed to the metal pot.

"With a kind of grease we boil out from the intestines of sharks and an oil that comes from one of the weeds in The Seafields."

"It sounds repulsive enough," said Peter.

"Witches' brews are always repulsive," said Tabor. "Otherwise they would never work."

"Modern witches try not to offend," said Peter. "Why don't you mix something else with it so you don't stink up the whole ship?"

Again Tabor laughed. "Pao has been working on that for about a year now. Last month she tried some of Rose's flower oil. But then, she's a witch of a different kind."

"She certainly is."

Tabor looked down at him, one foot resting on the lip of the cauldron, the other on a stubby wooden platform from which he could watch the boiling liquid.

"You look better," he said.

"I look better? What do you mean, I look better?"

"I mean you look better. Your skin is browner and you look more relaxed. Expecially around your eyes."

"Just getting my sea legs," said Peter. Suddenly the image of the eerie and beautiful Sargasso Fish flashed through his mind. The waving spines. The fins moving slowly over the weeds. He trembled for a moment as if a sudden chill had fallen in the air.

"I mean I do feel much better," he said quickly.

At dinner Peter noticed again that Pao was missing.

"You're not likely to see her for the next few days," said Tabor. "She's going to be very busy."

"Oh really?" He could feel the concern for her absence well up within him, and he cursed himself for it. What could it possibly matter? In a few days he would be gone.

"She's rehearsing for The Dance of The Nine Islands. She told you about that as I remember."

"Yes. A festival of some kind. But won't she be eating with us this week?"

"No. She sort of goes into seclusion. She eats and sleeps with The Madrids, and they all rehearse things from morning till night. But it's only for about four days. Then you'll see the dance. And then," he said with emphasis, "you'll have seen everything."

Raven, who was sitting across the table from him, suddenly looked up and stared at him. "Yes," he said, in a curious flat tone of voice that suggested an extreme hostility, "you'll see everything in a couple of days. Then the grand tour will be over and you'll be no better than the rest of us."

Bright bent over him and poured soup into his wooden bowl. Lines of pain narrowed her eyes and lifted the corners of her mouth. "Raven," she whispered, "you mustn't speak so harshly. Sutherland wants to be one of us. He means you no harm."

But Raven drank his bowl of soup in silence and then walked out of the galley, his hands thrust in his pockets, with a sort of swaggering unconcern that betrayed, or so it seemed to Peter, a painful self-consciousness.

After the evening meal he hurried down to the old bilander in whose hull he had hidden his dinghy. Carefully he examined everything. A square fitting in the bottom of the boat and an iron loop on the edge of the middle seat were designed to hold a mast, but the one he had found that day was too tall and thick at the base for a fourteen-foot dinghy. Perhaps he could cut it down and plane it at one end to fit the iron ring. Then too, he would need lines to hold it fast, lines for the sail, and something to stabilize the dinghy in compensation for the height of the sail: some sort of keel or perhaps a pair of outriggers.

The motor presented no problem. It clamped nicely against the flat stern of the dinghy. But of course he would need more gasoline if the motor were to do any good.

For an hour he wandered around in the adjacent wrecks, looking for the materials he needed. Once he thought he saw a man staring at him from far away in The Outland, a black figure standing in the shadow of a sloop. He could not be sure. It was dark when he returned to his dinghy, and nearly morning before he gave up his work and returned to his own schooner halfway up toward Northside.

There was still a great deal left to do and he was very tired. Tomorrow would be another long day. It was just as well, he thought, that Pao was not around. And yet he regretted her absence more than he was relieved by it, and he wondered how much his heart was really in his work. He could see now why some might prefer to stay here on The Drift. It was easy to give up. To breathe quietly and dream life away in peace here on this strange island of derelicts where the past and the present and the future were all transfixed in silence and in the changing images of the clouds.

The Drift was a place of—he could not find the right word in his mind. Indulgence, perhaps. A romantic indulgence in mystery and in the bizarre. The ships themselves were mysteries, mute testaments of dead ages and lost journeys. And then too there was something final and mysterious about the strange forces that had brought them together in this improbable place, unknown to the rest of the world. It was as if its secret were a token of some larger secret, some final hinge that would reveal another dimension of experience that he had never imagined, except perhaps in dreams. And then of course there was Pao. She was another part of the mystery. Pao with her man's shirt tied above her waist, her loose sailcloth shorts, her easy grace as she walked from ship to ship, raising her arms to balance on the narrow catwalks and leaning to one side on the slanting decks of the ruined ships. Pao who spoke many languages and who seemed to know sometimes what he was thinking and who, most of all, was incredibly beautiful. Her beauty was in itself a mystery. Her lovely dark eyes and her long black hair were enough to make anyone look twice, but in other ways she was quite ordinary. Her nose was too short and her cheeks, a bit too narrow. Miriam had certainly been a better looking woman from almost every point of view. And yet Pao was more beautiful. It was a distinction that somehow eluded him.

Even Tabor was, in his own quiet way, a mystery, for something about the man gave him a curious, pleasant feeling he could not place in his catalogue of emotions. Something about his short-trimmed beard, which he stroked occasionally, his weathered, brown face, his tall rangy figure, his easy way of walking that made Peter think of Saturday morning and a pair of tennis shoes, his easy way of leaning against things and cocking his head a little to one side as if the wind were blowing or as if he were trying to catch a whisper of sound somewhere below him. There was a special, informal grace about him, not the grace of an athlete or a dancer, but the grace of a man who was sure of himself, or at least a man who was sure of something.

He took off his shoes and threw himself into bed. How strange, he thought, that his mind was so full of images and ideas when he was so very tired, so close to sleep. Back home at Harrington University nothing ever occurred to him after eight o'clock, and sleep had always come in the midst of silence, a silence in which he often spent the time counting the number of cars passing in the street by his house or listening to his own heartbeats.

Chapter Eight

SHADOWGAMES

After his chores the next morning, he slept most of the afternoon. When he awoke he had the distinct memory of someone having been in his room. He lifted his head and saw a piece of seabread and a hyacinth on the table next to his bed. Pao again. Her small, wet footprints were still visible on the wooden floor.

After rinsing his face with water and walking out onto the deck, his head still heavy with sleep, he saw one of the most amazing things he was ever to see on The Drift. The children below his boat were walking on the water.

In the shadow of the large schooner adjacent to his own, seven or eight children ran back and forth in the water, shouting and screeching at each other. Their feet made a hollow *shadush* when they moved. He recognized several of them as the black-arm-band pirates who had raided a schooner the day before.

"Hello, Sutherland!" It was David and Michael, Tabor's children.

"Hello," said Peter. "I see you're—you're walking on water."

"Yes!"

"Well, that's fine. Who taught you to do that?"

"We learn by ourselves. All the children can do it."

"I see." Then he remembered that Bright had said something about weedwalking. Walking on weeds.

"I bet you're wondering how we do this," said Michael.

"The question had crossed my mind," said Peter, who was trying to maintain some semblance of rationality. He was beginning to feel very foolish. There must be some simple explanation.

Then the whole group of them ran across the water in a cloud of noisy splashes that sent spindrift tumbling everywhere in the air around them. Now that the children were out of the shadows he could see that they wore enormous wooden shoes. And then, with what seemed to him to be amazing strength for children, David and Michael scrambled up a rope arm over arm and leaped over the rail of his schooner.

"Hi!" they said together.

"Hi, yourself. Let me see your shoes."

They smiled and offered their shoes for his examination, and together they burst into an involved explanation of how they worked. The shoes were thin circles of wood about two feet in diameter. They were warped into shallow cups and worn inverted so as to give a slight buoyancy from the cushion of air trapped inside. Two leather straps that fitted through narrow slips near the center of the shoes bound their feet.

"We can't just walk anywhere," said Michael. "It has to be where there's weeds. The weeds hold you up for a second until you can take another step."

"I see. Can anyone learn to weedwalk?"

"Just the children," answered Michael. "Grownups get too big. Pao told us you can't weedwalk after you're twelve or thirteen if you're a boy. She says sometimes that girls can until they're fifteen. Unless someone gets them pregnant," he added as an earnest and thoughtful qualification. " 'Course you can't do much of anything then. Not until you get over it."

"I see," said Peter.

" 'Course grownups can do a lot of things that children can't do," said David. "Pao says it's not so bad when you can't weedwalk any more. She says then it gets more fun to read and sing and work on the dances for the festivals and stuff." Peter could see that for the sake of politeness the boy was trying to make the adult world sound attractive, or at least palatable, but that his heart was not in it.

"Pao says that even when you get old, there are things to do, like The Long Journey and things like that," said David.

"What's The Long Journey?"

"It's the other end of shadowgames," said Michael, who could not let his brother explain anything without his assistance. "It's where The Elders from all the clans go and sit together in circles and close their eyes and let their minds float away on silver cords."

"It's like sailing away to The Islands," said David. "Rose goes on The Long Journey every few days now. S'about all she does, now that she's got so old," he said doubtfully.

Peter smiled in a hopeless way, listening to the words of the two boys. "I see," he said.

Then one of the boys from the weedwalking group called them from somewhere around the side of the next boat.

"Shadowgames," said Michael. "Today it's our turn and we can play in English. I never get as many ideas in Spanish or French as I do in German and English. Do you know why that is, Sutherland?"

"I haven't the slightest," said Peter.

"Me neither," said Michael. He pushed his long, blond, wet hair out of his eyes. "The Madrids do everything different. They even play shadowgames underwater sometimes. It's different that way cause everything keeps moving and the forms don't stay the same. Pao says the ocean is like a crystal glass and that playing shadowgames underwater is like seeing into someone's mind."

"That's very interesting," said Peter, who was still trying to mask his confusion as best he could.

"Pao can do all sorts of things," said David. There was a tone of reverence in his voice. "She knows what the weather is going to be and she knows when new boats are coming to The Drift. The day before you came here she told Tabor—he's our father—that someone was coming. And she knows what people think. She says it all comes out of shadowgames. Is that true, Sutherland?"

"David, I just don't know. I don't even know what a shadowgame is."

"Gosh!" said Michael.

"It's cause he's from land," said David. "They do things different on land. You mustn't ask him so many questions," he added in a fierce, embarrassed whisper.

"But what did you do when you were little if you didn't play shadowgames or weedwalk?" persisted Michael, who was paying no attention to his brother.

Peter smiled. "I don't remember what I did when I was a child," he said. "I don't think I did much of anything."

It seemed that neither of them had heard or understood his answer. "We're going to play for a while by *The Mary Strattford* before dinner," said Michael. "C'm'on with us. You can follow over the boats." And in another minute they were sloshing off across the water to find their playmates.

Peter stared after them, wondering vaguely if they were real children. Judging by the size of them, they couldn't possibly be more than ten or eleven years old. How did they manage to speak so well and know so much at that age? Within him he felt the stirrings of his academic education, his position in the outside world as a teacher. What theory of child development, he wondered, would account for them? Their many languages, their inventions and their strange games? How was it that they seemed so advanced for their age, when they were left so much to themselves, with so little supervision? But perhaps the question was absurd. Dimly, he suspected that it betrayed him as a hopeless and ineffectual pedant. In his heart he suspected that most of the important things in life were not formally learned in schools; they were things one learned for oneself somewhere beyond classrooms and books.

He, of course, had never enjoyed teaching. And in a perverse way he had always been defensive about his own formal education and about education in general because, after high hopes, it seemed to have done so little for him as a student and as a teacher. He suspected that teaching was for those who felt deeply about others, and he knew now that he had never really cared much for anyone; he had only wanted others to care for him. He had wanted to gain friendship without ever giving it. Sometimes he had even wondered if in his finest moments he were really capable of love, of friendship, of compassion or sympathy. He could not help but feel now that in some ways Tabor's children were emotionally and intuitively more mature than he. It was a disturbing thought. God, how they made him want to throw away his whole life, to burn it or feed it to the sharks. How much clearer, how much more like water and wind he might have been if only, if only he had somehow lived his life in a different way, if he had only lived more freely, more openly, closer to himself and closer to other people.

Slowly he made his way to the deck of *The Mary Strattford*. It was nearly six by his watch, which he had set that morning by the sun. Then Bright appeared from out of the hatchway to call David and Michael.

"Dinner in just a few minutes!" she was saying. "When the sun touches the water you've got to come in!"

"All right," they said. "We're just going to play one more form. We'll be up soon as we finish."

The children sat like Indians in a circle of five on the deck of an English brig that lay one boat west of *The Mary Strattford*. When they saw Peter, Michael stood up and called out to him through cupped hands.

"Sutherland! Come play with us! We'll teach you shadowgames!"

"Shhhh," said David in a loud, furtive whisper. "Maybe he doesn't want to play."

"Sure he does. Don't you, Sutherland?"

"I don't know," said Peter. "It sounds too hard to learn in just a few minutes."

"We can teach you in a second!" said Michael.

"It doesn't take too long once you get the hang of it," said David. He looked up at him shyly.

Peter had never played with children, and he felt awkward and embarrassed. "Well," he said, "I suppose I could try."

When he had entered into the circle and squatted among them, Michael introduced him to the two dark-skinned, bright-smiling Madrid boys, and to a frail little girl with almond eyes whom the others called Blanca. Then he began to explain the game.

"It's done in five parts," he said. "First, someone thinks up a form. A form is a picture of something in your head, only it has to be something near you that everyone can look at. Then everyone thinks together—that's why we sit in a circle, so we can sort of make a circle with our minds. The second part is when someone has to answer the form with The First Image. That's something the form is like when you think about it inside your head. The third part is when someone else thinks up The Second Image. Pao calls that a mephador."

"A metaphor," said his brother.

"A metaphor," said Michael without blinking. "Then the fourth part is when the next in the circle has to bring the two images of the form together to make a new form by finding a Joinword. Then the last part is when the last one in the circle gives a clue to a story using the two images and The Joinword, and then everyone tries to guess the story. See how we play?"

"I don't think so," said Peter.

"No one could understand, the way Michael explains things," said David. "Let's just play. Then we can *show* you how it goes."

"Okay," said Michael, whose spirits apparently could not be dampened by any insult, and who still seemed peculiarly excited by the presence of an adult. "I'll start."

He begun to look about him in a slow, casual way. "Let's do the sails," he said finally. "My first form is the big sail on *The Mary Strattford*."

The second boy in the circle looked at the sail for a moment and then said, "The sail is like a bird."

A few moments later the third boy in the circle said, "The sail is like a ghost. It moves by an invisible power the way ghosts do. And besides, ghosts sometimes dress up in sails."

"You mean sheets," said David.

"Blanca, give us a Joinword," said Michael.

The little girl stared hard at the sail and her eyes narrowed. Her small bony shoulders hunched together, and she brought her knees up under her chin. It seemed that her whole body was intent and trembling upon the edge of that scrutiny. "A pre'storic bird," she said at last.

"That's cause 'bird' and 'ghost' are joined by 'pre'storic bird,'" whispered Michael. "Cause a ghost bird might be one that used to be but isn't any more except when you think of it. So the thought of it is like a ghost. D'you see?"

"Michael always has to explain everything too

much," said David. "It's much better if you don't explain."

"Let's go on," said Michael, ignoring his brother's objections. "David, it's your turn to make a story."

"It's a tale of time," said David.

"It's a tale of time," repeated Michael. "Now it's anyone's turn. Who can guess David's story?"

"I can see that one," said Blanca. The little girl closed her eyes and waved her hands in the air in great excitement. "There's a bird who flies through time instead of through the air. One day he comes to Now. But in Now he's a ghost because he doesn't really live now—he lives a million billion years ago cause he's a pre'storic bird. So now he rises like a ghost out of the water or maybe the sea of time and changes the way ships go by blowing on the sails."

"I see a sailor who finds a golden bird that takes him through time," said one of the Madrid boys.

"Blanca wins," said David. "My story was about a bird who flies through time and turns into a ghost who blows ships off their courses."

"Ships in different centuries all blown off course by the same bird," said Blanca. Her eyes were shining. "Oooh!" she said. "That's a good story! Maybe Ramirez can write a song for it!"

"Do you know Ramirez?" said Michael, looking up at Peter.

"I don't think so."

"He's The Bluewater Bard!" The boy grinned broadly, and all the children laughed. "Quick!" he said. "While we're going so good let's do another form!"

"There's no time," said David. "We have to go in for dinner now. Maybe—maybe Sutherland could come out with us after dinner. I mean if you're not busy."

" 'Course he's not busy," said Michael. "No one works after dinner. Not even Tabor."

As they walked over to *The Mary Strattford* the Madrid boys and Blanca waved good-bye, and when they were out of sight Michael reviewed the game once again:

"So if the form was sails again someone might say 'bow,' cause a bow shoots an arrow through the air like a sail makes a ship shoot through the water. And then someone else could say 'fire,' cause brown sails look like fire when the sun sets." He pointed to the brown sails of *The Mary Strattford* as the setting sun filled them with a flaming orange. "And then someone could make a Joinword by saying 'the sun sinking below the horizon,' cause it looks like a fiery bow. And then someone would make up a story about the sun using the idea of a bow made of fire."

"I see," said Peter.

"It sounds so awfully hard when you explain," said David. "Pao says that when you get real good at metaphors you get real good at feeling people with your mind and then pretty soon you don't have to talk so much if you don't want to."

"That's hard to believe," said Peter.

"It's hard to understand, but it's not hard to believe," said Michael, who tugged at Peter's sleeve in order to draw his attention away from his brother. "Believing is easy. I can believe anything!" he said proudly.

Chapter Nine

ROSE

At dinner he said very little. Pao was still missing, and that disturbed him. How long, he wondered, before he would see her again? Rose, the old woman, stared at him for minutes at a time during the meal. He felt uncomfortable in her presence. He was vaguely depressed.

While the others discussed ways of raising a schooner that had nearly sunk the previous night and Bright talked of a new vegetable The Vague Noires had discovered growing near The Bridge, Peter watched Tabor's children and wondered about the games they played. He understood now that shadowgames were games of the imagination that involved making up metaphors and stories. That much was obvious. But they also seemed to be guessing games that suggested the beginning of a kind of psychic power. And he had the impression from what the children had said that Pao and Tabor had some interest in these games and had helped teach the children how to play them. He suspected that shadowgames were a kind of education, a preparation for living on The Drift as an adult. It was part of a continuum, as Michael had suggested, that ended in something called The Long Journey. It all suggested a surrender to the inward power of things, whatever that might be, and a rejection of the outward power, the power of the world beyond The Drift, whatever that might be. It made him think of Pao and the silver whistle; it made him think of the whistle's hollow sound and the dark treasures that lay hidden in the third level of the old caravel. It was as if that day on the ancient ship they had been playing a kind of shadowgame.

When the meal was over, he and Tabor stayed behind at the table to talk, while Bright cleared the dishes. She said nothing at first, but her quick eyes often touched them, and she smiled faintly whenever Tabor spoke.

"Tabor, do you understand the games your children play?" Peter was saying.

"Pretty well. Why?"

"I'm not quite sure why they get so interested in them. Why do they love metaphors, for instance?"

"Metaphors have a great power with children. They show correspondences between things. Not the correspondence of logic or science, but the correspondence of feeling and sense. Children find that very mysterious and wonderful."

"I've never noticed that," said Peter.

"Of course you have," said Tabor. "Children see a lion's head or a castle in clouds and spirits in the waves and soldiers in a row of clothespins. They're forever pretending something is really something else. I think it may have to do with the way they learn words. Any new word is like a metaphor for a child because it brings so many things together for him under a single name. It has a sort of magic fluidity; words are not just counters for things. Beyond The Drift children lose that fluidity when they grow up; here we try to preserve it." He smiled. "I suppose that's something I learned indirectly from Pao," he said. "I'm supposed to be her teacher, but sometimes I think I learn more from her than she does from me."

Peter felt somehow that he had lost the thread of the conversation. "So in shadowgames the children learn to see relationships," he said lamely.

"Life is a series of metaphors," said Tabor. "A series of correspondences. The better you are at metaphors, the more you can bring into your circle of feeling and understanding. And the children begin to learn this when they play shadowgames. They come closer to the world, and they come closer to each other."

Bright, who had been listening to every word, was standing in the corner of the room washing plates in a wooden basin. "Pao told me about that once," she said timidly, half turning around from her work. "She said that metaphors are a way of feeling, a way of looking at everything that touches your life. She says that with them you can feel the places where things meet if you don't let the words put everything in different boxes."

She took off her apron and folded it and laid it carefully across her scrubbing board. "I think that to feel where things meet is what love means. Do you think that's true?"

Tabor looked up at her with great pleasure and surprise. "I think so," he said.

Peter smiled. "Well, from now on I'm going to confine myself to simple questions. Questions like, what's the name of the funny-looking orange vegetable we had for dinner tonight?"

Bright laughed. "That's not such a simple question either," she said. "It's the new one I was talking about that The Vague Noires found. Weren't you listening? Nobody knows where it came from and it doesn't have a name."

After dinner he stood for a few moments on the deck of *The Mary Strattford*, thinking about the tools and ropes and the new sail he had found near Driftsend and the work that lay ahead of him that evening. From across the deck came the creak of a rocking chair where Rose sat and stared at the brilliant orange clouds in the west, the last signs of the setting sun. After a while the silence between them became, for Peter, uncomfortable. And yet he did not walk away. It was strange, he thought, not to walk away. That was what he had always done, but now he could not. He watched the old lady and the sunset and listened to the sound of her rocking chair.

"It's a lovely sunset," he offered.

She made no answer.

"I suppose you've been here for many years," he said, trying again after a moment or two.

The old woman's head turned slowly, like an owl's to look at him. "I was here on The Eighth Day of Creation," she said. "That was when God made The Drift."

"I see."

"That must have been some time ago," she added in a more conversational tone. "But you see, my husband and I were only married a month ago and were on our honeymoon when we came here. It was just after The Great War. He was a captain in the Eighty-seventh Fusiliers. But he did not survive the wreck. One of the spars fell on him and broke his neck."

"I'm sorry," said Peter.

"He was a very passionate man. We would have had many children." Her eyes turned back to the orange clouds at the horizon. A faint, sudden smile cracked the corner of her mouth.

Peter watched the old woman curiously. "I understand you were Pao's teacher before Tabor," he said.

"Pao? Pay your debts and owe nothing." The old woman burst into cackling laughter. It reminded him of glass breaking.

"Pao," she said again. "Paolozzi. Yes of course I was her teacher. But when was that?"

"I don't know," said Peter. "I haven't been on The Drift very long."

At this she turned very quickly toward him as if he had startled her. An odd light grew in her eyes. "Are you from France then? Do you have a message for me from Benjamin? He said he would come back when the war was over and we would be married. He's a captain in the Eighty-seventh Fusiliers."

"I'm afraid I don't know him. But I'm sure you'll hear something very soon," said Peter quickly.

Then the light in her eyes went dead. "No," she said. "He's gone now. He didn't survive the wreck. One of the spars fell on him and broke his neck."

"I'm sorry to hear that."

"Don't be sorry. That was nearly sixty years ago. I've lived a long time without him, but I've never forgotten." And then for a while there was another silence between them.

Peter watched the old woman as she sat and rocked back and forth. She sat very erect in her chair like an old general watching troops pass in review. She wore a plain gray dress. Her arms were incredibly thin and withered, and the veins and tendons in her hands showed clearly through her yellowish, transparent skin.

"Where are you from?" she said, quite suddenly.

"I'm from Connecticut."

She was silent again for a moment. "Is that one of The Islands?" she queried.

"It's part of The United States."

"It must be out there somewhere," she said, pointing to the horizon. "All the islands and all the boats come from out there. People are born on ships that are bound to be wrecked. When the storm comes and the waves swamp the decks, some men drown and some manage to swim to the islands and some come here. There's nowhere else. Men make the ships and all the ships are wrecked in storms.

"That's why no one ever leaves The Drift," she said. "Everyone here is afraid of sails." Again she burst into her frightening laughter. "Perhaps it's better this way.

Did you ever look at the sea hyacinths around the ships?"

"Yes, I've noticed them."

"Strange how they look like Lotus," she said. "Very strange." Angain she laughed.

"Lotus?"

"This is The Land of The Lotus and you may or may not be Odysseus. I suspect that you are."

"My name is Peter Sutherland."

"I know what your name is, stupid boy. When I say you are Odysseus I don't mean your name is Odysseus. Are there flowers where you come from?"

"Flowers?"

"Come now, you must know what flowers are. Even Odysseus knows what flowers are. Roses, Gardenias, Lupine, Orchids—"

"Yes," said Peter, who was beginning to feel very awkward again, "there are flowers in Connecticut."

"Here there are flowers in the mind where you cannot see them fade. Eventually they may fade, but you cannot see them fade."

"There are flowers in the water by The Cliff," he offered.

"I mean the flowers that curl back into seeds," she said. "Not real flowers. Not that kind of real."

"Real flowers are the only kind I know."

"I daresay. Yes. You must be Odysseus." Again she laughed. "But what were you saying about Pao? She was a student of mine, you know. I gave her all my gifts. All my poor flowers."

"That was—that was certainly very nice of you," said Peter.

Rose looked at him with a lidless serpentine stare that withered him with its sudden contempt. "My but you are a stupid boy," she said. "But that's of no importance." She rose from her rocking chair and walked like a man, very lean and erect, toward the plank that led to the next ship. Suddenly she stopped and turned to look at him again.

"And when are you leaving?" she said.

"Leaving?"

"You're leaving The Drift. When are you planning to go?"

He was stunned. "I thought no one left The Drift," he managed to say.

She watched him but she did not answer.

"They would all stop me if I tried to leave," he said.

Again she made no reply.

"Does everyone know?" he said finally.

"Everyone knows you want to leave, but only Pao and I know you are leaving. Pao and I have a gift together. And all the children will have the gift. When you get back to the mainland, tell my husband where I am. Tell him I've been waiting all these years."

As she was about to leave, she turned back once more. A shadow crossed her face. "I keep forgetting," she said with the air of someone who has forgotten a ball of yarn. "He's dead, isn't he? Yes. Dead nearly sixty years."

Chapter Ten

THE SCARFACED MAN

The mornings settled into an easy routine. The work was pleasant and simple in a way that work had never been for him before. On his third morning in The Seafields, schools of jellyfish, drifting in from the outer reaches of The Sargasso Sea, began to invade the bands of clear water between the vegetation, and Reuben took great delight in pointing out the different varieties and colors. Peter had never seen jellyfish before, and he was fascinated by their subtle pastel hues and the way they floated at different levels, some just below the surface, others as much as two or three feet underwater, where they took on the ghostly shimmer of an illusion. Once he tried to lift one out of the water with sticks, but just as it reached the surface it broke into pieces and drifted away.

"Invariably they will do that," said Reuben. "It is their only way of escape."

"They have no other way," said Javitt.

Each time he returned from The Seafields he went a different way, hoping eventually to explore all of The

Drift, and each day he saw things he had not seen before: large grayish plants with a texture like velvet that grew in clumps down near The Outland; a classical figurehead on the prow of an ancient ship; a swarm of sundark children playing an elaborate game on a large blue board with pieces of colored wood. But on his third day's return from The Seafields he heard a terrible sawing sound somewhere nearby. He thought of the story that Pao had told him, David and Michael's tale of The Hatchmaker sawing hatches in the bottoms of boats which then sank during the night.

Suddenly he came upon the bow of a nineteenth-century schooner that loomed thirty feet above the sloop he was crossing. A young boy in a black shirt hung over the narrow ribbon of water below the schooner, one hand clinging to the rail, the other sawing away at the bowsprit with a large hacksaw. It was Raven.

"Hello," said Peter.

The boy turned suddenly, almost losing his narrow footing at the edge of the bow. For a moment Peter had the impression that he would leap down upon him like a giant bird swooping down to seize a squirrel. The boy's eyes glittered, but he did not speak.

"What are you doing?" said Peter.

"I'm sawing off the bowsprit," said Raven.

"I see. Any particular reason?"

"I want to see it crash into the water."

"What will that accomplish?" said Peter.

"Nothing," said Raven. "That's the whole point. My purpose is not to accomplish anything." He gave Peter an acid smile.

Peter smiled back. It was a lovely day and nothing, he promised himself, would dim his spirits. Not even Raven. "What will you not accomplish after you don't accomplish anything by sawing off the bowsprit?" he asked.

"I'll saw the whole goddamn boat in half," said Raven.

"Won't anyone mind?"

"This is my boat," said Raven. "Nobody can stop me from doing anything I want on my boat. Even Tabor said so."

"So this is your life's work?" said Peter.

"Not really. In a year or so I'll probably be an Outlander. They fight and steal women and raid The Southern Edge for supplies and sail around The Drift in rowboats and rafts. It doesn't make a lot of sense, but it's better than fooling around here making up songs and dances and staring at the moon."

For a moment they stared at each other, Peter looking up from the sloop, Raven hanging above him from the rail of the schooner. He had never really seen Raven before in the clear light of day, except at a distance. He was not an ugly boy, but something about his appearance was unsettling. His hair receded slightly above his temples to reveal a broad and prominent forehead, but his face was dominated by the long shock of black hair that fell down over one eye. His long narrow nose pointed to lips that were thin and bloodless. His small chin gave his head a triangular look, like the joker in a deck of cards.

Raven laid the saw on the deck, shifted his weight, and brushed the hair out of his eye. He was slender and very pale, but when he moved there was a sureness about him, an agility that was not frail or effeminate, but wolfish and careful.

"Haven't you got business somewhere?" he said.

"I was just going to lunch," said Peter. "Are you coming?"

"Not with you, Sutherland." He picked up his saw again and went back to work. Peter watched for a moment and then began his journey back to *The Mary Strattford*. A few seconds later he heard a loud crack and then a splash. The bowsprit had fallen into the water.

Raven laughed, and his laughter was high and brittle.

For a moment Peter remembered the small man with the knife, the Outlander who had tried to come up behind him.

"With a bomb I could do better," Raven shouted.

That afternoon, standing on the deck of his own ship, Peter caught a quick glimpse of Pao running across The Northside Cliff about twenty boats above him.

"Pao!"

She smiled and waved at him, but did not answer.

The evening of his third day at The Seafields he spent in the hull of the old bilander where his aluminum dinghy was hidden. He had borrowed a heavy bone needle and some thread from Bright, and he worked, again late into the night, at cutting a large sail down to a reasonable size and stitching the edges. Finally the lamp burned low and he was forced to give up for the evening. As he turned to leave the ship, he saw a face and broad shoulders framed in the hatchway above him. The face smiled in the dim lamplight. It was horribly discolored. It belonged to the Outlander he had knocked into the water four days earlier.

Footsteps sounded on the deck above him. Apparently the scarfaced man was not alone. For a moment Peter was frozen with terror. The Outlander's smile held him like a rabbit in the eyes of a wolf. When the man finally began to move down the stairs, Peter seized a claw hammer he had found in the motor launch and a large paddle he had confiscated from a schooner nearby. The Outlander stopped. He tossed his gaff hook from hand to hand and cocked his head to one side. Then two more heads appeared in the black hatchway above him.

He knew that if the first man got to the bottom of the stairs it would be the end of him. There would be no way then of keeping the rest of them from coming down, and he would have to fight three armed men in the cramped darkness of the hull. He glanced at his lamp. It was burning very low now. He would have to do something quickly.

Frantically he looked around the interior of the ship. The whole hull was a single open space meant simply for storage and sleeping. There was nowhere to hide and no other way out. There were other hatchways, but the stairs leading up to them had all rotted away. Suddenly he remembered the dinghy and the outboard motor. Perhaps—just perhaps—he could frighten them. It would depend on whether or not they had ever heard the sound of a motor.

He hurried back to the dinghy, which lay near the pointed end of the hull, and cried, "Diablo! Diablo!"—it was one of the seven or eight words he knew in Spanish—and pulled the cord to start the motor. It coughed once.

"Diablo! Diablo!" he shrieked, waving his hands in the air. He felt very silly, but he also felt very frightened.

All three men advanced to the bottom of the stairs as soon as they saw him retreat. But now they hesitated. The scarfaced man tried to urge the other two on, but they would not move. They stared at the motor hidden under the black tarpaulin.

"Diablo!" said Peter. He jerked the cord for the fourth time. Finally, under the urging of their leader, the two men began to move toward the dinghy, but just at that moment the motor sputtered to life. Peter pushed the throttle to the open position and then began jabbering at it and pointing to the three intruders. The noise in the narrow hull of the boat was deafening. The three men stared at the object still hidden under the black canvas, and their eyes grew wide with terror. In a second they had disappeared, the clatter of their footsteps sounding on the stairway and then against the wooden deck above him, everyone except the scarfaced man, who stood his ground and looked curiously and without fear at Peter. Then he smiled and nodded his head.

"Motor," he said finally. He poked at the motor with his hook. Then he set the hook under the edge of the tarpaulin and lifted it off. "Motor," he said again. "For to go away." Then he looked up and Peter saw his eye staring at him in the semi-darkness. Again the man shifted the hook from one hand to the other, and then suddenly he turned and walked up the wooden stairs that led to the deck.

Peter hesitated for a moment and then decided to follow him. On deck he saw the Outlanders scurrying in different directions over the walkways and boats that led back across the edge of their own world. One of them tripped over something and fell with a shriek into the water. The scarfaced man walked slowly from boat to boat. Once he looked back. Then he too disappeared into the darkness of The Outland.

When they were gone, Peter turned to look at the moonlight and the outline of ships against the night sky. All would have been peaceful and lovely again had it not been for the weird and anachronous grinding of the outboard motor that murdered the romantic silence. It was like a demon from another world.

A light went on somewhere near Northside. And then another. Quickly he ran down into the hull of the bilander and shut off the motor. When he returned to the deck he could hear voices, people calling and whispering and walking about in the dark.

Then the moon slipped behind a cloud and he saw nothing but four or five glimmerings of light from the yellow oil lamps. He knelt down and put his arms around his knees, hoping that no one would see him or come to investigate. Crouching there in the darkness he felt very much alone. He thought of Pao, whom he had not seen for several days except at a distance, and then only for a brief moment.

* * *

The next morning things went rather badly. No one spoke to him at breakfast, and later in The Seafields, Reuben and Javitt worked silently and avoided his glances. When he returned to *The Mary Strattford* for lunch, he took a longer way along The Southern Edge, and he saw Tabor and Raven inspecting the old wreck in which his dinghy was hidden. Raven had just come up from the hold and seemed very excited. He shouted something at Tabor, but Peter was too far away to hear what he was saying.

Perhaps now he would incur the resentment of everyone on The Drift. People here were very upset, he had gathered, by anything that broke with tradition or with routine. It was in some odd way a threat to all of them that he wished to leave and was taking steps toward doing so. He could not quite understand it. It was as if life here were only a gossamer fabric, easily torn, and the outside world a harsh and destructive force to be avoided at all cost. What was it that Rose had said? Something about how all the boats in the world are wrecked and how everyone on The Drift is afraid of sails. He remembered the dead, bitter certainty in her voice. It was something she seemed to understand very clearly, even in senility. Had she meant that The Drift was only a dream, a place for fearful people to avoid the storms of life? And yet that very morning it had seemed very real; his previous life at the university had been the dream, an improbable fantasy obliterated by the spell of the ancient ships and the windless isolation of the moment.

Now he could see *The Mary Strattford* eight boats ahead of him. Bright and Rose were sitting on the deck watching him approach. For a moment he considered skipping lunch and going directly to his own boat. He had a feeling that there would be a scene over his dinghy. It would be worth skipping a meal to avoid it.

The worst thing, he realized, was that his plan was now public knowledge. Perhaps someone would take measures to stop him. And of course the Outlanders would be back. The darkness, the element of surprise, and the black tarpaulin had worked temporarily to his advantage. But they had all seen the boat and they would soon overcome their fear of The Devil. He shook his head in disgust. Everything had gone well until last night. In a way he had even learned to enjoy his temporary exile on The Drift. Now everything would be different, and there was no telling what he might find when he went back into the hull of the old bilander. Perhaps they would hack everything to pieces. Then he would have to start all over, and it would be weeks before he could again find ways, and means of leaving The Sargasso Sea.

Then he remembered that the scarfaced man had not seemed at all frightened by the motor, and in an odd way he found that reassuring. He had seemed less hostile somehow, not the same man he had knocked into the water six days before. He had actually smiled, but not with that sadistic leer Peter remembered from his battle in The Outland. He realized now that he did not understand The Outlanders and could not really predict what they would do. He hunched his shoulders and put his hands in his pockets and gave up any further attempts at meditation. Perhaps, he thought, they would just leave him alone.

At lunch Bright talked incessantly of food and sewing and a new shadowgame the children had invented, but no one else spoke. Finally when the meal was nearly over, Raven looked up from his plate and stared at Peter in a deliberate, hostile way, and smiled.

"Tabor and I saw your boat and your motor today," he said. "What do you plan to do with them?" It was a direct challenge. Everyone stopped eating and looked up at him, waiting for his answer.

"Never mind that," said Bright quickly. "Wait until he sees Pao in The Dance of The Nine Islands. Two days from now he won't be interested in motors anymore."

She smiled with a kind of hesitant expectancy when everyone turned to look at her. Then Tabor laughed.

"She's right," he said. "Pao has a much better shape than an outboard motor."

Then they all began to laugh. Reuben laughed hardest of all; huge tears of mirth rolled down his cheeks. It seemed to Peter that they were tears of relief and happiness, and he did not understand how such a simple remark could change everything.

"Won't be interested in motors anymore," said Reuben, who seemed now on the verge of strangulation. His face was beet red and he quivered silently.

"No interest in motors," agreed Javitt, who seemed a little confused by all the laughter. Then he scratched his stubbly chin and thought for a moment, and then he jabbed Peter on the shoulder to attract his attention.

"I saw a motor on a boat once about a year ago," he said. It was only the second time Peter had ever heard him speak except to echo Reuben. "Do they really help the sails?" he asked. "Or are they just for making scary noises?"

Chapter Eleven

DRIFTSEND

That afternoon the sky was cloudless, like a blue mirror. It made him think of the days he had spent sailing, the days before his ship sank and he had drifted into The Sargasso Sea. But after an hour or two a light wind blew across the water, and for Peter it was a mild shock. A dead calm had engulfed The Drift ever since he had arrived, except for an hour or so the day he and Pao had gone exploring. And now the atmosphere had changed. It was as if the wind, blowing from all the latitudes of the earth, brought news of the world beyond and broke the inward stillness of things, the timeless sleep that settled everywhere like dust on the water and on the old ships.

He felt very restless. Pao had virtually disappeared now for four days, and in spite of all there was to do and see he was at loose ends without her and found her image and her voice in his mind while he ate, before he slept, and during his walks to and from The Seafields. There were things everywhere to remind him of her: the shirt he wore, the seabread and the flowers on his dresser—and the conversations of the children were filled with references to her. It seemed that she had left her mark everywhere, most of all upon him. Tomorrow he would see her again; tomorrow was the day of the festival for which she had been preparing in secret. But today he felt restless and alone. Today the sky was a mask; the glittering water, a vague mystery; and beyond the point of Driftsend two Outlanders in long beards were sailing in a wide circle around The Drift on a raft rigged with a large gaff sail. He could hear their voices, blurred echoes across the water. He watched the red fishing bobbins trailing in their wake. Suddenly he longed to be with them.

He was reluctant now to go back to his dinghy during the daytime. There was no point in creating friction. His position, he felt, was awkward enough as it stood. There were a number of other things that needed doing. First, he might spend some more time looking for gasoline. He had explored all of the small motor launches two days before and had found nothing. His best chance now would be in searching the clipper ships, some of which, he suspected, carried auxiliary engines. At least that would give him something to do. And besides, he had longed to explore the clipper ships at Driftsend, the forbidden zone at the east end of The Drift where The Hatchmaker played his music. The sound of that playing haunted him even in the long afternoons when all was silent save for the merest gauze of wind and the cry of birds. The Hatchmaker had become a kind of focal point in his mind for many things. He suspected in some intuitive way that The Hatchmaker was the key to his ambivalence, his inability to make up his mind about the meaning or purpose of The Drift.

Meaning and purpose. Somehow the words seemed absurd. Peter had always been fond of categorical distinctions, his ability to put things in different boxes. But The Drift was baffling, a fantasy world that denied categories. It left him not with categories of meaning, but only with impressions, notions of how to feel his way through a kind of labyrinth. He smiled, thinking how difficult it was for a structured, self-conscious person like himself to live in a world without precedents. And so he was thrown back on intuition, and this, he thought, was the essence of dangerous living. He did not know why he wanted to explore the clipper ships, but there it was: an urge that he knew, somehow, would clarify this vague impression that he could not put into words, this sense of mystery, this feeling that the burnished sky hovering in the halcyon calm above The Sargasso Sea was really the eye of some mystic vision, the calm center of a maelstrom, the epiphany of some inward state of being.

It was two o'clock when he stood on the deck of an old scow and looked across to the three clipper ships at Driftsend. The nearest one, listing slightly to starboard, faced north and south, while the other two, resting their sterns against the starboard side of the first, fell together into a kind of arrow pointing east. All three were very different from the older boats he had explored with Pao. They were lower, more streamlined, and their rigging was of heavy wire instead of rope. He noticed that no one had taken any of the sails for clothing and that the deck ropes were still coiled near the masts where the crews had left them. Apparently no one had boarded any of them for a long time. For how long, he wondered, had these ships been forbidden in the mythology of The Drift?

He hesitated for a long moment before boarding the first ship. Three of its sails were partly unfurled, and they billowed now in the waning wind. The ship heaved with the billowing, like a sleeping giant dreaming of a journey.

The clipper seemed in good condition from the outside, except for one of the masts that had collapsed across the scow he was standing on. Years ago someone had planed it flat to form a walkway. Slowly he moved across, careful not to look down until the mast broadened at the base, and then leaped to the deck of the first ship at Driftsend.

For a moment he stood in that new silence, not knowing where to go. The boards creaked under him. He stood in the shadowy yellow light of a half-furled sail, listening to the faint wind and to the blurred shouts of children and women who seemed a thousand miles away. It was like the feeling he had had on board the old caravel that he and Pao had explored. He regretted now that she was not with him. Strange, he thought, how the atmosphere of the old boats affected him. It was as if they were haunted.

Slowly he walked across the deck. He noticed that many of the lines were still intact, although they had rusted very badly. Occasionally he would pull one to see the point of a sail begin to unfurl, or to hear a wooden spar groan under the sudden weight.

Then on the poop deck he saw something that almost made him cry out in delight: a large screw propeller with two blades missing and a long section of the drive shaft. So there *was* an auxiliary engine, and that meant gasoline. He thought for a moment he could smell it somewhere in the depths of the ship.

The nearest hatch revealed a wide stairway that led down to a wooden landing, then doubled back upon itself into the darkness of a long wooden corridor. He lit a match. The tilting corridor led down further toward midships. There, probably, would be the galley and the sailors' bunks. The other way led back to a series of rooms that looked like officers' quarters.

He lit another match, his last, and walked slowly along the passageway, sometimes balancing himself on the slanted floor by holding one hand against the wall. Slowly his eyes adjusted to the dim light.

The first room he entered was very large. An enormous map of the world showing sea currents, winds, and depth soundings covered most of one wall. The map, set in a fluted mahogany frame, was made of varnished yellow paper marked with a fine network of cracks and small peelings. From the opposite wall, diffused columns of yellow light poured through large portholes. The floor was littered with maps, newspapers, books, pieces of leather, and a dozen wooden chairs lying on their sides and backs. In the center of the room stood a long oak table. At one end of it he noticed an iron astrolabe, and at the other end, a beautiful astral globe set in an elaborate bronze stand. By turning wheels near its base, it could be tilted to any angle. The globe was painted in black and the stars and planets in silver. The belt of the constellations ran through its center, each figure outlined in a different color. A bright blue silhouetted the figure of Sagittarius the Archer; his arrow shot far out into the painted curve of the cosmos, out beyond The Northern Cross, beyond Cepheus, The North Star, and Andromeda.

He took a deep breath. His mind had been turning inward like an Archimedes' spiral, and for a few seconds he had forgotten where he was. He straightened up and looked around him. A piece of newspaper responded to a sudden wisp of wind from one of the open portholes. It drifted for a moment like a ghost in the yellow air. He bent over and picked it up. It was *The London Times,* July 22, 1900.

He stood in the middle of the room and listened to the creaking of the boat. He thought again of the arrow of Sagittarius on its way past The North Star. The starry god and his arrows, trapped on the curve of a starglobe like the figures on the urn in the Keats' ode.

Then he heard a noise somewhere down the corridor outside the room. A door closing. Perhaps, he thought, it was the wind. He listened. Somewhere in one of the rooms he heard the thud of footsteps, and then quite suddenly, an impossible jangle of sounds, like a chorus of xylophones terribly out of tune. It seemed much louder and somewhat different at this close distance, but it was still unmistakable: the music of The Hatchmaker.

An unreasonable panic swept over him, and then almost immediately he felt very foolish. Whatever the sound was, it was almost certainly nothing dangerous. He could not believe that the ship was really haunted, or even inhabited. Slowly he made his way down the corridor until the noise was very loud all around him. But where did it come from? He opened one door after another, but they revealed nothing but cabins and storerooms, long since deserted. Perhaps, he thought, it came from another level of the ship somewhere below or above him.

He found the old wooden staircase again and walked down to the third level, the dark hold of the clipper ship. For a long time he groped around in a black labyrinth of boxes and kegs in a broad, uncompartmented area that seemed to take up most of the hold. Many times he stumbled into things he could not recognize, things that clattered across the floor when he kicked them, or fell over like corpses or sacks of grain. In some places water had seeped through the boards and collected in large pools.

He had assumed that his eyes would eventually adjust to the dim light; he realized now that he was in almost total darkness. That and the sloshing of the water made him very uneasy. How incredibly stupid he had been to come down here without a lamp. He turned back, trying to retrace his steps, but soon realized he was lost—lost in the black, watery vaults of an ancient ship where no one ever went. He cursed himself again as he felt the darkness closing in upon him. He was alone now with the sound his feet made in the water and a vague smell of oil and gasoline and decaying potatoes.

Suddenly he realized that for an uncertain time—a minute or perhaps a half hour—he had not heard the music of The Hatchmaker. Even that would have given him some sense of direction, something to move toward.

For a while he wandered about in the dark, slowly growing more desperate. Once he thought he heard footsteps somewhere behind him.

Suddenly he cracked his head on a door and stumbled into a small room lit by three lamps. The sudden light confounded him, and he raised his hand to his eyes and sucked in his breath. He listened fearfully, waiting for something ominous to descend upon him, but he heard only the creaking and gurgling of the ship.

The room appeared to be an officer's cabin. A single bunk stood in one corner, a bookshelf on the opposite wall, and a model of a whaling ship on a large desk near the center of the room. At one corner of the deck, steam rose from a plate of beans and fish that someone had left unfinished. The odor of the warm food filled the room. It was true then. Someone actually lived at Driftsend. He took a step forward into the room, stopped and listened. Then, for the second time, he heard footsteps, this time very close. They came from just beyond the door on the other side of the room. He knew that in a moment the door would open and he would find himself face to face with—the inevitable answer came unbidden into his mind—The Hatchmaker.

But the door did not open and the footsteps faded away into another corridor. Peter had no heart to follow them. He took two of the three lamps and went back into the dark bowels of the ship. In a few minutes he found the stairway, climbed it, and emerged with an infinite sense of relief into the cool, early evening. There was no sound anywhere. The wind had vanished with the sun across the horizon.

The next morning he told his story at breakfast.

"You must have been terrified," said Bright. "Just terrified." Her eyes were very wide. Her hands seemed almost to tremble as she gathered the breakfast dishes on a large wooden tray.

"It was frightening," said Peter. "I'd heard the stories

about The Hatchmaker, but I didn't really expect to find anyone."

"Is he more than twelve feet tall?" said Michael, his voice shrill with excitement.

"He didn't really see The Hatchmaker," said David. "He only heard footsteps. Why don't you listen with your ears?"

"Did he sound more than twelve feet tall?" said Michael.

"Some say The Hatchmaker is like a snake," said Reuben in a kind of rattling *sotto voce*. "And when he uncoils himself, why he's longer than the boat he lives on at Driftsend."

"Even longer than that," said Javitt.

Rose smiled. It was the first time Peter had ever seen her smile. "He's only a man," she said sleepily. And then she closed her eyes and put her hands over her forehead, and when she spoke again it seemed to be from a great distance. "Tall," she said. "Yes. Very tall with black hair like Benjamin. And such a fine musician!" There was a strange enthusiasm in her quavering voice.

Tabor looked at her with sudden interest. "Rose, when did you know The Hatchmaker?" he asked. "How long ago?"

"Did he live with one of the clans?" said Michael.

But the old woman did not answer. She sat motionless, her fingers pressed against her forehead.

"She's going on The Long Journey," said David in a whisper. "She doesn't need The Circle of Elders so much now—she can do it all by herself."

Bright smiled at the boy and nodded, and then turned back to Peter. "But what were you doing at Driftsend in the first place? Didn't you know it's a forbidden place?"

"No, I didn't," he lied. "I was just curious about The Hatchmaker."

But when the talk had ended Tabor led him out onto the deck, out of earshot of Bright and the others who lounged in the morning sun. "What were you really looking for?" he said.

"Gasoline."

Tabor was silent for a moment. He looked very sad. "You still intend to leave then?"

"If The Outlanders don't wreck or steal my aluminum dinghy."

"I think it's safe for the moment," he said.

"It's not safe at all," said Peter, who did not understand why Tabor was smiling. "Everyone knows where it is now."

"It's safe for the moment. But I strongly suggest that you don't try to leave The Drift. People will get very angry. They'll even try to stop you."

Together they walked up toward The Cliff and stared out over the sunlit ocean. Peter could feel the anger rising in his throat. What business was it of Tabor's, he wondered, what business was it of anyone's, what right did any of them have to stand in his way? It was bad enough that no one helped, that no one in all these years had ever repaired any of the boats for sailing.

"I did come here by accident," he said, choosing his words very carefully. "And my whole life is back in The United States. I'm not getting in anyone's way by rescuing my own boat or borrowing some sails from a deserted ship that belongs to nobody. I really don't see that you have anything to say about it."

"There are very strong traditions against leaving The Drift," said Tabor. "Every year all the clans meet and review the common law. Every year they say that it's forbidden to sail out beyond the horizon because the world is an evil place of storms where men fight and kill each other and waste their lives on vanity and ambition. Eventually, they say, the outside world will find peace, and when that happens a great man in a white ship will discover The Drift and lead everyone back to land. But until that time everyone must wait."

"And is that what you believe?" said Peter. He could

not suppress an angry smile. "Do you think that someday the world will heal itself of evil and a man will come in a white boat? Is that why you're against my leaving?"

Tabor looked out across the water. "No," he said.

"The world is full of good and evil, but I daresay it's the same on The Drift. You have your Outlanders too. But that isn't the point, really. The point is that everyone here is expected to think and feel the same way. It's a kind of creeping, benevolent dictatorship that passes itself off as The Free Life simply because there isn't much to do here and hardly anyone is responsible for anything. I'm just beginning to understand that, and for me it makes their whole thesis about The Drift as a retreat from an evil world look rather shabby."

"I'm not going to argue with you," said Tabor. "But I think there is a kind of freedom here that is very rare in the outside world. Almost everyone who comes here finds it sooner or later. I think you're finding it already."

"Well that's just fine," said Peter, who was not really listening. "I'm not allowed to go back to my own life because the natives are superstitious about boats. So much for my freedom!" But then he saw a strange look in Tabor's eyes, a look of resignation and sadness that he did not understand.

"I'm not trying to offend anyone," he said helplessly. "You least of all. I just want to go home. Surely that's not such an unreasonable desire, even from your point of view."

"No," said Tabor quietly. "I suppose not."

Peter was surprised that he did not argue the point further. He wondered what Tabor was thinking. "There must be more to all this," he said, trying now to sound interested. "There must be something you haven't told me that keeps people here. What is it that everyone is really afraid of?"

Tabor was quiet for several moments. He hunched

over the bow rail of the boat, watched the seabirds, the slow movement of the ships, the glinting of the morning sun on the rivers of green water that moved slowly between the boats. "The open sea. Storms. Sailing out into the world," he said finally.

"But one must sail out into the world. There's nothing else to do in life."

"Here no one sails anywhere. You've noticed that none of the boats are ever used as boats. But there is another ocean we sail here on The Drift, a stranger ocean that lies beyond the oceans that sailors know."

"And what do you use for sails on such an ocean?"

Tabor smiled. "The mind is a kind of sail," he answered. "The wind blows it where we wish to go."

"But what wind could there be in such an ocean? I mean, an ocean where nothing really moves and no one really travels anywhere, an ocean without commerce to real places?"

"The things you touch with your senses are like the wind," said Tabor. "That's Pao's way of putting it. She says that to see something truly is an act of perception and that when that happens, you move as if your sails were full of wind."

"That's rather poetic, but I'm not sure—"

"It's a very simple thing," said Tabor. "It's only the difference between seeing something actively and seeing it passively. It's what the children learn to do with metaphors in shadowgames. It's the way Pao looks at things."

Peter thought again of Pao and the old caravel. Well, that had been a lovely afternoon, but it was not really relevant. The Drift was in many ways charming and mysterious, but surely the world was larger than a square mile of derelict wrecks; his part of it was over a thousand miles away. But before he could say anything further, Bright appeared in the hatchway of *The Mary Strattford* and began waving at them.

"Hurry up!" she said. "You're going to miss everything!"

"Miss what?" said Peter. "I'm supposed to work this morning down in The Seafields. Reuben and Javitt are waiting for me."

"Theres no work today!" said Bright. "Reuben and Javitt are down at the meeting place with everyone else!" She was shouting now to make herself heard over the distance.

Peter and Tabor made their way back toward *The Mary Strattford*. "I don't understand," said Peter. "What's going on?"

"Today is a holiday," said Tabor. "I nearly forgot."

Then his two children appeared from nowhere and began tugging at his sleeves. "Come on, Tabor," said Michael. "We want to see the trees and the monsters and everything. Is Pao going to take off her clothes this time?"

Tabor began to laugh. "Hush," he said. "You both talk too much."

"Hurry up!" said Bright as she went off with a group of Bluewater children toward the western side of The Drift. "You'll miss The Dance of The Nine Islands!"

Chapter Twelve

THE DANCE OF THE NINE ISLANDS

Tabor led him westward to a place midway between The Cliff and The Outland that Peter had seen before. It was the meeting place called Twoboats that Pao had showed him during his third day on The Drift. A platform nearly a hundred feet square had been made from the decks of two ships joined together by carpenters. The masts had been removed, a large area painted blue, and as he watched, some men arranged two layers of netting in a large circle across the painted space.

At the stern of one ship he saw again the long slide that led down somewhere toward The Southern Edge.

Within the blue circle of paint and netting were nine black tarpaulins which hid queer, lumpy forms that Peter could not identify. They were arranged in a kind of star shape that stretched about seventy feet from one side to the other. The netting was carefully laid around the edges of the tarpaulins. Once, for the briefest instant, he thought he saw one of the dark shapes move under its canvas covering.

"What's under the tarpaulins?" he asked.

"You'll find out when the dance begins," said Tabor. "I don't want to spoil it for you."

"When does it start?"

"In a half hour or so. As soon as all the clans get here." And then he shouted something in Spanish to a group of young men who had just arrived at the other end of the boat. They laughed and shouted something back to him. "It won't be long now," he said to Peter. "Here come The Bluewaters."

Many people had already arrived. They sat in a large circle now around the edges of the blue space on an arrangement of kegs and boxes, dividing themselves into five groups, corresponding to their clans. Peter and Tabor sat near Bright, Tabor's children, and the other Mary Strattfords. Across from them was The Vague Noire clan of French Canadians and Germans. The Bluewater and Conquistador Blanco clans sat to his left. To his right were The Madrids, by far the largest group. In this clan the people were all dark-skinned and blackhaired. Some of them, Tabor believed, were descendants of Spanish explorers that had come to The Drift hundreds of years ago. Others were Brazilians, Portuguese, and Cubans. The Madrid children were especially noisy. They climbed all over each other and over their parents, played elaborate shadowgames, and chattered in shrill, staccato voices.

Each clan, Tabor explained, had certain customs that were peculiar to it, and each had a section of The Drift that it marked off for its own: The Mary Strattfords and The Madrids formed two sides of a large wedge whose broad side included all of The Northside Cliff and whose point came almost exactly to the center of The Drift. The Vague Noires lived in the southeast quadrant along the east or Mary Strattford side of the wedge, while the Conquistador Blancos lived along The Seafields below The Madrids. The Bluewaters, famous for their music, held a strip along the south and southwest that led up to The Bridge, the narrow western point of

The Drift where all the musicians gathered in the evenings. But generally speaking, the territorial divisions were vague, and there were no restrictions on trespassing or taking things from different ships. In fact, the idea of owning ships or groups of ships was in itself a very nominal concept, practically meaningless except as it applied to the clanboats.

"Each of the clans," Tabor was saying, "has its own character. That's a much more important thing than the geographical boundaries. We Mary Strattfords, for example, are considered to be the leaders and organizers for most of the important activities, in spite of our small numbers. The Madrids, on the other hand, are the most creative and outgoing, and there is also a standing joke about them being the best seducers and lovers, because they have so many children. The Bluewaters are the best musicians; they play their songs to anyone who will listen. The Conquistador Blancos are the cooks and wine makers. They make a yellowish alcoholic drink out of God knows what that's very popular, though I don't especially care for it. The Vague Noires are very nice to everyone, but they stay mostly to themselves except on festival days. I think this is partly because their language, more than any of the others, is a mixture of many tongues, and it's very hard to understand. Only the children can speak it perfectly."

Then Peter noticed that one of the barrels in the Madrid section stood apart from all the others in that it was painted a bright blue. Presently a tall, dark-skinned man with long white hair took his place on it. He carried a trio of hand drums.

"Listen," said Tabor. "It's beginning." And with that he moved away to another place where a large barrel provided him a better vantage point. He waved to Peter and then pointed to the old man.

But to Peter it did not seem that anything in particular had begun. Everyone waved to the man with the drums and called out to him, but the old man did not answer or acknowledge their greeting in any way. He stared at the blue floor in front of him. Presently, amid the noise of the children and the voices of the adults chattering in three or four languages, he began to play. At first he could not be heard over all the commotion, but after a minute or so the beating grew louder. The young men in The Madrid clan began to listen; then gradually the others fell silent. Soon the man on the blue barrel was the focal point of the entire gathering. His small drums had little resonance, but in the silence their sound began to grow in Peter's mind. The first drum made a very sharp sound; the other two were muffled and soft, forming a contrapuntal pattern of echoes. After ten minutes everyone was silent. Everyone listened to the drums.

Then Pao appeared at the edge of the circle. He had never seen her look more beautiful. Her long black hair was braided and fixed in a loop at the back of her head. She wore a pair of black trousers and a man's white shirt. She stood for a moment without moving, and then for a brief instant the drums stopped.

"The Dance of The Nine Islands," she said.

Then the drums began beating again, this time much faster than before. Pao began to dance. Peter could tell from her dress and from her mannish gestures as she pushed an imaginary boat into the water that she was playing the part of a man, a voyager across a painted blue ocean. Her dance progressed in a series of undulating motions. Her whole body rolled from side to side with the pitch and yawl of her ship. Several times she raised her arms together out in front of her, closed her fingers, and then swung gently on the weight of an imaginary line. Her eyes closed. Slowly she danced toward the first tarpaulin, stepping sideways, then rising on her toes, then sinking and stepping back in the swell and deep of the waves of that netted blue ocean. Once she opened her eyes and peered out toward the horizon; another time she glanced upward to the point of her sail and then shielded her eyes to see the position of the sun. Always she moved at an oblique angle, never forward, never sideways. Slowly the billowing slant of her imaginary sail carried her on toward the first tarpaulin. The drums became the sound of wind and the sound of water.

She stopped near the edge of the tarpaulin.

"The Island of The Twelve Golden Fruit Trees, where oranges hang like burning lamps." Her voice was like the drums and the water and the wind.

With these words, the twelve trees threw off their tarpaulin and slowly rose to their feet. They were dressed in green. Each wore a crown of green weeds, and a pair of bright orange spheres hung from a short length of twine held in each hand. Their dance moved in a slow, wide circle around the edge of their island. They made low sighing noises. The arms and trunks of the trees swayed, each, it seemed, responding to a different wind, for the complex pattern of their dance moved their branches into a myriad of clustering, many-pointed shapes, like a series of slow starbursts.

The sailor moved around the island, gazing at the twelve trees and the golden fruit that swung from their branches. Once she tried to land, but the trees very gently blocked her way. Once she tried to seize one of the oranges, but the trees smiled and lifted their branches up out of reach. Regretfully the sailor sailed away. The twelve trees closed their eyes, murmured in a sleep of voices, pulled their tarpaulin back over them, and sank into silence.

Her second journey took her again into the open sea. For several minutes she sailed in wide circles until she reached the second island.

"The Island of Flowers In Profusion, where The White Spirits dance in The Immortal Fields."

Here nine men dressed in white hoods arose, threw off their tarpaulin, and began a long procession across the island. The procession consisted of three rows that intersected each other at odd angles. The regularity of the procession was broken when occasionally one figure would turn his head and wait for another to cross his path, or when, quite suddenly, one figure would leap into the air and raise his arms above his head. All of The White Spirits moved in small quick steps that gave a ghostly oriental sense of gliding rather than walking. Occasionally one of them would smile at the sailor, who was still circling the island. Once the sailor tried to land, but one of the spirits shook his head and blocked the way with his arms.

The third journey took the sailor to the third island.

"The Island of The White Clown of The Mountain, who made the oceans from his own breathing and plucked stars from the sky to make The Nine Islands," cried the sailor.

The Island of The White Clown was taller than any of the others. The tarpaulin peaked nearly eight feet above the ocean. Under it, a single figure slowly began to move. When the tarpaulin fell away it revealed a man sitting on a high stool of blue and silver, dressed on a loose-fitting robe that fell to the ground in a white pool of linen. In one hand he held a small silver harp that had no strings. A ghostly white paint covered his face except for one large symmetrical tear, a spot of bright blue, that fell from the corner of one eye.

The sailor anchored a few feet offshore and shielded his eyes against the white eminence of the great figure sitting on his throne. Slowly The White Clown played his hands across the empty wedge of the harp and cocked his ear to catch the soundless melody, and all the shapes beneath all the canvases began to sway to the music. Then he sang in a high, reedy voice. His singing was a sprightly jumble of syllables that ended at regular intervals with an inexplicably mournful "tra-la, tra-la." When his song was over, he smiled at the sailor, reached into his mouth, and pulled out a silver key. He turned it in the sunlight so that its reflection made a tiny spot of light that moved across the water, around the boat, and finally rested on the sailor's forehead. Then The White Clown threw his key toward the boat, reached down behind him, and drew the dark canvas over himself and over his island.

The sailor caught the silver key in his hand. He turned it over and over, and then slowly sailed away to the fourth island.

"The First Island of Fire."

Here a man dressed all in red stood in the center of the island, writhing like a flame. His arms turned and bent in many directions. His fingers stretched open and pointed to the sailor. His nails undulated like fingers of fire, and the mask he wore peaked above his head in a fiery pinnacle. Looking neither to the left nor the right, the sailor carefully guided his ship along the shoreline of that dangerous island. Once he brushed against the fiery fingers. Still he did not turn his head or look behind him.

The sailor's fifth journey brought him to the fifth island.

"The Island of The Winds, where the air whistles through the rocks and caves." This time the sailor spoke more softly and in a more natural way. The ritual intonation in his voice had disappeared.

At the fifth island the sailor himself removed the tarpaulin. Beneath it were fourteen figures, all painted gray, except for their hands, and all naked, except for loincloths. They sat, kneeled or squatted in weird angular positions, some with their shoulders hunched, some with an elbow protruding, some curled up in balls, some with large loops made with outstretched arms. None of them moved.

The sailor pulled his boat toward the shore, dropped an imaginary anchor, and landed. Slowly, curiously, he picked his way among the gray, sleeping forms, shielding his eyes against the wind. Occasionally he would sit on one of them, lean his chin in his hand, and contemplate the sea. Once he pushed one of the rocks with his foot and watched it roll head over heels into the water. "Splash," said the rock. And the other rocks laughed very softly.

The sailor's sixth journey took him to the sixth island.

"The Island of The Old Enchantress, who sings to all the men who live on all the islands," she said.

The sailor reached beneath the canvas and pulled out a five-foot pole fixed to a wooden stand. A foot or so from the top of the pole was a small spar from which fluttered a square piece of sailcloth. When the sailor removed this apparatus, the whole canvas collapsed, for there was no one underneath.

Carefully the sailor set the sail at the edge of the island. Then, much to Peter's discomfort, he removed his shirt, and the illusion of the sailor was no more. Pao then wrapped the sleeves of her shirt around the T-spar in such a way that they hung on either side like arms. When this was done she crawled under the tarpaulin.

When, after a moment of stillness, she threw off the tarpaulin and stared at the sail stand and the shirt, Peter began to understand. The sail was the boat, the shirt represented the sailor, and Pao was now The Enchantress.

In spite of her nakedness, the dance did not at first seem very immodest. It consisted mostly of rapid turns made about a small point of space, broken by a series of attitudes in which she would remain absolutely still except for a flowerlike movement of her wrists and fingers. It was the dance of an enchantress, but the enchantment was not exclusively a sexual enchantment. At various times during the sequence, she produced objects out of nowhere like a magician; the objects seemed in some way to be a part of the meaning of the dance. First, an ancient lamp which she lit with an imaginary brand and then threw into the water. Later, a silk scarf of many bright streaks of color. When she finally began to move toward the sailor, it trailed behind her like a wake, and Peter thought of Iris, the messenger of the gods, whose thousand-mile cloak was the rainbow that mortals saw after her long journeys through the sky. Once she produced the key from her own mouth that The White Clown had given her, and threw it toward the sailor's boat. Once she found a wooden flute floating in the water and on it she played a slow oriental melody.

Finally The Enchantress pulled the boat to the shore of her island and began to dance around it. Now her motion was more overtly seductive. She picked up the two sleeves of the shirt and began to sway back and forth, rocking the boat and the sailor from one side to another. Slowly she drew it toward the center of the island.

Peter did not quite understand what the parts of the dance signified or how they went together, and yet he felt a unity in all the disparate images. The lamp, the scarf, and the key had, he supposed, some sort of metaphysical significance, and now all these things echoed, like variations on a theme, in the slow seduction of the sailor. The dance seemed to mean that the mystery of man and woman together was the mystery of all things: the lamplight of all wisdom, the color of all beautiful images, the key to man's search for another world that would somehow be a revelation of human purpose. The power and intensity of her lovemaking was like the spinning of heat and energy in that first whirling place on the first day of creation. For man, the wonder of woman. For woman, the ecstasy of surrender in which she rises finally to conquer her lover.

But somewhere in this dance of passion and creation he sensed curious, comic sadness that he could not quite identify or name. It made him think of the large blue tear painted on the cheek of The White Clown.

Then the drums stopped. Then a short sputter of drumbeats. Then silence again. Then three sharp beats in uneven rhythm. Against this pattern of silence and sudden, irregular beats, The Enchantress stood in a kind of tense uncertainty that seemed like a fusion of action and inaction. Once, her head turned. Once, the arch of her foot lifted as she shifted her weight from one foot to the other. Once, she pressed her fingers against her legs, stretching them and then relaxing. Then, in what seemed to be a continuous motion, The Enchantress circled one leg and one arm around the puppet sailor and the mast of his ship, slid to the ground, turned the boat over on its side with her leg, and pulled the black tarpaulin over her, the boat, and the sailor.

For Peter, the last three journeys were an anticlimax. And yet, like the others, they were intensely interesting. It was only that now his feeling, if not his mind, was beginning to slide away from the dancing. It was as if he were falling from a great distance into a pool of dark water where Pao waited for him.

Pao's seventh journey, once again as the sailor, brought her to "The Island of The Ten Giants, who tend their gardens and their sheepfold." She mingled with the giants, worked with them, watched the cycle of the seasons passing from winter to spring and from planting time to harvest time. After a while the giants carried her back to her ship and again she was on her way.

Next came a second Island of Fire, where again she navigated near the shore of an island where her ship barely avoided the flaming fingers of another fire monster, this time a larger and more ferocious one.

Next came "The Island of Unending Night, where The Black Narwhales eat the heads of the fishermen of all The Islands."

Here the tarpaulin was not removed. Not by Pao, who sailed three times around the black shore, not by the dark shapes that moved and groaned and laughed beneath the tarpaulin. Sometimes one of them would rise up so that his form was partly visible beneath the covering: a pointed head. The black semblance of a draped arm. At the end of her third circling, Pao pointed her ship back into the open sea.

"The Island of The Twelve Golden Fruit Trees, where oranges hang like burning lamps," she cried.

She had come full circle from paradise to earth to hell and then back to paradise. Now the trees repeated their dance, and one of them removed a green branch from his head and threw it to Pao. She caught it and raised her arms above her head. Then she went to the center of the ocean, stood for a moment in silence, and then pulled a gold pin from the coil of hair looped at the back of her head. Her long hair tumbled down.

"Let us make our circle for The Dance of The Nine Islands," she said, "for it is the circle and the dance of all our fears and all our desires."

With that, all the creatures of all the islands—the trees, the spirits, The White Clown, the rocks, the giants, the fire monsters, and The Black Narwhales—threw off their tarpaulins, and joined Pao in the center of the blue circle. The drums beat louder. Pao was now the center of the dancing spiral that wound and then unwound and then wound again. Soon everyone in the audience had joined the dance. They sang, waved their arms in the air, and Peter was borne up among them like a cork rising on a giant wave. It was impossible, unthinkable, to resist the momentum of their dancing and their singing. The spiral wound, unwound into a circle, and then wound into a spiral again. And in the center of the spiral, Pao whirled like a dervish until one of the young men caught her.

The dancers shouted and leaped into the air, and finally, after a space of time that he could not measure, people began to fall away from the dance, sprawling across the netted blue circle, and the spiral of shouting dancers disintegrated into broken lines that wheeled every which way. The drums continued for a minute or so, then settled into a long, arhythmical roll of sound, then stopped. The last few dancers had fallen to the deck of the ship. No one moved. There was no sound but the sound of heavy breathing, the distant cries of birds, and the creaking of wood.

After a while Peter opened his eyes. He felt he had awakened from a long sleep filled with strange dreams. Tabor was gone. Several of the others were leaving. Pao sat on a rolled-up canvas near the center of a sprawled circle of dancers and talked quietly to three young men from The Madrid clan.

At the stern he noticed a young girl going down the slide followed by a young man. He went to it and peered over the edge. The chute plunged down between two large boats and from where he stood he could see no further. Beyond the curve of those two ships he heard a sound that reminded him of Pao's laughter. He thought again of her dancing, of her inward world lost in the books of an old Spanish ship and in the shadow-games and dances of her enchanted mind. Now she was with the others. She was the leader of the dancers and he was clearly an outsider. He wished now that things might be as they had been four days earlier, but that intimacy, he felt, would never be recaptured. Pao was too securely a part of her own world and he could never be a part of it for long. He knew now that she and Tabor would never leave The Drift; it was their whole life; his lay on a continent somewhere to the west, beyond The Sargasso Sea and the vast ocean that lay beyond it.

It was with a sense of regret that he turned away from the wooden slide and the laughter that echoed from somewhere below him. The sound of it was a bitter taste in his mind. Pao. Paolozzi, the princess of mystery, now forever beyond his reach. Perhaps he had never wanted anyone in his life as much as he wanted Pao. At first, she had seemed to be only an enchanting child with a childlike curiosity about strangers. Then she became a young woman whose beauty and intelligence and flattering attentiveness had been diverting for a while. And now? He could not believe that it was only a desire for something that was suddenly unattainable. No, he had loved her almost from the beginning. It seemed now that for days, for weeks, for years he had been waiting for her.

"Hello," she said.

He turned around. She had been standing a few feet behind him. Her lips were open slightly, and for a moment her eyes seemed fearful or apprehensive. She stepped forward and put her hand on his shoulder. The touch made him shudder.

"Are you cold?" she said.

"No, Pao, I'm not cold."

"Then take your shoes off. And your shirt. We'll go down the slide together."

A long silence of desire and anxiety welled in his throat and made his voice tremble.

"What's at the end of the slide?" He watched her take off her shoes. He could not stop watching her.

"A pool," she said. And with that she disappeared over the edge.

He removed his shirt and his shoes, set himself on the lip of the slide, and let go. He saw Pao vanish around the edge of the boat about twenty feet ahead of him.

The slide was very long and very smooth. It consisted of a series of long, curved wooden sections that had apparently been worn and buffed by constant use. It descended very gradually and the momentum carried him along very slowly. He had the sense that any moment he would stop, but the angle of incline was just enough to keep him moving. It was a curious feeling.

Gradually he descended below the first level of ships. At first he could see the cabins and the sails and the lifeboats. Then he sank deeper, turning between the dark hulls that were shielded from the sunlight. Noises began to reverberate in the semi-darkness. Water lapping against the boats seemed to blur and fade in a hundred directions in the shadowy green light. Time was slow.

The dizzy slide moved downward inexorably toward the dark water, toward the pool that Pao had promised would be at the end of it.

Once, he looked up and recognized the broken railing of the schooner from which he had seen the slide several days earlier. He saw himself standing on the edge of the boat, peering down into the shadows. He waved to his former self, and the ghost in his imagination waved back and shook its head in consternation.

Suddenly the boats fell away and he came out into a burst of light just an instant before he plunged into the cool water. Pao was there waiting for him. A giant splash of white foam, and then they sank together to the bottom of the pool, their arms around each other. He felt that they would never come up again. It would be an eternity of death and they would plunge together to the bottom of the ocean and to the heart of things beyond the circle of the ocean currents and beyond even the circle of time.

For what seemed to be a very long time they swam together in the deep water. The pool was made of an enormous net suspended between three boats near The Southern Edge. It was perhaps a hundred feet across, lifting into a shallow line of water near its edges. Together they swam down to the deepest point in the center of the net. Slowly the net undulated to the movements of the water. Long strands of seaweed and the roots of flat-petaled seaflowers clung to the heavy cords of hemp, waving in the slow currents and transforming the net into a green web that held them there in the deep silence.

Pao touched his shoulder and pointed through the net to a school of yellow fish that skittered like bright coins falling through the water. Their tiny faces held looks of perpetual amazement. When Pao moved, some turned to look at her, while others darted away.

And then, far beneath them, Peter saw a large gray shape drifting north. Once it stopped and turned upward. And through forty of fifty fathoms of water he imagined his eyes met the eyes of the shark. It was a fearful confrontation, even though the shark was lost in an unknown and endless world far below him. For a moment he felt unhinged. It was as if he might fall into the deep world. But the beast was far away, the green web was strong between them, the water was cool and green and soothing. He put his arms around Pao and together they drifted to the surface.

"I was almost out of air," he said.

"So was I," she said.

"Another minute and we might never have come up."

"It would have been a good death," said Pao.

"Yes," he said. "I was thinking that too."

"I wanted to swim all the way down to the shark," she said. "Did you see the shark?"

"Yes. He would have eaten us."

"Sharks are beautiful," she said. "There's no reason to be afraid of sharks. When they swim deep they never bother anything."

He looked at her floating there in the green water. He could think of nothing else to say. He was sick with desire for her. A young man and a woman at the other end of the pool were talking quietly, and their voices reverberated across the water. The air was still bright. He watched Pao moving her arms in the green water.

"Are you that much in love with me?" said Pao.

"Yes."

She swam closer to him and touched his shoulder with her white hands. "Are you trembling?"

"Yes."

"Are you in love with me?" she asked again.

"Yes."

"The sharks have eaten your tongue again," she said.

"Not the sharks," he said. "There are things much larger and more beautiful than sharks. Things that can eat you alive."

"And have you been eaten alive?" She pressed herself against him and bit him very gently on the shoulder. He closed his arms around her in the water and together they began to sink for a second time toward the bottom of the pool. After a while Pao caught herself, and with two strokes brought them both back to the surface. She swam to the edge of the net. Peter followed her. She lifted herself out of the pool, her arms and legs dripping with the green water. Her black hair fell around her neck and down the front of her white shirt in a thick shining river of darkness.

"Where would you like to take me?" she said very softly.

He took her hand and led her back up toward The Cliff to his own boat. The shadows of masts and sails were long now. The afternoon light was fading. When they were inside the cabin and when the door was closed he kissed her on the mouth.

She began to weep. "I thought you would never love me," she said. "For so many days I thought you never would. We have only a few days before you sail away. But now at least . . ."

She lay back on the bed and pulled him down to her. He could feel his desire for her drawing him into the hollow silence of her mouth and into the coolness of her body, that was still dripping wet and smelling of seawater. Nothing else mattered. He was sinking now into the green labyrinth of his senses, and the world of his own mind and his own past shattered, broke away like a continent disintegrating somewhere beyond the horizons of The Sargasso Sea.

Chapter Thirteen

A MARRIAGE

AND A HISTORY LESSON

It was nearly morning when he awoke. Pao lay curled around him, her leg pressed between his, her head resting on his shoulder, her long hair across his chest. He lifted his head and looked for a moment out his window. A touch of color wavered in the east. There was not a sound anywhere. His head fell back on the pillow. Pao murmured something in her sleep and drew her hand slowly across his face.

"What did you say?" he whispered.

"Donmove," she said. "Snotimetogetup."

He put his arms around her.

"Umm," she said.

He thought of his dinghy lying in the hull of the old wreck. Probably by now it had been torn apart or stolen by the Outlanders. No matter. He would stay here on The Drift. He would live with Pao and they would have their children here away from the world. Here where all life was a feast of the imagination and the days passed in a never-changing season.

Pao was very warm in his arms. He closed his eyes

and listened for the sound of the world, but there was nothing, only an immense stillness that rested like a white balm in the center of his mind.

An hour later he awoke again. Gently he disengaged himself from Pao and got dressed. Before he left for his morning's work he pulled the sheet back over her and kissed her on the temple.

He worked steadily that morning with Reuben and Javitt until nearly eleven-thirty, and by that time he was ravenously hungry. As they made their way back toward *The Mary Strattford* he heard, very faintly, the sounds of The Hatchmaker from Driftsend, and between the boats he saw David and Michael weedwalking. The *shadush, shadush* of their wooden weedshoes melted into the atonal melodies from Driftsend. When he waved to them they waved back and shouted and ran in a quick, foaming circle of water.

"Listen to The Hatchmaker," said David, cupping his hands and calling up to him.

"He's playing lunch music," cried Michael in a loud, piercing voice.

"But The Hatchmaker doesn't eat lunch," said David. "He's a ghost, and ghosts don't eat anything."

"I know that," said the other impatiently. "So 'stead, he had lunch music. Isn't that right, Sutherland?"

"I guess so," said Peter.

"His music is like shadowgames," Michael persisted. "He plays with music like a game. For ghosts, things in the air like music take the place of real things like eating and breathing."

His brother frowned. "Sometimes we skip lunch to play shadowgames," he said doubtfully as the two of them shadushed away toward Northside, "but that's different."

Michael laughed and shouted something at his brother as they disappeared around the edge of a New Bedford whaler.

At the noon meal Peter noticed that Pao and Raven were both missing. With as much of a casual tone as he could muster, he asked where they were.

"I don't know where Raven is," said Bright. "But Pao is taking a nap."

"At this time of day?"

"Well," said Bright, "she's not used to making love all night long."

His fork fell out of his fingers and dropped with a noisy clatter to his plate. His face turned scarlet. Desperately he looked up at her. She was smiling at him benevolently. Reuben and Javitt continued eating. Rose was sitting very erect in her chair, staring out of one of the portholes. The children were playing with their food at the other end of the table. It was as if nothing of any real interest had been said.

"I see," said Peter in a voice that was barely audible.

He turned to Tabor, who sat next to him. Tabor was busily eating the last of his scallops, but the faintest trace of a smile lifted the corners of his mouth.

"What's so damned funny?" said Peter.

Tabor turned to him with a look of injured innocence. But the smile was still there. "Funny?" he said. "Is something funny?"

"How did Bright find out?" he whispered.

"We all saw Pao come out of your cabin this morning at about ten o'clock," said Tabor in a voice that to Peter seemed much too loud. "It's been a wonder to everyone that it didn't happen sooner. You really have quite marvelous powers of restraint. Herculean, I would say."

Peter flushed again and made a desperate gesture with his hand for Tabor to keep silent.

"But everyone knows," said Tabor. "Even her friends from The Madrid."

"That's impossible," said Peter in a furious whisper. "They don't even know who I am."

"They all know you. They've even made up a little

song about you and Pao that someone is going to sing at the next festival."

Peter blushed for the third time. He opened his mouth but he could think of nothing to say.

"Pao is very popular with The Madrids," Tabor continued breezily. "She always works with them on songs and dances." Judiciously he stabbed the last scallop in his bowl and dipped it into a little cup of yellow sauce.

"But isn't anyone the least bit annoyed?" said Peter. "When people found out that I was working on my own dinghy no one would speak to me. I was an outcast nearly all day."

Tabor laughed. "Yes," he said. "Nearly all day."

"But now that I've abducted one of the daughters of the clan, no one seems to mind."

"Well, if you feel you should be punished, I suppose we might manage to think up something," said Tabor. "But really I think we'd all feel pretty silly. Especially now that you're married."

"I'm what!"

Now everyone, much to Peter's discomfort, was taking an interest in the conversation. Reuben and Javitt were smiling in a fatherly, patronizing way that suggested amusement at the antics of a child. Bright was trying very hard not to laugh. Even the children were watching him. Only Rose had maintained her senile unconcern. She continued to stare fiercely out the same porthole.

"You're married," said Tabor. "When two people love each other and live together they're married. You do love Pao, don't you?"

Everyone stopped eating and waited for his answer. They all stared at him, and for a moment he imagined they were holding their breath. "This is ridiculous!" he muttered. And then, without meaning to, he smiled foolishly.

"This has all been a plot," he said with what was left of his embarrassed anger, knowing that it was too late now to make an issue of anything. "You've all been in on it! You've all taken advantage of the fact that I'm alone here and you've all been . . ." He had run out of words. He had never felt quite so stupid. ". . . in on it," he concluded. Everyone was still staring at him. Suddenly he remembered that someone had asked him a question.

"Of course I love Pao," he said miserably. "Everybody loves Pao. Is there any reason why I should be an exception?" There was a general cheer, and the children applauded. Then everyone went back to eating. When he got up to leave, Bright threw her arms around him and gave him a large, wet kiss on his cheek.

"You'll be very happy," she said. There were tears in her eyes. "Pao is such a wonderful girl." Peter smiled in a boyish way and shook her hand awkwardly with both of his hands.

"She is wonderful," he said.

Outside he saw Tabor making his way toward Northside. He was still smiling, and that made Peter furious. But then he remembered that Tabor was always smiling or nearly smiling. He was a curious sort of person. It was as if nearly everything in his life struck him as vaguely humorous. At a distance Peter had always admired and respected people with a sense of humor. Humor and wit had always seemed to him to be a kind of magic. Perhaps that was one reason why he respected Tabor and in a curious way felt drawn to him.

On the way back to his own schooner he happened to look down into the narrow space between the boats, and for a moment he saw something that almost made him laugh: three tennis balls bobbing in the green water, just below the surface. He imagined that in a few hours or days they would probably sink to the bottom of the ocean.

"Tennis, anyone?" he said out loud.

No one answered.

A week passed. In the mornings he worked in The Seafields, in the afternoons he worked with Tabor on the old boats, and in the early evenings he would sit on The Northside Cliff and listen to the weird sounds of The Hatchmaker, watch the children's games, or walk with Pao across Northside or through one of the ancient ships. At night they would make love fiercely, and in the mornings Pao would timidly ask him if married women were always so terribly sore and so terribly happy.

Sometimes in the morning the rare, light wind that lasted only an hour or so would change directions, and he would watch long lines of Sargasso Weeds break up and then reassemble in new lines along the new direction of the wind. Sometimes hundreds of glassy, leaf-shaped creatures would float past The Southern Edge, just beyond the inside borders of The Seafields. Sometimes a school of sea horses would move about in the weed-choked water between the boats. Sometimes in the evening the musicians from Bluewater and Conquistador Blanco would wander singly or in two or threes down by The Southern Edge, singing songs until the moon set. Sometimes the children would weedwalk at night with torches, making chains of fire across the water that made him think of Chinese dragons, a weird complement to the cold, night-burning luminescence of the micro-organisms that lived everywhere in the weeds. And so the days and nights passed in a blur of sensations, and Pao was with him always. Her shadow seemed to touch everything he saw, everything he imagined.

Often Tabor, Peter, and Pao would talk together late in the afternoon when the sun was near the water. For hours Peter would tell them of his past life—his empty childhood, his empty marriage, his struggle through graduate school at a third-rate university, his career at Harrington University. Sometimes he would send them into fits of laughter at the absurdities of his former life; sometimes they would listen sadly, reliving with him the frustrations of his loneliness and his disappointments. Pao, of course, was intensely interested in his account of his old life, but often she did not understand. What, she wondered, was a Chevrolet? And what was a bank loan? And how did water run through pipes? And in a symphony orchestra, why did so many people want to play their instruments all at the same time? How did buildings stand up? Did land end suddenly like the edge of a boat or did it gradually get mushy like porridge and then turn to water? Why did he teach new students every year and give up the old ones, and how did all the young girls keep from falling in love with him?

It seemed to him that Pao and Tabor were his first true friends, and as time passed he could feel their influence upon him; he could feel himself changing, deepening into a person he hardly recognized. It was a lovely time, the best he had ever known.

One day on The Northside Cliff, Tabor called him over to the port side of an old schooner to watch a school of large green fish that nibbled at the weeds near the stern.

"I've been thinking," he said. "Now that you've been married for seven days you ought to have a permanent and responsible job of some sort."

Peter smiled. "Like what?"

"Well, like, why don't you write a book?"

"A book? Out here?" You can't be serious."

"I am serious. I thought we might collaborate on a book about The Drift."

"What could we possibly say about it that anyone would believe?"

"You forget that the only readers would be people living right here."

"Then why write it in the first place?"

"I think it might be enlightening for all of us," said Tabor. "Many of us have no clear idea about where we are or where The Drift came from or who lived here before we did. I was thinking of a sort of history that would give an account of its time and place in the world."

"But I don't know anything about the history of The Drift. I've been here less than three weeks. I wouldn't know where to begin."

"I have a lot of research material," said Tabor. "Ships' logs, diaries, letters, drawings, all sorts of written records. Some of it goes back over three hundred years. And then too I have a lot of museum pieces: guns, lamps, furniture, toilet articles, things I've gathered together into a sort of display room in one of the big whaling ships near The Bridge."

"Sounds as if you have the project well under way."

"I've done a lot of collecting and organizing, but I need a second opinion. One more educated than my own. Also I need someone who can write decently. I know six languages but I have no sense of style when it comes to writing things down."

"It does sound like an interesting project," admitted Peter, "but sort of futile. An unpublished book about an unknown place that no one would read."

"There are scriveners over at Bluewater who would make copies so that everyone on The Drift could read it. But even if no one read it, even if you and I were the only ones, I still think it would be worth the doing."

Peter watched the green fish swimming just beneath the surface of the water. Worth doing, he thought. What made things worth doing? He had often dreamed of writing a book, a brilliant work of imaginative scholarship that would set the academic world on fire, something that would bring him fame, money, and admiration. Would that have been worth doing?

When he was twenty-eight he had dreamed of writing such a work, and shortly after he had accepted his teaching position at Harrington University he began gathering notes for a book about family life in ancient Egypt. But after two years of hard work his interest in the project began to wane. He had amassed a total of two thousand five hundred and seventy-three note cards, and he had not the faintest idea what to do with them. What did one do with facts? Why, one organized them into a pattern of some sort and produced a book. But for Peter the organization was not forthcoming. And then one morning when he began using his notes for a series of lectures in his survey course in ancient history, a young man in the fourth row had asked him what significance Egyptian family life had in terms of the general course of Egyptian history. The question, he remembered, had been rather awkwardly phrased in the halting manner of a confused but sincere young man who wanted to know where Egyptian family life belonged in his semester notes. And Peter was dumfounded. It became clear to him at that moment that he had no real understanding of Egyptian history, and that history in general was for him little more than a collection of facts arranged chronologically. Why, he wondered, had it taken him so long to realize that he would never really be a historian?

He picked up a broken piece of iron railing and tossed it into the water. The green fish that he and Tabor had been watching darted away in a silent explosion of color. Perhaps if somehow he had managed to write that book, perhaps then things would have turned out differently. But even as thoughts of money and recognition and power passed through his mind, he knew that these were not always the essential things. There were better reasons for writing books, better reasons for a lifetime of study, better reasons for being alive. Perhaps for the first time in his life he was beginning to understand that.

The green fish had come back and were skittering near the surface in an enormous cloudy pool. It seemed that the splash from the piece of iron railing had not frightened them away but had attracted more of them. He stared into the water for a long time without speaking.

"Tell me about The Drift," he said finally. "What was it like here hundreds of years ago?"

"Hundred of years ago?" Tabor lit his pipe and puffed and smiled with pleasure. And in turn, Peter smiled inwardly, for he knew that Tabor's great joy in life was long conversations.

"Only a few of the logs and diaries go back that far," he began. "I've only finished one of them, a fragment of a journal by a sea captain named Faulkland."

"What does it say?"

"It's very fragmentary. I'm not even sure about the order of the pages. He talks about old galleons filled with spices and gilded furniture where a few men lived like oriental emperors. They had servants and chamber music in the evenings, and balls and elaborate torchlight ceremonies or celebrations of some kind that moved in double lines from one boat to another. But only a few lived this way. Most of the people, and there were apparently hundreds of them, fished and collected seaweed, or worked for the rich captains of the galleons and capital ships. Faulkland also mentions a strange group of men dressed in sailcloth who called themselves The Servants of The New Atlantis. He says they were originally thieves and perverts bound for a penal colony somewhere in The New World. When their ship was wrecked in a storm they escaped and killed their guards a week or so before they came to The Drift. They worshiped the sea and bathed in a fishnet pool as an act of purification. So far I've had to take Faulkland's word for all this. There doesn't seem to be a shred of evidence to prove any of it. Nothing but the fact that parts of some very old boats still exist, which does prove at least that The Drift was here three or four hundred years ago."

"I don't understand. You think the diary may be a hoax?"

Tabor shrugged his shoulders. "Perhaps not a hoax exactly. But it's just possible that Faulkland was amusing himself by writing a romance. The style seems—I don't know—perhaps too literary to be a diary. Perhaps it was something to entertain his friends when he got back home. His reference to the 'New Atlantis' cult may have some satiric intent. Perhaps he had read Francis Bacon. But then on the other hand it may refer in some way to the notion that Atlantis lies somewhere beneath The Sargasso Sea. The Drift, then, would become a kind of New Atlantis."

"You mentioned his going home," said Peter. "Did you mean that at one time people could leave The Drift?"

"Yes. They were continually repairing boats, and every few months one of the captains would sail away with a hundred or two hundred people. They would row for a hundred miles and then the wind would carry them to The New World or back to England, depending on whether they had rowed north or south. But apparently the number of derelicts floating in more than equaled the number that sailed away."

"I see."

"Recently I've been trying to trace down some evidence for Faulkland's diary. He mentions, for example, that there was a Poet of The Drift, a man they called Damian, who wrote fifty volumes of poems on all subjects. But so far I haven't uncovered any of his works. Faulkland writes that Damian spent most of his time with The Servants of The New Atlantis, and like them he refused to leave The Drift. The Servants stayed because they were slowly gaining control and because there was nothing for them in The Old World except prison or the noose, but I suspect that Damian may have had other reasons. The diary says that Damian could improvise verse on any subject for an hour at a time and that most people thought he was made or possessed by angels or the devil.

"The closest I ever came to verifying even a small

part of this came about ten years ago. One of the divers from the old Daybreak Clan discovered a galleon caught in the weeds about twenty feet under his own boat. It was filled with the remains of books and ships' logs; apparently it had been a sort of library. The diver brought back a sample. I went down the next day, but the galleon had sunk during the night. Apparently he had cut through the weed beds that held it up. When I went under I saw the boat about a hundred feet or so below me. It was just barely visible."

Peter was silent for a moment. He pictured the boat in his mind, a boat filled with the works of a lost poet, sinking into the green silence of forever. "What about the book the diver brought back?" he said finally.

"Just a pair of swollen wooden boards and a pulpy lump of paper. There were some smudges of ink, but no visible letters. But there was something interesting about the boards. The words '*je suis*' were carved on the inside of one of them, and under them, the letter *D*."

"*D* for Damian," said Peter.

"It's possible," said Tabor. "That is, if there ever was such a man."

"But what happened to everything?" said Peter. "I mean to the rulers, and The Servants of The New Atlantis and the hundreds of people?"

"There's a legend that around this time—three hundred and twenty years ago—there was a great storm on The Drift, the only one that's ever been recorded here. It sank hundreds of boats and killed hundreds of people. In a young girl's diary there's a story about how her parents were killed in The Great Disaster of sixteen thirty-seven. Perhaps that was it. Apparently only a few dozen people survived, and since then no one has ventured out into the sea. We swim in net pools and some of us can dive ninety or more feet under the boats, and the children go weedwalking, but no one sails out into the open sea.

"The girl—I think her name was Mary Bellamy—writes that afterwards The Priests of The New Atlantis (as they then began to call themselves) told a story about how the spirits of the sea had made The Drift and had brought the storm to punish those who had tried to escape. Finally, when the feudal captains died off and The Priests gained power, it was forbidden for anyone to leave. Of course The Priests had good reason to avoid contact with the outside world."

"So the great storm changed everything," said Peter.

"Perhaps it did," said Tabor. "That is, if there really was a storm."

Together they walked across a narrow bridge that led down from Northside back toward *The Mary Strattford*. "So how about it?" said Tabor.

"How about what?"

"The book, remember? That's how all this started. I've been trying to enchant you with the mysteries we might solve and with the secrets we might uncover. Have I succeeded?" He held out his large brown hand and waited for an answer. Peter took his hand and smiled.

"Wonderful," said Tabor. "It's a bargain then. You know, I think we're going to have some interesting times together."

"I'm sure we will," said Peter. "But I think perhaps we ought to put this off until—well—until I get used to being married."

Tabor laughed. "I understand," he said. "I won't bother you until the honeymoon is over. But then," he added with a look of mock resignation, "your honeymoon may never end at the rate it's going. In which case we'll never get anything done."

As Peter walked back to his own schooner to look for Pao, he heard someone shouting from The Cliff. It was a Madrid pointing out into the sea. At *The Mary Strattford*, Bright, Reuben, and Javitt were straining to catch his words. Peter made a funnel with his hands and called out to them: "What is it? What's he saying?"

"It's a ship!" siad Bright. "A ship on the north horizon!"

Chapter Fourteen

THE SHARK

Tabor and Peter sat on the edge of The Cliff and watched the ship for nearly five hours. In that time it circled The Drift twice. At first it dipped and bobbed at the edge of the horizon, a gray and hazy silhouette in the afternoon sun. Tabor's eyes never seemed to leave that dim, elusive shape, and he passed the time by telling stories of other ships that had come to The Drift in other times—tales of half-crazed seamen, of strange treasures, of empty and soundless ships with no trace of life and clues of disaster that had baffled him for years.

By the next afternoon the ship had made several more circles and was much nearer. Peter could see now that it was an old fishing boat, a three-master sloop with two jibs and gaff rigging. It listed badly to the port side, and there were no signs of life on deck. From the poop fluttered a flag that he did not recognize: blue and white stripes with a white square in one corner that contained an emblematic sun.

"Any signs of life?" said Peter.

Tabor surveyed the stricken ship through his binoculars. "I don't see anything moving," he answered. "Part of the ship is charred and the lifeboats are gone. But there may be things we can use. Sometimes we find fishing equipment and tools."

"Yes. But I was hoping there would be people. News from the world."

Tabor looked at him. "Yes," he said slowly. "I often hope for news from the world."

Peter watched the sloop make its slow journey around The Drift. "Perhaps someday we may all go back to that world," he said.

"Perhaps someday you will, my friend," said Tabor. "I've always said that no one leaves The Drift, but perhaps you will."

"And why not you too? You're a strong man, and much of your life still lies ahead of you."

Tabor smiled and put his large hand on Peter's shoulder. "My life ended years ago," he said. "And all my strength lies in the fact that I've accepted defeat. Perhaps that's the difference between us."

"But I don't understand that," said Peter. "What could ever have defeated someone like you?"

Tabor was still smiling, but Peter could see clearly now the melancholy that had always been a part of that smile. "The war," he said. "Watching young men burning to death in the oil slicks of the ships I torpedoed. Fighting for a hopeless and wrongheaded cause. Depth charges. Water leaking into compartments. The death of all my friends. Days on a raft. A lovely woman I met on The Drift who died when our second child was born. Middle age. Many, many things, I'm afraid." He stared out into The Sargasso Sea and watched the derelict ship that with every passing came closer to The Northside Cliff.

Four boats below The Cliff, The Elders—embarked on The Long Journey—dropped hands and arose one by one from their closed, silent circle. Slowly they made their way up to where Peter and Tabor were sitting, to watch the ship from the world beyond The Drift.

"It's my husband," said Rose with an air of triumphant finality. "He's come at last."

A few minutes after The Elders had gone back to The Long Journey, Peter felt a small hand press his shoulder. Behind him he saw a beautiful face and a long streaming of black hair. Pao.

"What do you think of the new boat?" she said, looking into his eyes, letting him know that she cared nothing for boats.

"Oh, it's a fine boat," he answered. "A lovely boat."

Tabor smiled at them. "I think I may go down to have a closer look. I'll see both of you later," he said.

And soon Tabor, Reuben, Javitt, and three men from The Madrid had managed with the aid of ropes and Reuben's raft to bring the new ship to the edge of The Cliff. Peter and Pao watched from above, while below the others explored it. Soon it was clear that everyone was rather disappointed; the boat was nearly empty.

"There's nothing much here except this," said Tabor, calling up to them after the others had gone. In his arms he held a pair of aqualungs and a black rubber diving suit. "Do you know how to use these things?"

Peter nodded.

"Then how about coming down here and giving us all a demonstration?" He waved in the direction of the dozens of men and women who sat along the edge of The Cliff, people who had come to watch the men who had secured and then explored the old sloop.

Peter and Pao made their way down the incline of small broken sailing ships to the place where Tabor waited for them. It had been years since he had been deep-sea diving with Miriam, but the equipment looked familiar after he had lifted it and turned it over in his hands. "It's really very simple," he explained as he removed his trousers and crawled into the rubber suit.

"You breathe through the rubber mouthpiece and you adjust the flow of air by turning this lever. The whole thing fits over your back."

"And you can breathe underwater?" said Pao in a whisper of suspicion and disbelief.

Peter laughed. "You can breathe underwater."

"You mean you could just stay down for days and days and never come up?"

"No, the air gives out after a few hours."

"But how do those things hold enough air for all that breathing?" she persisted, still not convinced.

"The air is compressed. That is to say, the important part of it that we breathe is compressed. It's called oxygen."

"Compressed?" said Pao.

"Yes, it's, well, compressed." He made a gesture with his two hands.

"A lot of air is pushed together into a small space," said Tabor. He smiled and put his arm around her shoulder. "Air is thin and you can put a lot of it in a small space if you push hard enough."

"I don't believe it," said Pao, reddening at Peter's laughter. "How could anyone push all that air into these funny tubes?"

"A machine does it," said Peter, hoping that she would not ask how the machine worked, or who made such machines.

She was silent for a while. "I guess I don't know anything about machines," she said finally. "Tabor will have to teach me about machines."

"Tabor will teach you nothing about machines," said Tabor. "Tabor hates machines, and besides he is no longer your teacher."

"Teaching and loving," she said. "You teach everyone and you love everyone. Those are the two things that come naturally to you."

Tabor looked down at her, but he said nothing.

"That's a fine compliment," said Peter after a moment. "I was always such a bad teacher and such a bad lover."

"How completely you've changed," said Pao. She put her hands around his shoulders in back of his neck, and drew him against her.

"Ugh," she said. "How can one make love to a metal monster?"

"Aqualungs are not for loving," he said. "They're for swimming."

"Then swim," said Pao. "Show us how it works."

"Why don't you explore the underside of The Drift?" said Tabor. "None of us has ever really seen it very clearly."

"Give me fifteen minutes," said Peter. "If I don't come up be sure to call the coast guard."

"Wait!" said Pao.

"What is it?"

"I—I don't know. Be careful. Don't let that metal thing drag you down. Don't let anything hurt you." She kissed him.

Peter balanced on the edge of the listing boat, setting himself for the plunge into cool water.

"We'll be waiting right here," said Pao.

Then Peter remembered their swim in the netted pool. "Why don't you come with me? You could stay under for a minute or so."

"Not in the thick weeds. No. You go alone this time. We'll be waiting right here."

An enormous splash and then he felt himself sinking in the green water, while the bubbles from his aqualung gurgled upward through the thick weeds.

At first he could see next to nothing; the weeds caressed him, parted silently where he moved forward, and obscured everything beyond a hand's reach. The, quite suddenly, he found himself in a kind of wavering corridor of green that branched off in several directions. Then the lane where he traveled began to close and he felt a moment of panic, as if somehow the wall of weeds, moving in the unpredictable and subtle currents, would crush him.

For a while he traveled again in the green blindness until he came all at once into an open space. For a hundred yards or so all around him the weeds thinned into drifting strands and chains, and in the wavering light from above he could see parts of the underside of The Drift quite clearly. It was an amazing sight. Dozens, perhaps hundreds of ancient ships, almost completely enveloped in the mass of weeds near the surface, lay submerged at odd angles. Most of them had lost all detail in the overgrowth of vegetation and appeared only as long shapes that heaved slightly in the current. He saw now that The Drift was like an iceberg: a small piece showing above water and a vast pyramidal structure widening below the surface.

He swam in large circles, trying to see other parts of The Drift, but soon the weeds had moved inward in large drifting islands, and his vision was partly obscured. Then the water below him suddenly cleared and again he could see for hundreds of feet. The endlessness of the ocean filled him with a kind of fearful rapture. He thought again of Pao and the netted pool. But now there was no net to guard him against that infinity, that frightening expanse of mystery and imagination.

Three hundred feet below him hovered the remains of a twelfth-century warship. Its forecastle and sterncastle were plainly visible. What, he wondered, was holding it up so far beneath the weeds? It was like a miracle, a ghost risen from its graveyard thousands of feet below.

At that moment he saw the shark.

Somehow he was sure it was the same shark he had seen in the netted pool. A bleary smudge of gray far below him, it nosed back and forth, sometimes changing directions very suddenly like a caged tiger. He had a strange feeling now that he had lived through all this before. It was as if the time he had dipped his face into the water and seen the shark from his dinghy, the time he had swum with Pao, and now were all the same moment, repeated in different settings. The shark was an image, a hieroglyph in some forgotten language. And on each occasion the image of the moment had drawn him deeper into the water and into the secret resources of his own mind.

Slowly the shark moved upward. It seemed aware of him now. Its turnings and gyrations always brought it closer to where he treaded water, breathing through the aqualung, which sent bursts of silver bubbles oscillating, spiraling toward the surface, surface that was now no more than a diffused lambency far above him. He could sense the great power, the great freedom and grace of the thing that was coming toward him. It was less than two hundred feet below him now. He could see its lidless eyes staring at him.

Peter began to breathe very deeply. Inside him he felt a great roaring silence, a rapture, a sense of the immortality of the sea that moved like an invisible spirit, a dark wind, everywhere around him. He waited a minute or two longer, treading water and listening to the bubbles, and then he swam down to meet the shark.

He moved his feet in a slow undulating rhythm and parted the water in front of him with his hands. It seemed to him that he was very deep now. The water was darker and the glimmering of light from far above was a shifting of yellowish green, an elusive thing. Then he wondered where the shark was. He turned around in the space of water where he was suspended, but there was nothing but a great pressure against his body, a silence, a numbing coldness. Dimly he realized that he was breathing too often and too deeply.

Then an enormous gray shape brushed against him, turning him over in the water. It wheeled around and began circling him. Th great pointed nose, the rows of teeth in the moonshaped mouth, the gill slits, the forked tail, the malevolent eyes—he saw them all and he felt curious, strangely unafraid. Such an enormous and evil thing, he thought. Evil, and yet it would not attack him, but only circled and waited. Evil and yet not evil. Like a ghost of something he had always feared which suddenly, in a strange new light, had become more an object of fascination than fear.

The shark was the most beautiful thing he had ever seen. Like a giant wave, like the roaring locomotives he had dreamed about and feared as a boy, like a great ship sailing in the space between the stars, like a mythical beast or a prehistoric sail-backed reptile swimming in the ocean. A great universal force that seemed, with its brute beauty, its danger, and its infinite strength, to lie behind everything, behind all the pleasure and pain of the world, behind all that he had ever hoped or dreamed. How beautiful, he thought. And how incredibly grotesque.

"Have you ever been eaten alive?" Pao had once asked him. Perhaps that was what was happening. His whole life was being eaten, devoured, ingested, and changed into something that he had never clearly imagined before. Now the shark was moving toward him, its forked tail swinging back and forth, and it seemed that the water became grainy and disconnected. Something was roaring in his ears. He could see nothing but the face of the shark very near his own, the gray face with its mouth half open. With trembling hands he reached out and touched the jaw and the gill of the great beast, and as he did so it turned and plunged toward the bottom of the sea at such a speed that in a moments's time it was only a gray smear below him. And for a long moment after it had disappeared he could feel the rubbery flesh in his hands, the jaw of the great shark.

He knew that it was time now for him to go back to the world above, but he had no desire to do so. He felt that he was slowly dying, sinking to the bottom of the ocean. Strange lights were bursting everywhere in his mind and in the grainy water, and soon he was aware of nothing but the sound of bubbles rising a thousand miles to the surface.

Chapter Fifteen

NIGHTSONGS

For a long time it seemed that he was drifting in the deep water. The current rolled his body over and over, and sometimes the fish would nibble curiously at him. One day a pair of half-hungry sharks tore at him in a desultory way, and another time a dolphin nosed him to the surface, and rolled him over and over. By the end of September the current had carried him to Bermuda.

His head was missing now as well as one of his arms and most of both legs. His swollen body had assumed an altogether inhuman shape, a blue and red fruit with dark creases where shreds of the rubber diving suit still circled his body.

"Mummy," said the little girl in the white bathing suit. "Come see what I found."

"What is it, Rachel honey?" The mother lay under a large green umbrella.

"Big rubber fish," said the little girl. She made a big circle with her small arms to emphasize the "big."

"Later, honey," said her mother. "Mummy was up late last night and she's going to sleep for a while."

"It's so blue, Mummy," the little girl persisted. "Like sky."

"Blue?" The word made her mother vaguely uneasy. "What is it, honey? A rubber swan or something like that?"

"Uh-uh. S'like a fish. Only it's all big and s'got pretty colors."

Her mother sat up and looked at her. "Is it something dead, honey? Don't play with dead things."

"Dead?" The idea had not occurred to her. "It smells funny," she offered.

Rachel went back down the beach to her new toy. It lolled back and forth very gently in the foam. It was the most beautiful thing she had ever seen in all the four years of her life, and the sight of it filled her with delight and wonder. It was like a fish, like a whale, like a tree trunk, like a funny colored balloon that you blow up and squeeze into shapes with your fingers.

Then a wave came and the blue and red shape turned over and Rachel saw an arm with gray fingers, and she thought that perhaps most of all it reminded her of a person. And then she imagined that at one time it really had been a person, and that the sea had changed it, given it the colors and the shapes that belonged to the sea, and that this was only the end of a long trip that had begun on the other side of the water where the sun was.

She reached down and touched the shoulder of the thing she had found in the water. It was very pleasant to touch, like all things that came from the water: smooth stones, soft driftwood, spongy weeds, the water itself that went out everywhere as far as she could see. And the colors were so pretty. They made her think of big, bright flowers she had once seen growing somewhere in a tree stump.

But suddenly Rachel was terrified. Her mother was

standing behind her screaming, clutching at her, trying to drag her across the sand, away from the bright thing that lay on the beach.

"Sutherland! Are you all right?"

It was Pao's voice. The sound wavered in his ears as they lifted him out of the water.

"Sutherland! Are you all right?"

Tabor laid him on the deck and removed the breathing tube from his mouth. "He went down too far," said Tabor. "The pressure and the drop in temperature were too much for him."

"Is he going to be sick?" said Pao.

"Yes. Very."

"But is he going to be all right?"

"I think so. He's got the bends, but he doesn't look too bad."

Peter opened his eyes. Tabor's face wavered in front of him. He blinked several times until the image was clear. "How long—how long was I down there?" His voice was a thin whisper.

"Only a little while," said Pao. She took his hand and pressed it between hers. "Are you all right? You look so blue."

Blue, he thought. Such a pretty color. But the word made him uneasy. He had dreamed something about blue that he could not remember.

"I don't know. I think so. I saw a shark."

"Sharks won't hurt you," said Pao.

"Sharks will tear your legs off if they have a mind to," said Tabor. "It depends on what you do and how hungry they are. Why didn't you come up when you saw him?"

"Sharks won't hurt you," said Pao. "But I was worried because you were gone so long. I didn't really think you could stay under with your metal tubes. I thought —I thought you were dead."

"I'm all right," said Peter. But he could not sit up by

himself, and he felt very sick and very cold. His fingers and his feet felt numb and the bones behind his ears ached. For a moment he wanted to throw up.

"I went down too far," he said. "And when it was time, I didn't want to come up at all. And then for a second I must have passed out, and then I remember coming up, trying to stay beneath my bubbles, but I came up too fast."

"Nitrogen narcosis," said Tabor. "You're lucky to be alive at all. I never should have let you go down there by yourself."

Pao and Tabor helped him to his feet, and together they started back toward *The Mary Strattford*.

"For God's sake, tell us what happened," said Tabor. "Tell us about the shark."

The warm boards of the boats felt good beneath him as he walked, dripping wet, from ship to ship. Slowly his head began to clear and the nausea began to ease. "I'm not sure what I can say about it," said Peter. "Everything was strange. Sort of, well, rapturous. The shark was swimming toward me, so I swam down to meet him. I had a feeling he wouldn't hurt me. I had the feeling that nothing could hurt me, or that if something did, it wouldn't matter. It was as if—" But he could not find the words.

"It was as if the shark were not really a fish, but something else," said Tabor. But Tabor did not look happy.

"Yes," said Peter. "As if it were something else." For a few moments he thought about the shark, trying to remember why he had gone down to meet it, why he had reached out to touch it. It seemed now to have happened to a long time ago. "Or as if it were a person in disguise," he said. "A person who wanted me to go somewhere. No, that's not quite it. The shark seemed to be a representation, an emblem of something. Does that make sense?"

"Finally," said Pao.

"Finally what?" said Peter.

"Finally you are learning what the children know. You're learning about shadowgames."

Tabor looked at her in surprise. "Shadowgames!" he said. "You don't seem to realize that he might have been killed. The shark might have torn him apart!"

When he reached *The Mary Strattford* he was still very weak, and the sight and smell of food suddenly made him violently ill. Bright helped him into the kitchen where he threw up into a large washbasin and then lay down on a mattress in the corner where she napped sometimes during the day. An hour later he felt much better.

When the meal in the other room was over, Pao came into the kitchen and bent over him. There were tears in her eyes. "If anything had happened to you I would have died," she said. "I would never have danced again for anyone."

He smiled weakly and reached up to touch her. His hand felt cold and damp against her cheek. He trembled. "I feel better," he said.

"Would you like something to eat?"

"Yes."

She brought him a small bowl of yellow vegetables and a piece of fish, something that Reuben had caught that morning. They talked quietly for a while, holding hands, listening to the soporific murmur of the water against the hull of the boat that lay beneath *The Mary Strattford*.

"Let's go to The Bridge," said Pao. "All the clans will be there this evening for the Nightsongs."

"Will you sing tonight?"

"No," she said. "I told everyone that I would not be singing tonight and that I—that we would not be staying very long." She touched his arm and looked down at her own feet.

* * *

Musicians from all the clans had gathered on The Bridge that evening to play their music. First, one group would sing or play, and then another would take its place when the first had exhausted its repertoire. When the sun set, a dark-haired Madrid girl came with a dozen torches, and there was music that went on for hours into the night, music that moved and changed like the flickering of diamondlight in the black eyes of the singers. Soon many torches warmed and illuminated the cheeks and shoulders of everyone who gathered within their circle of light. He sat with Pao and they held hands and listened to the music.

Many of the songs were composed by a slender, hawk-faced young man, a Bluewater, who looked something like Raven. He sang in a reedy voice that reminded him of a clarinet. His songs were based on modes that never involved more than four or five notes, and he accompanied himself with a mandolin-like instrument upon which he plucked a bass continuo pattern of parallel fifths and sixths. Peter noticed that many of the other young singers had learned his songs or had written others that were imitative. Other songs that sounded like slow English ballads were sung by small groups of singers, sometimes in two or three part harmony. Still others were quick songs, like sailors' jigs or medieval dances, sung by two or three people and accompanied by drums made of small wooden kegs held between the knees. Others were instrumentals, complicated pieces that involved a slow counterpoint between two guitars and a mandolin or two lutes and a guitar. Sometimes they imitated classical fugue or canon forms. Others were songs that everyone seemed to know, songs that everyone sang in unison.

Many were love songs. Others were songs of adventure on the sea, of strange voyages to mythical places that reminded him of The Dance of The Nine Islands. One was a ballad about a land beyond the stars. Another told of a goddess of the sea who on her wedding night wove a robe of seafoam to enchant her mortal husband. Another told about how, a hundred years ago, The East Bridge was two hundred miles long and reached almost to The Land of Bermuda. Still another described a city made of coral that lay at the bottom of the ocean somewhere beneath The Drift:

> Swim down with me, my love,
> Where the fish are wan and pale
> And waving weeds are dark
> And light is sure to fail;
> For far beneath, I know a coral city
> Where all The Elders stay,
> And wait for us to make our downward way,
> And wait for us to make our downward way.

And still another told of a giant bird that comes at night to bring dreams to children:

> Coo, my little one, coo, my love:
> The Blackbird has a thousand journeys
>   which he nightly keeps,
> And nothing in his world is really what it seems;
> His cloudy wings touch everything that sleeps.
> And the shadows of his wings are filled with dreams.
> Coo, my little one, coo, my love.

As the music played on and on, he closed his eyes, and his mind began to wander. He thought again of the shark. Pao had told him once that sharks were beautiful. But sharks had teeth and they lived in a deep world where Peter could not breathe and where everything was dark. A shark can tear your legs off, Tabor had said. Yes. It had been a moment of insanity, that moment when he swam down to meet the shark. The singers were singing of love, of blackbirds carrying dreams, of kingdoms at the bottom of the sea, but only an hour or two earlier he might well have been torn apart by a mindless beast.

Together they listened to the music for an hour and then made their way back to Peter's schooner. The Nightsongs faded behind them, blurring into the sound of the water. It was Pao's music, and it was the music of the ancient boats. But as they lay in bed together he heard, in the moments before they embraced, sounds that were not a part of those things that had enchanted him. It was an alien murmuring, a discordant melody that cut across the wavering romantic fragments that still drifted in from the torchlight singers forty or fifty boats away. And it occurred to him that there were really two kinds of music on The Drift: there was the music of the people and the boats, and there was also the music of The Hatchmaker.

Chapter Sixteen

RAVEN

When the sun broke across the horizon and a shaft of light from the porthole above the instrument panel touched his cheek, he woke abruptly, and in that sightless moment before his waking mind had lifted out of his sleep, his dream continued. He was drowning. He could not find the rubber breathing tube, and he struggled desperately against the heavy water that would not let him breathe or move his arms. Suddenly he struck Pao on the ear, and she moaned, turning in her sleep.

Then he opened his eyes. The room came back to him, silent and familiar. He breathed deeply, closed his eyes, and slept for another hour. When he awoke again, Pao was gone.

There was an overflow of supplies on *The Mary Strattford* from the previous day's harvest, and so there was no work to be done that morning in The Seafields. Peter felt very much at loose ends. He wandered up toward Northside looking for Pao, who had not appeared for breakfast.

"Sustenance," said Reuben, clucking his disapproval. "Nourishment and sustenance are the keys of life. Man cannot sing, dance, or work without three meals a day. Pao will come to no good end if she neglects her stomach."

"Her stomach," said Javitt, nodding in agreement.

The two old men followed him for a while, then settled down on the slanting deck of an eighteenth-century English ship of the line, crossed their legs, and began to play a game with Tarot cards on the warm sunlit boards.

Peter wandered on by himself. He still felt queer about what had happened the previous day. He was of course an inexperienced diver; perhaps he had breathed too quickly and hyperventilated. That and the pressure and the drop in temperature at that depth seemed to have produced a very strange state of mind. The Rapture of The Deep, they called it. The whole experience made him uneasy, but of course it was only a single incident to set against days and days of happiness. It was as if he had been made over, changed into a creature of a different species, or as if he were asleep, dreaming of a faraway land where there was no time, no death, no struggle against the impossible odds of mortality. The dream had a logic of its own, as dreams will, and the beauty, the warmth, and the deceptive reasonableness of everything around him made the waking world, the world beyond The Drift, seem unreal and remote and filled with absurd conflicts.

He remembered once when he had been only twelve years old he had dreamed of a world in which everyone lived in trees. Sap, leaves, and bark had provided all the necessities of life, and everyone lived in a great forest where it was perpetually autumn and the brown and gold and crimson leaves gathered in huge drifts upon which he and his companions played endlessly. For several hours that morning it had seemed like an eminently sensible arrangement, so much so that at breakfast, when he saw his father reading the financial page of *The New York Times,* his mother cooking Mother's Oats, and the gray kitchen walls of the old brownstone apartment, he had burst out laughing at the tenor of his own life, a breach of etiquette for which he was severely reprimanded; and often now he had a similar urge to laugh when he thought of his old life at Harrington University, when he thought of Miriam, Harry Ranton, and Dr. Ratcliffe, when he thought of the tennis courts where he went to show his summer tan and, in rare and shy moments, agreed to play tennis with a pretty undergraduate coed or prove his masculinity by soundly trouncing the fourth-seeded member of the college tennis team.

It had been such a futile life, tiring and somehow mindless. He had always been pushed by forces he had never understood, forces that destroyed his will and his vision. Now he was in so many ways a different person. Seldom now did anything ever tire him, and everything, it seemed, was a source of profound interest. People were interesting. There had been a time when, in his own secret way, he had needed people very much and had been terribly concerned about the impression he made upon them; but he never wondered about them, about what they thought or felt, and he had never really trusted anyone. Now all that was changed. His love for Pao and Tabor, his interest in the children's games, in the bold arts and strange beliefs of the adults, in the mystery of the ancient boats and their forgotten cargoes —all this had sent his mind in so many new directions that he was now less aware of his own feelings as such, and less conscious of himself as an intellect painfully set apart from the world around him. He was alive now in a way he had never been before.

But the episode with the shark disturbed him. And there was something else: a moment of lost consciousness, a dream that he could not remember.

All at once he found himself at The Southern Edge.

What, he wondered, had brought him to this part of The Drift? Then he remembered the dinghy. He had not seen it in over a week now, not since before The Dance of The Nine Islands. He thought about the sail, the motor, and all his homemade rigging. Probably by now The Outlanders had destroyed all of it or had taken it for their own purposes. Still, it might be interesting to take a look. He had spent a lot of time working on it. He might have used it to sail around The Drift and perhaps someday if he had changed his mind, perhaps then he could have persuaded Pao and Tabor to come with him back to—the phrase came into his mind quite naturally—The Island of Connecticut.

He had to admit that even now there was doubt in his mind. Granted, his old life was absurd. But dimly he realized that there might also be something rather profoundly absurd about spending forty or fifty years on an island of derelict ships.

He stepped down into the dark hatchway of the old bilander where he had hidden his dinghy. Slowly his eyes adjusted to the dim light. To his great surprise, the dinghy was just as he had left it. And the sails, the motor, and the five gallons were all there. But when he moved forward to get a closer look, he saw a figure sitting near the point of the hull. His muscles froze. It was a trap. That was why they left everything as it was. He whirled around, raising his arm to ward off an expected blow, but there was no one anywhere behind him, no one anywhere else in the ship. Puzzled, he stared at the single figure crouching in the hull. Why would one Outlander lie in wait for him? But perhaps it was not an Outlander.

"Who's there?" he said finally.

The small figure rose off its haunches and walked toward him. In one hand he held a knife, and in the other, a long paddle.

"Raven!"

The figure recognized him and lowered his weapons. For a moment they stared at each other.

"I thought you'd never come," said Raven. "It's been eight nights now."

"I don't understand. What are you doing here?"

"I'm defending your boat," he answered.

"I still don't understand. Why should you guard my dinghy? I thought you rather disliked me."

"You're right about that," said the boy in a matter-of-fact tone. "I hate you."

Peter looked at the boy, trying to decipher in his face the meaning of his hatred. Raven was trembling now. His long hair fell over his eyes and he brushed it away.

"Did someone make you do this?" said Peter.

"Nobody makes me do anything. I do just what I like."

"That's marvelous," said Peter. "You must be very happy."

The boy glared at him. Then his eyes darted from one thing to another and his lips trembled as if he were trying to find words.

"Now look," said Peter. "You've got to tell me what this is all about. If I've offended you in some way I'm very sorry."

"You're sorry. That's pretty good. Well listen, if you're really sorry, why don't you get out of here? I mean, way out of here like back to the moon or wherever you came from."

"Is that why you've guarded my boat? So I'll have a way of leaving?"

"You bet it is. I even stole some food from Bright and a net and some clothes and an extra paddle. So now you got everything you need." The boy stared at him fiercely and then threw the paddle across the hull. It landed with an enormous clatter that seemed to please him. He closed the blade on his knife and put it in his pocket. "I had lots of time down here," he said quietly. "So I finished what you started. I made outriggers so you could use your sail, and I fixed all your lines. So you can leave anytime." Again he pushed the long shock of black hair out of his eyes. He seemed on the verge of tears now. He looked so young, so raw-boned and angular, so very vulnerable. He was even younger than Pao.

Pao? Could that be it?

"Pao," he said out loud. The boy winced. The word was like a blow in the face. So that *was* it. He should have suspected it long ago.

"What about Pao?" said Raven.

"You're in love with her," said Peter.

The boy stiffened. "Love!" he said. It was a cry of pain. "I don't love anyone!" Then he began to shake and cry out in a wordless, incoherent way. He rushed at Peter, swinging his fists, beating at the air like a drowning man. A blow glanced off Peter's temple and he staggered backward against the old wooden steps leading up to the hatch. A sharp pain shot through his head, but he had the presence of mind not to cry out or strike back.

Raven stopped all at once, gasping for breath. It was as if he had suddenly come out of a seizure.

"I'm sorry," said Peter very quietly. "I'm really very sorry."

"You're sorry about everything," said Raven.

"And thanks for pocketing your hardware. Otherwise, we might really have hurt each other."

"Don't thank me for anything."

"I only meant that it showed a certain amount of good sense."

"I don't have any sense," said Raven, whose fury had turned suddenly upon himself. "I don't have sense about anything and I don't know anything about anything."

"Tabor says you're one of his best men."

"You're lying."

"I'm not. He told me that when you began to skip work three days ago. He says he misses you."

"Nobody misses me. Do you know what the other boys over at Madrid call me?"

"What do they call you?"

"Seaweed."

"Hmmm. Well, your problem then is to find better, nastier names for them. You know, like Blowfish, Bilgewater, Fishguts—"

Raven tried very hard not to smile, and suddenly Peter felt enormously pleased with himself. "Come on," he said, putting his arm around the boy's shoulder, "let's get back to *The Mary Strattford* before all the food is gone and we both starve to death."

On the way he learned that one of The Outlanders had tried to get down the hatch two days before, but that Raven had beaten him off. Since then they had left him alone. He could not help thinking what an act of courage and hatred it had been. One lonely boy spending eight nights in the black hull of a creaking old ship, waiting with his pocketknife and his paddle for The Outlanders. He felt a surge of admiration and pity.

"Would you be happier here if I went away?" said Peter.

Raven shook his head. "Probably not. I've never been happy here. I hate shadowgames and dances and all those things. I work on the boats. But there isn't anything else. It's always the same, like being in a cage. Someday I'll kill someone and then they'll put me on The Outland. And that'll be the end of me. No one lives more than a few years on The Outland."

"Why don't you like the shadowgames and dances?" said Peter after he had thought about what Raven had said.

"Because they don't mean anything," said Raven.

Before they had gone very far they heard behind them the sound of splashing water and paddles slapping against wood. Raven smiled and pointed his finger to a place perhaps a hundred yards away, beyond the near edge of The Outland.

"Look!" he said. "They have their own dances and games, just like Pao and The Madrids."

When Peter turned to follow the direction of Raven's finger, he saw a large flat-bottomed barge, apparently built from scraps of other ships, where eight scarred and bearded men, all stripped to the waist, were shouting and waving their arms in the air like children. The scarfaced man was among them, beating his paddle against the barge and jumping up and down. There seemed to be no pattern or focus to what they were doing, and from that distance they reminded Peter of ants trapped in a glass jar running in all directions.

"It gets more organized after a while," said Raven. "Watch."

"We'd better get back to *The Mary Strattford*," said Peter. "We're going to miss dinner."

"Wait a minute," said Raven. "See what they're doing?"

He led Peter two boats closer to The Southern Edge where they could get a better view, and from there they watched for what seemed to be the better part of an hour. As they stood there, clouds of mist began to form and roll slowly inward from the far side of The Outland.

The Outlanders played three games while a dwarfish, white-haired old man with one leg missing beat out an even rhythm on a drum. One side of his chest caved inward, as if the ribs had been removed, and was covered with purple scars. The first game was something Raven called Ropes and Knives. The contestants received long knives which they held in their right hands. Then a one-foot length of rope was tied first to the right wrist and then to the left ankle of each man, so that they were forced to bend over and hobble at each other like crippled beasts, flailing and pushing with their left hands, lifting their legs and leaping awkwardly when they saw openings to lunge with their knives. The first man to slash the other's chest was declared the winner. The second game, Paddles and Rafts, involved teams of two men, one to paddle and steer a small round craft and the other to strike out against his opponents and their rafts with a long oar. The winner was declared when three of the four teams had been dumped into the water amid cheers and shrill whistles and stamping of feet and loud cries of despair. The third game was a free-for-all called Stinking Fish. To Peter it was a weird variation of vaudeville's pie in the face. The scarfaced man brought a large wooden table of fish to the center of the barge, and then each of the eight men chose the largest fish he could find and proceeded to use it as a weapon against his fellows. The game was played amid a kind of screaming, frantic laughter that all but incapacitated those who played. One man simply rolled around the barge, hugging his huge dead fish and giggling. The scarfaced man was perhaps the most aggressive of the Stinking Fish combatants. He had the largest weapon of all, and after a few moments he managed to sneak up behind a small dark man who was busily swinging at someone else, and with a prodigious heave he struck him squarely on top of the head with such force that viscera and pieces of fish flew every which way, drowning his victim in fish parts and spraying everyone nearby with blood. With that, the scarfaced man leaped into the air, laughing and shrieking at his fallen opponent.

Peter noticed then that other people had gathered on other ships to watch the games of The Outlanders. They talked very quietly. Hardly anyone moved. They made him think of the reticent uncertainty of children watching lions at a carnival, their fear of the roars and the open jaws and the sharp teeth set against their faith in cages and steel bars.

"It's nearly done now," said Raven. "This part is called The Dance of Friends and Enemies." But it was not a dance at all, as far as Peter could tell. The Outlanders were simply shouting and running around again, everybody slapping everyone else and shaking everyone else's hand. And then quite suddenly it was over. The scarred, bearded men dropped their hooks and fish and knives onto their four small rafts and slowly paddled their way into the rolling mist, like elves in a fairy story drifting off into the land of sleep. They talked quietly now. Their faces were calm. Just once, the scarfaced man turned and smiled at the men from The Drift who had watched them. Casually, with the air of a boy skipping stones on a lake at sunset, he threw an iron boat hook at the silent watchers. It fell far short, clattering on a ship's deck somewhere at the edge of The Outland. He waved once and then turned back just as his raft began to disappear in the mist.

The large flat-bottomed barge was empty now except for the crippled dwarf and his drum, who had fallen asleep together—the drum silent, the old man wheezing and sighing in a dream of peace.

When they got back to *The Mary Strattford*, Pao was standing at the stern of the ship, waving at them.

"Sutherland! Did you see The Outlanders? Did you see what they were doing?"

"Raven and I watched for a while," he said.

"It's terrible all the things they do," said Pao. She threw her arms around him, ignoring Raven. "Come inside. I saved you something to eat."

Peter looked back at Raven, who had already turned away and was walking across a narrow plank to the next boat. "But I sort of enjoy watching The Outlanders," he said, gently pulling away from her as Raven disappeared.

"It was like The Black Mass," she said very seriously. "Tabor told me once about The Black Mass."

"A celebration of evil? I don't think so. I can't take them that seriously. It's true, they're very grotesque and very cruel, even to each other. But in a strange way, I almost like them."

"How can you?" she demanded. "They're like—they're like hatchetmen!"

Peter smiled at Pao's newly acquired allusion. "Perhaps," he said.

Pao looked at him and then at the boat where Raven had gone. "I should have said something to Raven," she said.

"Yes. That would have been nice."

"And—and how can I say it? I like to watch The Outlanders too, but it hurts me to think that I do." She seemed to look far beyond him, and then turned her head slowly and rested it against his chest and put her arms around him again.

"Why should I feel that way?" she asked. "Why should the truth ever be painful?"

"Why? My God, the world is full of facts that are painful. But you wouldn't know about that. Your world is so perfect, so spontaneous and complementary to itself. You don't know anything about pain."

"You have taught me much about pain already," she said. "Perhaps even now there are things—things I can see in the future that I cannot believe because they are too painful. But why should that be? I used to think that the whole world was an extension of my desire and that I was an extension of the world's desire and that all things were a part of one thing."

"Perhaps that's true."

"But there are The Outlanders. And there are other things that may happen that I—I do not wish to happen."

"What are you afraid of?" said Peter.

"Never mind. I only meant that the shadowgames, the songs and the dances, the torchlight ceremonies, The Long Journey of The Elders, all the things we love here on The Drift make a circle that is perhaps not as large as—that is, a circle that does not admit to certain things that are—really unpleasant." Pao closed her eyes and turned her head slowly. She seemed very unhappy.

"In The Middle Ages," he said, "people thought of life as something that moved on a wheel passing between extremes of fortune and misfortune. Like the passing of the seasons."

"Yes, but there are no seasons on The Drift," she said. "We do not think of seasons here."

She trembled and pressed herself against him and kissed him on the mouth. "Let's go to your boat," she said.

"Now? At this time in the afternoon? We'll miss dinner." But already he could feel himself assenting to the touch of her hands, to the feel of her breasts against him. She was so young, he thought. So lovely and so perfect.

"Seasons and times of day," she said, trying to smile. "People from land are so concerned with things at the proper time. But love has an appetite that knows no season or time of day. Isn't that true, Sutherland? Isn't that true even on land?"

He gathered her black hair in his hands and pulled so that her head fell backward, and then he kissed her on her throat and on her ear and cheek, and finally on her mouth.

"I love you," he said.

Chapter Seventeen

ECHOES AND LOOMINGS

The sun was near its zenith when he woke the next morning. Pao, he remembered, had whispered something in his ear an hour earlier, something he could not remember. She was gone now. Every morning, it seemed, she woke before him and was seldom seen by anyone before the noon meal.

But on his way to *The Mary Strattford* that morning he saw her walking, six or seven boats above him near Northside. She carried a large bag of something on her back. He waved to her and when she saw him she shifted the weight of it to one hip so that she could wave back with one hand. He called out to her, but she was gone before the sound left his lips.

That afternoon Pao was missing at lunch and Bright seemed unusually quiet. She seemed preoccupied, and when the meal was nearly over she looked up at Peter.

"I'm worried about Rose," she said in a low voice. "She's been on The Long Journey for nearly two days now and I don't think she's stopped but once for meals.

Sutherland, could you go and see if she'll come up for an hour or so? Tell her I've got some hot soup and seabread. She'll listen to a man more than a woman. I don't believe she's heard ten words I've said to her in the last ten months."

"She'll be all right," said Michael, who was beating a rhythm in his empty wooden bowl with a spoon and smiling expectantly at his brother. "Nothing can hurt Rose."

"Rose will die if she doesn't eat," said Tabor. "She's got to eat just like everybody else."

"Ordinarily I'd ask Tabor," said Bright. "But he promised The Bluewaters he would supervise the work on one of their ships this afternoon."

"Is she still up near The Northside Cliff where we brought in the new ship?" asked Peter.

Bright nodded. "I think so. She used to bring The Elders together in different places all over The Drift, but now she almost always goes to the same place for The Long Journey."

When the meal was over he crossed the five boats that separated *The Mary Strattford* from The Cliff. From there he could see a circle of seventeen men and women sitting together and holding hands three boats to the southwest. As he drew nearer he could hear the murmur of their low voices repeating vague syllables over and over in a wordless jumble, and then a space of silence. Then slowly it rose again, a tide of sound like the moan of the wind. As he watched, he slowly became aware of the motion of their bodies, a subtle movement that rose and fell with the wave of their voices, a slow leaning to one side and then a leaning forward. It was as if they were blown by a ghostly breeze no one else could feel.

Suddenly Rose looked up and stared at him. The effect was so startling that for a moment Peter could not remember why he had come.

"Bright thinks it's time for me to eat," she said, staring at him in that flat, unblinking way that had always made him uncomfortable. "Very well. We must all render unto Caesar."

"She has some hot soup and seabread," said Peter, who no longer bothered to wonder how Rose and Pao knew what was in his mind.

"Give me your hand," she said, extending a white, bony claw with five fingers. Her hand was very smooth and very cold, and for an instant he thought of the cool, rubbery nose of the shark he had reached out to touch during that strange time underwater.

The old woman stared into his eyes. "Plants," she said.

"Plants?" said Peter.

"Plants," she answered. "You have always shown such a remarkable interest in plants. You and your friend Odysseus."

Peter nodded. "I remember now," he said. "You were asking me about flowers one day on *The Mary Strattford*."

"Such a remarkable memory," said the old woman, spitting out the words. "A mind like a filing cabinet. Did you know that the stems and leaves of Sargasso Plants are not really stems and leaves at all?"

"Bright mentioned something about that," said Peter.

"Sargassum is simply a form of algae," she continued. "A simple plant, really. No sperms, no ova. It simply grows at one end and rots at the other. An open chain of cells that never ends. A maze of rooms that never becomes a house."

Peter looked at her, wondering what he was expected to say. "It seems to grow everywhere," he offered.

She sighed. "I suppose I really should not be so contemptuous of you and your kind," she said. "You have a good brain and a good heart and it's not your fault you were born in a world where nothing moves."

Peter smiled. All at once he realized that he was no longer afraid of Rose. More and more she seemed to be a person, no longer a mythological figure in an illusion called The Drift. "Are you saying that Sargasso Plants are like The Drift itself?" he said.

She looked at him sharply, surprised at his question. "They have the form of a complex entity, but they are not complex in function," she said. "But that is not the important thing. The important thing is that the weeds move with The Drift, The Drift moves with the sea, the sea moves with the spin of all the seas, and all the seas together move with the moving earth which revolves in the circle of the solar system which turns its larger circle in The Milky Way Galaxy. All forms of life and existence are only forms of motion," she concluded. "To stop moving is to stop living, to stop existing. That is what I taught when I was the teacher of all the children on The Drift."

"Everything is a form of motion?" said Peter. The idea had never occurred to him before.

"Small moving things divide into smaller moving things," she said, "until finally there is no matter at all. Nothing but the essence of motion and energy itself."

"Like an electron," said Peter, hoping, smiling in his hope, that Rose had never heard of electrons.

"Never mind that!" she snapped furiously, hissing the words through her teeth. "On land you people always move about so as to remain still. On The Drift people remain still so as to move about. Do you understand that? That's why The Drift is a land of metaphors. A metaphor is an act between two images that never stops moving. In your world," she added, "there are only dead metaphors. Which is worse than none at all. You have frozen everything into categories that you walk into and examine like tombs."

Just then Peter had an image of himself standing for years in the middle of a river that was always raging at flood time, trying with all his strength not to be swept away by the violent current. The whole world, it seemed, was awash with motion in that turbulent place, but he, for the sake of responsibility, propriety, efficiency, and other dead metaphors, had tried to remain calm, to ignore the current of his senses, to save himself from the life around him which he had always viewed with so much apprehension and fear.

"What happens to people who try to deny the principle of motion?" he said.

"Today on The Long Journey we all lived on The Island of Arabia," she said. "I saw white horses with hoofs of silver flashing in the sun. And dark-skinned men with scimitars and hanks of hair."

"I was asking you about your idea of motion," said Peter wearily.

"The men in Arabia are very passionate," she continued. "If I had stayed, I would have had many children. In just two days I built an empire and was raped by a black prince of Ecbatana. But I don't suppose anything will come of it."

Peter smiled. "It would be inconvenient if something came of it," he said. "I mean, with your husband so far away in—is it London?"

But Rose did not answer. It was as if a light had gone out somewhere behind her eyes. Carefully he guided her along the decks of ships, across planks, over bridges that spanned the short spaces of greenish water. In five minutes they were within sight of *The Mary Strattford*.

"I was the teacher of all the children," she said suddenly. "Did I tell you that? One day I discovered that reality has three parts and so I became the teacher of all the children. I spent years organizing schools all over The Drift. Seven forms and six subjects in each form two in sense, two in thought, and two in dreams. Every day I would rise at moonset and meditate upon my lessons until morning. Then I would teach two hours at each of the five schools. The Conquistador Blancos called me Doña Rose, The Lady of Learning."

Her hand trembled for a moment as he guided her from one boat to the next. "Those were proud days for me," she whispered. She followed him passively, moving like a tower of ivory floating on water. She was, he thought, a senile queen walking to her tomb.

"I never had children of my own," she said after another long silence. "You see, my husband has been gone for some time now. There was a shipwreck and we were separated. Yes, a shipwreck. I remember it quite clearly now. A spar fell and broke his neck."

On *The Mary Strattford,* Bright and Tabor's two children were playing with silver pieces on a green board, and as Peter and Rose approached, the three of them looked up and smiled. Raven sat some distance away, perched on a rail, staring off into space.

"We need a new rule for this game," said Michael. "Something to keep my brother from bringing his gold crown in before The Third Circle."

Rose looked at the children, first at Peter and then at Michael; then her arm stiffened and she pulled away from Peter's guiding hand. "Where are you taking me?" she demanded.

"You're home," said Bright. "This is *The Mary Strattford.*"

The old woman exhaled sharply and then walked toward the hatchway. "Sutherland would have made a good pupil," she said. "But I'm afraid he cannot be one of us for long." She lifted her long skirts so as to follow Bright down into the galley.

"What did she mean, I wouldn't be with you for long?"

Michael moved one of the silver pieces of eight and then looked up. "Rose is a smart lady, but she doesn't always make too much sense," he said. "Pao says she remembers that when she was a little girl Rose was different. She says Rose used to be the most important person on The Drift."

"She was always the same stupid old lady," said Raven from his perch on the rail. "She's never been anything but an old lady."

"Don't be nasty," said Peter. "Why don't you sit down and play—whatever it is they're playing?"

"If you want to play," said Michael, "we can give you a silver outflank on seventeen."

"No thanks."

"We always ask him to play," said David, "but he never wants to."

"I hate games," said Raven.

"Let's go for a walk then," said Peter.

Raven hesitated, looking first at the boys and then at Peter. "No thanks," he said at last. "I'll go by myself."

"Let him do what he wants," said Michael.

"Don't worry about him. Come play with us," said David. "We need someone to take Bright's place."

"Hooray!" said Michael, who hated delays of any kind. "Sutherland can play for Bright until she comes back!"

But just then Bright returned from the galley. "No," she said. "Go after him. Someone should go after him, and you're the only one he'll really talk to."

"Perhaps I should," said Peter. "Perhaps I can do something for him."

Three ships away, Raven's slender form was still visible, the tails of his black shirt waving behind him as he ran.

"Wait!" said Peter. But his voice was lost over the long distance, and Raven did not look back. He ran along the rail of a large schooner and peered over the point of the bow, trying to keep Raven's black shirt in view.

He followed him across the great caravel and the barquentine that he and Pao had explored, it seemed so very long ago, and then on almost to The Bridge at the western edge of The Drift. This was strange territory for Peter, consisting largely of small oriental trading ships and several large Chinese junks.

"Stay away!" cried Raven, still a hundred feet ahead of him. "Stay away or I'll kill you!"

Then he remembered how Raven had guarded his aluminum dinghy on those long and dark nights, alone with only a long paddle and a knife. Now somehow he felt responsible for him, and for a moment it seemed that Raven was someone very close to him. Perhaps someone he had known or imagined a long time ago.

I'm not going to Harrington University, said the Raven in Peter's mind. I'm not going to wear a blue suit and sit around at all your silly parties at the country club and study medieval history and play the violin and dance the rhumba.

Then what do you want to do? he asked the voice in his mind.

I don't know, the voice answered. I just want to get away from all this. I want to go home.

But now the real Raven had doubled back along The Southern Edge, past the green and yellow Seafields where he and Reuben and Javitt worked nearly every day. And then for a while he disappeared completely, and Peter followed almost by instinct, listening to the vague thud of footfalls, sensing where the boy had gone almost by smell or by the damp impressions his feet on the wooden boards. Why do I bother? he asked himself. And with that question he stopped running and looked around him. He was lost now, and Raven was nowhere to be seen.

He climbed halfway up the catwalk of a nearby brig and looked around. Three boats to his left he saw the stage called Twoboats where Pao had done The Dance of The Nine Islands. High and to his right he could barely make out the outline of *The Mary Strattford*. And below him, only a boat away, he saw Raven walking very slowly, looking behind him every few feet. Suddenly he looked up and saw Peter hanging from the catwalk.

"Stay away or I'll kill you!" he shouted.

Peter looked down and smiled and waved with one hand. He wondered what he could do to get Raven to take himself less seriously. "You couldn't kill a crippled sea gull!" he shouted back. "Now just wait a minute—I want to talk to you!"

Raven smiled, pleased at Peter's feigned anger. "You'll have to catch me," he said, leaping from one boat to the next, his black arms outstretched like wings.

Peter scrambled quickly down the catwalk and then hurried across to the old fishing scow from which Raven had shouted at him. In the corner of his eye he saw a black shape dart into a doorway, but when he reached the cabin it was empty, as were the sleeping and storage quarters below. But in exploring the small ship he saw that rotting boards had fallen out of the hull in the forward storage compartment, making a jagged hole large enough for a man to jump through. Outside lay the overturned hull of another nameless ship, upon which part of the fishing scow rested. Peter leaped through the hole, slid for a moment on the slippery, curved surface of the greenish hull, and lost his balance. From above him came the sound of raucous laughter. Peter shaded his eyes, looked up, and saw Raven's black outline against the sun, a dark profile shaking with laughter at the rail of a ship that loomed high on the side opposite the fishing scow.

"You'll never catch me," he screeched. "You're too clumsy and too old."

Peter winced at the "clumsy" and "old," but still he managed to answer in good spirit: "I'm a thunderball of fire and grace!" he cried. "You're as good as caught!"

"Bilgewater! Fishguts!" cried Raven, and he was gone!

When he reached the deck of the ship, Raven was two boats ahead of him again. But now the boy seemed tired. Even at that distance Peter could see his chest heaving and hear the flatfooted thud of his feet on the boards. When he reached Twoboats, he stopped and listened. Again Raven seemed to have disappeared. For long moments he blinked and looked about him; the world was bleak and dazzled because he had looked into the sun where Raven had laughed.

Then the boy appeared from behind a pile of barrels, the ones that had been arranged days and days ago in a circle around the painted ocean and The Nine Islands. Peter ducked behind the remains of a shearer mast and watched as Raven looked slowly about him, his hands open and loose as if they were sense organs listening, resting easily on the air. Then he turned and slowly let himself go over the lip of the slide that led to Pao's pool.

Peter followed, remembering the dance and the pool and the first night he and Pao had spent together. He moved again with that curious slowness of motion that he remembered so clearly, a soundless sliding always on the verge of a stop. And then quite unexpectedly Raven stood up a few yards ahead of him on the slide, and with an enormous leap caught hold of a rope dangling from the dark side of a large caravel, at the point where the slide turned into the reverberating chambers of greenish darkness between the boats, that hushed place of shadows just before the slide emptied into the pool.

Peter caught the edges of the slide and stopped himself. Raven was only a few feet above him now, slowly pulling himself up the rope toward a large hole in the girdle of the caravel. He waited until the boy disappeared into the hole, then he too stood up on the slide, jumped, caught the rope, and began to ropewalk up the slippery hull of the old vessel. A minute or two later he swung through the hole into what seemed to be a large captain's cabin.

Raven was sprawled in an old chair in one corner of the room. He did not look up when Peter entered.

"So you followed me all the way," he said in an even tone that betrayed nothing. "I saw you coming up, but I didn't have the energy to cut the rope or stab you as you came through the hole. I was too tired."

"Well," said Peter, "I'm grateful for that. I'd hate to fall all that distance."

"Nothing to be afraid of," said Raven. "The worst that happens is that you break your neck." He glanced in a listless way around his room, kicked over a pile of books near his foot, and sighed deeply.

When Peter was satisfied that Raven had settled into a relatively peaceful mood, he began to look around the room. Above the doorway was a sign painted in red ink that said "Raven's Eyrie," and beyond that lay a pile of ancient furniture, a woman's satin gown, a bronze cuspidor, two carved legs from a smashed table, and other things that Raven had apparently thrown out of the room into the hallway that led to other compartments and to stairs leading up to the gun deck. In Raven's corner of the room stood his large wooden chair piled high with cushions, a table with a dozen old copies of *Popular Mechanics,* and a tall floor lamp, its cord lying in a useless tangle under the chair. At the opposite end of the room lay a stuffed blackbird with some of its feathers removed and glued together in what looked like a crude attempt at a headdress, three other chairs, and an outboard motor half torn down, its parts scattered over the floor in piles of rust.

"I was trying to fix it," he said. "But I didn't have the right tools. You need the right tools to fix things."

Maps and diagrams clipped out of magazines and newspapers were tacked in a sprawling crazy-quilt pattern all over the walls of the room: political and geographical maps of Europe and South America, blueprint drawings of motors, railroad engines, airplanes, bridges, and buildings, and diagrams of German military campaigns.

"Once I wanted to form a new clan or a club or something," said Raven absently, staring into space like a boy with nothing to do on Sunday afternoon. "I was going to call it The Explorer's Club. But no one would join."

Suddenly from beyond the doorway came the sound of rats. Peter turned and saw five of them skittering along the wall, stopping, eyeing him with their flaming, cloudy eyes.

Raven smiled. "Well, I guess I shouldn't say no one." He reached into his pocket and brought out a matchbox filled with crumbs of boiled fish. The rats began to mew and cheep and run around Raven's chair, and then, to Peter's horror, they scratched and crawled their way up a sprawl of pillows and magazines, and from there they jumped into the boy's lap.

"There you are, clubmembers," said Raven, holding the pieces of fish above the rats, dropping them one by one.

The plump gray creatures bobbed and tumbled awkwardly in Raven's lap for the morsels of fish, then waved their noses in the air and twitched their whiskers, waiting for the next piece to fall. Peter had always hated rodents of any kind, but he watched, morbidly fascinated, as the pale, slender boy in the black shirt fed his small, wild-eyed guests.

"The thing I really like about rats is that if I don't feed them often enough they come up and bite my fingers. That's exactly what I'd do if I was a rat."

"But you're not a rat," said Peter.

Raven looked up from his hungry friends and smiled. "I'm not so sure. Anyway, I'm not interested in being human any more."

Peter pulled a chair up to within a few feet of Raven, sat down on the arm so that his feet would rest on the seat some distance above the floor, and waited for the grotesque meal to end.

"You know," said Raven, "there was never any arrangement between me and Pao. It's not that you interrupted anything when you came to The Drift."

"But you've always loved her."

Raven made a face at the word "love." "She never made fun of me the way the Madrid and Conquistador boys did," he said. "She sort of ignored me. I guess that was much worse."

"Why did she ignore you?"

"How should I know? She—well—she doesn't like people like me. She likes the Madrids and The Bluewaters because they sing and dance. Things like that."

"Then I wonder why she got to be so fond of me. I don't sing and dance and I'm much older than she is."

Raven smiled at the euphemism. "She's *fond* of you cause you're different. You've lived in places that no one here has hardly ever seen. You've got powers she doesn't have."

"What powers?"

"I don't know. That's what Tabor says that she says. You're 'The Beautiful Stranger'—that's a song she wrote when she was only twelve years old. She says she knew even then that you were coming."

Soon the rats finished eating and went elsewhere, looking for food. Peter descended from his cramped position on his chair and sat down. Raven smiled at his fear of the little creatures, but it was not a contemptuous smile. "You're not like anybody around here," he said.

"Why not?"

"I don't know exactly. Are you musical?"

"Am I musical? No, not especially. What's that got to do with it?"

"Everybody on The Drift is *extremely* musical. I'm more like The Outlanders. I like to fight and explore and make things."

"Some people say that's what history is all about," said Peter. "But why do you like to fight? Why are The Outlanders always fighting?"

"I s'pose cause there isn't much else to do," said Raven. "And besides, you feel better afterwards. It makes everything sort of peaceful inside you for a while."

"I suppose for some people—" But then he could not

finish the sentence, for Raven's sake. For some people fighting is like loving, he thought. For some desperate people combat is the only way to make contact, the only way to touch the life of another human being, the only way to define oneself in terms of the respect or hatred of others. In a sense, his life had been like that. A fierce, unhappy game of things to be won or lost from other people or from the world, a game that he had never played very well and whose victories had been like dust in his mouth.

Raven slouched in his chair and stared sightlessly into the hallway where his rats had vanished in search of food. Finally he reached underneath his chair and carefully, slowly, withdrew a large red guitar. He fondled it for a moment like a blind child, and then he began to play, to strum the strings in a chordless, incoherent way. Sometimes he would hum to himself and sometimes he would bark or chuckle or make obscene noises. "Raven plays to while away his days," he bleated once in a tuneless voice, and then smiled his hangman's smile. The noise of his voice and his guitar reminded Peter of something that he could not give a name to, something very familiar.

"Ever notice that guitars always have a hole right in the middle?" he said halfway through his concert. "That's pretty funny! No lid or anything, just a hole in the middle! And when you look, there's nothing inside! Just an empty box that makes sounds! Just a silly box of wood filled with twangs and strums that you can't put anything in because the wires are in the way!" He laughed and then he played louder, working his hand like a claw across the strings and shouting something incoherent about girls with figures like guitars.

Peter listened, and he sensed more clearly now the ambiguity and contradiction that seemed to be a part of everything Raven did and said. His clumsy, mawkish performance on the red guitar was a gesture of contempt for the music he could not play, for a life he could never lead. But it was also a rhapsody of self hatred, a way to dramatize his own ineptness and isolation by destroying the image of himself as a human being. It made Peter think of the rats that Raven courted as friends; it made him think of Raven's own ship that he was methodically sawing into pieces. But all this was, in a curious and unexpected way, a contradiction to something almost affirmative in that dark, jangled music. To Peter it seemed quite evident: a submerged reverence in the way Raven sometimes lowered his head when he tried to play, staring at the strings as if they were hieroglyphs in some forgotten tongue, and in the way his sardonic smile dissolved for brief moments into wistfulness. Peter imagined for an instant that he could read the boy's mind: *If I could really play, why then...*

Suddenly Raven stopped. His eyes filled with tears. "I'm not very musical," he said.

Peter put his hand on the boy's shoulder. "Never mind. There are other things in the world besides music."

Raven started at the hand on his shoulder and then pulled away, stung by Peter's compassion. His face turned red. Then he laughed and put the big end of the guitar under his shoulder and began to make terrible faces and groan melodramatically and stagger in a wide circle.

"A guitar is just a crutch!" he shouted in a wild, comic voice. As he banged and limped around the room, a terrified rat scurried out of one corner and disappeared beneath the broken furniture outside the cabin door.

"Look!" cried Raven. "I'm crippled!"

Then he laughed in a selfconscious way. Suddenly the charade was over and he stood in the center of the room, looking at Peter. The red guitar dangled from one hand in front of him. It was like a garment that hid his nakedness. There was a long silence, broken only by the sound of the boy's breathing.

215

"It's time to go back now," said Peter quietly, hardly daring to speak, afraid now of breaking the fragile equilibrium between them. "Bright will be wanting to know if you're all right."

When they were halfway back to *The Mary Strattford,* he remembered what the sound of Raven's guitar had reminded him of: The Hatchmaker.

At dinner he noticed again that Pao was missing.

"About ten days after a woman on The Drift begins to live with a man she moves all her belongings to his boat," said Bright. "The Bluewaters call that The Second Marriage. So I fancy she's been busy all day collecting things, being that she's lived in so many places. She told me she would see you sometime after dinner," she added in a conciliatory tone.

Raven looked up from his plate of fish and prawns. His eyes were filled with tears, but he did not speak.

"I saw her down at the water gathering sea hyacinths," said Tabor. "She said she wanted something nice for the brass bowl on your dresser."

"Pao has always been one to fix things up," said Bright.

"But there was something odd," said Tabor. "She looked rather sad."

"Sad?"

"Yes. I asked her what was wrong. She said she'd tell me tomorrow morning."

Then Rose stopped eating and turned to look at Tabor. "Tomorrow morning," repeated the old woman fiercely.

"When did you see her?" said Peter.

"About two hours ago," said Tabor.

"That's funny," said Peter. "I saw her for a second late this morning and she looked very—" But then he could not remember whether she had looked happy or unhappy. Had she smiled? He remembered that she had waved to him, but he could not see her face in his mind's eye, and when he tried to isolate her look at that moment he saw only a mirror, a shimmer of water in which nothing reflected. He remembered her hand and the movement of her body as she shifted the weight of her bundle to one hip, nothing more. Suddenly a strange image crossed his mind. Pao was a star made from mirrors of water, a star receding faster than the speed of light, moving out of his galaxy and into the void beyond it.

"—radiant, I should think," said Bright, finishing his sentence. "Tabor, you must have been mistaken."

"Perhaps I was," said Tabor.

Rose was still staring at Peter. She folded her arms and made no attempt to finish her dinner. When he looked up he could not avoid her eyes.

When the meal was over he hurried back to his own ship. There were indeed water hyacinths in his brass bowl, and the cabin had been scrubbed so that the wood smelled new and wet. And there were long curtains made from sailcloth hanging from the windows. On his bed lay a note:

> My Dear One—I will be back in two hours. I am gathering the last of my things. If you are here when I get back I will never let you go. This is a warning.
> Pao

He smiled when he read the note. But then almost immediately the words seemed to suggest a second meaning. What had she been thinking when Tabor saw her? He read the note again. "If you are here when I get back—"

He wandered out onto the deck of his schooner. The Hatchmaker was playing again, and he listened for a moment to the sound of his jangled music. Suddenly he was very restless; the idea of waiting two hours for Pao was unthinkable. Where had she gone? It was strange, he thought, that in all the time he had known her he had never thought to ask where she lived on The Drift. He had the impression, now that he thought about it, that she lived in several places. The children had said something about that once. It would probably be nearly impossible to find her before she came back in her own time.

Still, he had a terrible urge to do something. It was the same feeling he had the day he wandered into The Outland to retrieve his dinghy. He thought of the dinghy, ready now for its long and dangerous voyage, and he thought of The Hatchmaker and the mad sounds he made from the clipper ship at Driftsend. It would only be a matter of going back and searching through the ship for some sort of fuel; he was sure it was there somewhere. The whole place smelled of it. But this time he would not be so stupid; this time he would bring one of the hurricane lamps from his cabin.

He smiled. How easily his mind slipped back into the old groove. The old woman's ramblings, Raven's bitterness, and the episode with the rats had awakened something in him, the vague suspicion that he was somehow trapped, caught in a drugged sleep from which he could not awaken. Such things made him think in a vague way of the shark and of the blue dream he could never seem to remember.

He shaded his eyes and looked up at the sun that was sinking swiftly toward the horizon. Only a few minutes had passed. Pao would not return for at least an hour and a half. There was plenty of time. He knew somehow that his own feeling about The Drift would never be quite clear until he felt certain about the possibility of a return to his old life, a possibility that the discovery of gasoline would clearly establish, and until he knew something more about that strange musician, that summation of all the mysteries on The Drift, The Hatchmaker. Perhaps just a few minutes with a lamp would reveal a great deal about both.

The sun touched the horizon. It would be dark now in less than an hour. He brought a lamp from his cabin and then made his way toward Driftsend.

Chapter Eighteen

THE HATCHMAKER

As he walked down the stairs, the smell of moldering wood reminded him of his last adventure on The Hatchmaker's ship. He lifted his lamp. The yellow light made an uneven shadowy glow down the stairs and along the corridors.

Walking through the rooms and compartments below the second deck he could see that things had changed. The captain's cabin had been cleaned; the hallways were strewn with chairs that had not been there before. Once more he felt sure that someone lived here. But who? Who was The Hatchmaker? Who was this man no one had ever seen, this creature who produced his impossible sounds at all hours of the day and night?

The music, if indeed it was music, was very loud now. It seemed to come from everywhere, but after a while he sensed that its source was somewhere below him. After a short search he found a hatchway that led down to the fourth deck.

Here he was in absolute darkness except for the light from his lamp. Suddenly, with a turn in the corridor, he came upon a torch, fixed to the wall in an iron brazier, that sent a flickering illumination down the passageway. The music seemed very close now. It was no longer a jangling blur of vaguely melodic sounds, but a series of distinctly separate but wavering tones set against a hollow skittering and knocking that made him think of small animals running around in a dark room. He was almost sure now that it was a musical instrument of some kind—perhaps a harpsichord or a piano that was terribly out of tune.

He opened a door somewhere near the bow of the ship. Inside, the tilted floor was awash with water and a kind of green slime. When the boat heaved a little, the water ran across the floor toward him and then receded to the far side of the room, sloshing against the wall. On the far wall of the large room was another torch mounted in a brazier and another doorway opening into another room. He walked through the lake of green water, stood at the threshold of that doorway, and looked inside. Several moments passed before he realized that he was staring at The Hatchmaker.

It was a large room filled with boxes, mud, tin cans, rotting clumbs of garbage, and strips of newspaper floating in the water like dead whitefish. The overpowering stench held him at the brink of nausea. In one corner of the room sat an ancient grand piano that looked to be nearly ten feet long. Its legs were carved into Corinthian pillars and its feet into the claws of a griffin. The room and the piano seemed somehow familiar. He was sure that in his blind journey two weeks earlier he had been here. He remembered how the legs of the piano had creaked when he had blundered into them in the darkness. But then he had not known what it was.

On the piano was an old seaman's lamp, and sitting behind it an incredibly ancient man, who looked even older than Rose. He was dressed in a formal suit of black tails, very worn and very dirty. The old man was playing a four part fugue, parhaps something by Bach, but the notes of the piano wavered like a very bad tape recording; the instrument was so badly out of tune that it was impossible to distinguish any diatonic line of melody or harmony.

The old man played with great fury. The notes tumbled out of the wrecked piano like inharmonious demons come to plague him. Then he saw Peter standing in the doorway. His ancient hands poised above the piano, trembling, and the music echoed and died in the dark, watery silence. The light from the lamp played across his withered face and left his eyes sunk in deep pools of shadow. He was a ghost, an incredible caricature of a man.

"Who are you?" said the Hatchmaker. His voice was a piece of tinfoil crinkling in a black box.

"Peter Sutherland." He answered in a kind of croak that betrayed his terror. "Who are you?"

The old man cackled horribly. "Who am I? Who am I, you say? Why I'm The Hatchmaker. Surely you knew that!"

Peter stared at him. "You're really The Hatchmaker?" he said finally.

"Really? In reality? My God, who knows who I really am? I'm nobody, perhaps. A ghost of someone."

The old man stood up and sloshed through the greenish water toward him. The light from the two lamps, Peter's and The Hatchmaker's, made pools of wavering yellow in a sea of green. Instinctively Peter drew back.

"Don't be afraid," said the old man. "I won't hurt you. I couldn't hurt anyone any more."

"What are you doing here?" said Peter.

"I'm playing the piano. I play at least three hours every day. Perhaps you've heard me."

"Yes," said Peter. "Everyone hears you."

The old man cackled again. "I daresay they wonder what it is," he said. "The salt air ruined the tone years ago and the sounding board is cracked in a dozen places and the felts are all worn and I have no way to tune it any more. How does it sound to you?"

"It—it sounds very good," said Peter.

"It sounds monstrous," said the old man. "The strings are snapping one by one. For some notes all three strings are gone. I have no E-flat or D or C any more in the middle register. But I can still hear them in my mind when I play. Perhaps it's better that way. I can hear the tones very clearly, just as they used to be."

The Hatchmaker slowly shook his head back and forth. "But soon all the strings will be gone," he said.

"Then what will you do?"

"Play the piano of course."

"Without any strings?"

"Told you I can hear the notes in my mind. Very curious to know what the Bach chaconne sounds like when there's just the clicking of the wooden hammers and the sound of the water rolling around in the cabins. Perhaps then I'll have some peace. The piano will be in tune again and I can play and play until I drop." He laughed again in his high, breaking voice.

"And I'll never hit another wrong note. With no sound there'll be no wrong notes, don't you see?"

Peter stared curiously at the old man. The terror had left him now. In his mind he heard the hollow sound of the wooden hammers striking out at nothing.

"But I don't understand why you stay here alone. Don't you ever get lonely? And what do you eat?"

"The Outlanders bring me things during the day sometimes, and I come out on deck at night to pick them up. And besides, I've hundreds of cans of things that I took before I went into hiding here forty years ago." The Hatchmaker stared at him and smiled. His eyes glittered in the lamplight. He seemed oddly excited by Peter's presence.

"Lonely?" he said. "Of course I get lonely. But what's out there to relieve a man's loneliness? A lot of poor fish running around like children. Half of them don't even know there's a world beyond The Drift."

"They seem to be very happy," said Peter.

"They're happy like moron children," he answered. "They all make me sick."

"Then why didn't you try to get away?"

"Tried three times. The first time, my wife and our child were killed in a storm and the boat washed back to The Drift." The old man began to tremble and tears welled in his eyes.

"I'm very sorry," said Peter.

"That was over forty years ago," he said. "Don't remember what they looked like any more. Or even how I felt about them. But I know that her name was Elizabeth and when I say her name over and over again I sometimes hear the rustle of a blue silk dress and then I began to cry. Strange to cry about something you can't even remember." The old man was standing very close to him now. Peter could hear the sound of his breathing and see beyond the shadows of his brow into his flittering, unsteady eyes.

"Second time I tried to get away, the boat sank about a mile out. Third time, I got sick and had to row back. I was alone those last two times. Always alone. Tried hard to get some of the others to help me with one of the big boats. Could have gone to England, but no, they were always too frightened. The sea will get us, they always said. Better just to stay here and wait for help. Fools. They knew there was no help coming. All spineless fools."

"What happened then?"

"They all hated me. Couldn't stand being reminded of the other world. Couldn't stand being reminded they were all cowards. Finally made me stay on one of the small boats." He burst again into his cackling laughter. "I," he continued, nearly strangling on his own good humor, "was the first Outlander."

"You mean they made you an Outlander just because you tried to get them all to leave The Drift?"

"That and my grumpy disposition."

"And so you escaped and came here?"

"Came one night and began to play the piano. Everyone thought I was a ghost. Once in a while someone would come to investigate, but I always hid behind the door and hit them over the head with a hammer and threw them into the sea. And then the piano got out of tune and the music began to sound strange and then no one ever came after that. Except once."

"Who came?" He listened to the old man's reedy voice. He had forgotten what time it was.

"Someone came to The Drift one day in an old fishing boat that had a motor. He had three children and a wife back on The Island of Pennsylvania. He wanted to go back. He came to me. Someone told him I was The God of The Drift and that only I could let him go. I gave him fuel and some cans of beef and sent him away. Everyone saw him leave the next morning. Don't know if he made it back, but no one ever saw him again."

Fuel, thought Peter. Then he stared at the lamp burning on the piano. It smelled of gasoline. "Where did you get the fuel?" he asked.

"That night before I came here I filled a big raft with food and tools and rope and everything I could think of that I might need. The fools always stay inside at night. It was like stealing pies from kitchen windows. I must have made about seventeen trips."

The old man was beginning to tire. He wheezed and made his way back through the green water to his piano. He sat down and rested his head on the music board.

"How long have you been here?" said Peter.

"Don't know," the old man croaked. "Came in eighteen ninety-three. What year is it now?"

"Nineteen sixty-seven."

"My God," said the old man, who began to weep again. "All those years. All those wasted years."

"How old were you when you came here?" said Peter.

"I was only twenty-three. Whole life in front of me. I was a pianist going on tour with an orchestra in South America. Our clipper rammed an iceberg in The North Atlantic, but after it split in two the hull kept floating. There were about thirty of us hanging onto that piece of wood for about seven weeks. We managed to salvage some things that were floating around in the water, and it wasn't too bad until the last seven days or so. Fifteen died the last seven days. Our baby was born right then in the middle of everything. Right there on the side of the hull with all the people around. Somehow we managed to keep it alive. Some of the men wanted—they wanted to eat the baby. You see, we ate the last of our shoes that week and there was nothing else for anyone. But my wife stabbed one of them in the eye with her hatpin and he screamed and fell into the water and after that they all left us alone."

The old man began to cry again. "Elizabeth was so brave," he said. "So fierce and so brave and so loving. Her name was Elizabeth. Did I tell you that? Her name was Elizabeth Harkman."

And then for a while the old man said nothing. He played at his piano. The music sounded something like a piano sonata by Mozart that Peter had once played when he was a child, but he could not be sure.

"How is it out there?" he said when he had finished. "Are any of the old people left?"

"I don't know," said Peter. "Did you know Tabor? Or Bright?"

"No."

"Or Rose?"

"Rose? Rose Greenwood? Yes, of course I knew Rose. My God, is that old horse still alive? She must be nearly as old as I am. Rose was in love with me after she got over her husband's death, but God, I could never stand her. Is she still The Great Oracle of *The Mary Strattford?*"

Peter smiled. "I guess so."

"Yes. That's Rose. She'll never change. She can read your mind, you know. The last I heard, twenty years ago, she was teaching all the children to read minds. That's what happens when you spend five hundred years away from the world. Everything goes to the mind. She was the most mental woman I ever knew. Ever wonder how people set their watches on The Drift? They ask Rose. Rose tells time by moon and sun and stars. The children used to say that she could change time—make it longer or shorter. I don't doubt it. She was all mind and intuition, that woman. But in a way she was just like all the others. Weak. Foolish. Afraid of the horizon. Afraid of anything that wasn't wrecked up on The Drift."

Then Peter remembered that Rose had once been Pao's teacher. What was it Rose had once said about giving Pao all her poor gifts?

"The Drift was a little different when I was young," The Hatchmaker was saying. He began to mumble now, talking more to himself than to Peter. "There were some old carracks and even part of a medieval warship over near The Bridge. Things change on The Drift. But the State of Things never changes even if Things do. Hah! You live old but you rot early. All the people, all the boats. Everything slips underwater without really sinking. And everything sinks without really slipping underwater. Does that make sense?" He paused for a moment to tap his fingers. "Can't be sure," he said after a moment. "I haven't thought clearly about anything for years."

"But The Drift is very lovely," said Peter. "I've been happy here."

"Yes. Very lovely." The old man coughed and then spit into the water. "Lovely like the white bellies of dead fish floating in the water. Lovely like a green fungus. Listen, boy, you want to know what's kept me from getting senile all these years? Hate. You don't get senile as long as you've something to hate. I'm insane, you understand. I've been quite alone and I've read ten thousand books in the last forty years and I'm quite insane. Sometimes I go out in my rowboat at night and howl at people."

"But I love one of the girls from *The Mary Strattford*," said Peter. It was another part of him now that was speaking, a part that was sinking, receding across a great distance. But in his mind he could still reach out and touch the beautiful image made of water. Pao. The lovely girl who had read his mind.

"You love her now," said the old man. "But in twenty-five years she'll be like Rose. Rose was senile at forty. Never saw the world after a while. Never saw anything outside her own mind. Ever see the old ones sitting around staring at nothing for hours? It's like their eyes have turned up into their heads. They speak with their minds and they go on dreams together that last for days and days sometimes. And finally that's all there is. They get fat and they sit there in a pool of their own urine and they smell bad and they dream. And someone comes to feed them. And most of them are not even fifty."

Peter remembered the old people sitting in a circle, like children playing shadowgames. He had seen The Long Journey many times.

"You don't believe in the value of dreams then?" said Peter.

"Of course I do, boy. You forget I'm a musician. Music is the dream of sound. It's a world apart, as they say. Dreams are wonderful things, but not if you live your life so that none of them can ever come true, not even a little. Rose and the others, they ruined everything. If they had all worked together they could have gone home, and Elizabeth and I could have grown old together in England. But no. The old priestess would never allow that. Hah!"

The Hatchmaker looked up at the walls and ceiling of the compartment and then down at the green water. He smiled a thin, sad smile and then nodded his head. "Once last year," he said, "I was out on deck at night and I saw a man floating in the weeds. Drowned, but the weeds wouldn't let him sink. He looked, well, sort of poetic. Peaceful, like he was dreaming of something. The trouble was that he had turned blue and swelled up something awful. Not a pretty sight. Not pretty at all."

Peter kept staring at the old man. He stared at the small folds of white skin above his eyes, at his jowls and neck, at the deep wrinkles that creased his forehead and cheeks, and he thought about the blue man in the water. Suddenly he felt sick. Suddenly he wanted to leave The Drift forever.

"Do you have any more gasoline?" he said.

"Gasoline? Have all sorts of gasoline."

"Could you give me some?" Peter was not sure what he was about to say, but he could feel the urgency of the words forming in his mind. "I've got to get back into The North Equatorial Current."

"How do they feel about your leaving?"

"Everyone was upset at first. But now they think I'm going to stay because of the girl."

The old man laughed and waved his hands in the air. "Marvelous," he said. "They'll never forgive you. They'll eat their hearts out."

"But can you let me have some gasoline?"

"There's sixty gallons over in the corner." He pointed to a dark part of the room where the water sloshed against some metal jerrycans. "If that's not enough, you can have some from upstairs. You see, I still get out at night once in a while to steal things. At one time or another I've stolen most everything that's of any value on The Drift."

Peter went to the corner of the room and found three

twenty-gallon containers. "One of these would be fine. I think it's all I'll need."

"Well I must say you're not very greedy," said The Hatchmaker. "Greed has always been one of my failings." He laughed his terrible laugh. "And all my failings have had time to develop like fugues here on this miserable graveyard. You see I'm just like everyone else here in one way. I've wasted away too."

He raised his hands to still the objection that Peter never made. "Yes I have," he said. "Just like the others. Even the music is wasted away. All the salt air and all those cracks in the sounding board. Do you have a wrench?"

"A wrench?"

"Something to tune the piano with. You'd think that on the whole of The Drift there'd be at least one wrench. It would sound a little better if only I had a wrench."

"I'm sorry," said Peter.

Again the old man began to mumble, and his eyes lost their focus. He seemed to have forgotten that Peter was still there, hesitating at the doorway with his can of gasoline.

"Even so, there's something left in the music," he was saying. "Something that's not a part of them. That's why they're afraid of me. I still remember the old world, even after all these years. And the music remembers too. Bach. Vivaldi. Scriabin. Sibelius. The music even remembers some things that I've forgotten. I have to listen sometimes with my other ear, the one inside my head."

"I have to go now," said Peter. "Thanks for the gasoline. I needed the gasoline very much."

The old man suddenly took notice of him again. He stood up at the piano. His face was lost in shadows. "I make you uncomfortable, don't I?"

"No. Not at all. It's just that I have to go now. Thanks for the gasoline."

"It's all right. I make everyone uncomfortable. I'm an ugly, ancient old man. Should have died years ago. Be gone soon and then I'll be no bother to anyone."

Peter looked at him helplessly. There was nothing to say.

"You're doing the right thing," said The Hatchmaker. "I can see what you are in your eyes. They'd hate you too if you stayed too long. You'd be an Outlander, like all the other good men."

"Do you know The Outlanders?"

"They come here to trade with me sometimes. Think of me as their leader. The Revered One. Yes, I know The Outlanders very well. They spoke of you once. Old Grayfish told me you were a man of great courage. That's what I see now in your eyes. That's why they'd hate you on The Drift if you stayed too long. They hate anyone who lives as a man should live."

"But The Outlanders attacked me," said Peter.

"Yes. They test you by trying to kill you. It's their way, ugly monsters that they are. They knew if you lived to stay here you'd soon be one of them. Brighteye —he's the one you dumped into the water—he rather likes you. He knows about motors and he knows you're trying to get off The Drift."

The old man began to chuckle. "You scared the others," he said. "Most of them never heard motors. They told Grayfish about The Devil that roared in the boat. He laughed for nearly an hour. If he'd been along you wouldn't have gotten off so easy."

"I really have to go now," said Peter.

"Of course you do," said The Hatchmaker.

"Thanks for the gasoline."

"You said that before," said The Hatchmaker.

The old man was still standing at the piano. He did not look directly at Peter. His head was tilted away toward the shadows in the far corner of the room where Peter had found the gasoline. His white fingers rested on the black frame above the keyboard. He was like a blind man feeling his way, his head turned away a little from the direction of his movement, his hands reassured by the touch of familiar objects.

"I'd like to go with you," he said, "but I'm too old now. I'd never live through the journey and I don't want to die on the open sea. Better to stay here. I'll die here at the piano where I've lived for all these years."

"Good-bye," said Peter.

"Good-bye," said the old man. "I'd hoped you might come back again. You see, it's very lonely here and I've enjoyed our little talk. The Outlanders don't talk much. But you won't be back, will you?"

Peter hesitated before answering. "No," he said. "I won't be back."

"Well good-bye then. And have a good journey."

The old man raised his hand to wave, and from across the room Peter saw the shadow of his hand cast by the flickering lamplight on the wall behind the piano. He closed the door and made his way back upstairs.

"Good-bye," wailed the old man from the dark room, his voice rising like a ghost through the wooden compartments and passageways of the ship.

When Peter reached the deck he gasped for air. It was as if he had not breathed for hours. Inside, he was sick with pity. He looked up at the stars and felt the cool, windless night against his face. Then he looked down at all the broken ships around him, and his pity opened like a river to engulf everything on The Drift.

Then, slowly, his pity turned to loathing. Had he been mad? Would he have given his whole life to live here in this hopeless ruin? His whole life given for a song? He thought of the old man and the ruined fingers that had played a ruined melody for sixty years. He thought of Raven's bitterness and his council of rats. He thought of Tabor's passive spirit and of the old ones who sat in their circles for days without stirring. He thought of the shark to whom he had nearly given his life. It was as if he had walked in his sleep to the edge of some fearful cliff and had tried, in the logic of dreams, to give his life for the joy of plummeting through the windy air, for the joy of being a meteor, a heavenly body whose destiny it is to burn fiercely and then break apart, to dissipate and become one with the air and the earth. It seemed now that he was standing, fully awake, at the edge of that cliff and looking down at the broken, misshapen things below him.

Yes, he thought, it was all madness. Perhaps even his love for Pao was a perversion of normal love, a longing for youth and for the young manhood that he had never fulfilled, mixed with a regressive, incestual passion for the daughter he had never had, that phantom child through whom, in the furthest reaches of his unconscious, his youth had been twice lost: once by time and again in his childless middle age.

As he made his way down toward The Southern Edge, it occurred to him that there would be no way to explain all this and no hope of anyone coming with him even if there were enough provisions and enough room in his aluminum dinghy to hold them. He would never be able to face Tabor and Pao in the morning, and a confrontation with Raven would be even more difficult. There was only one thing to do. He would leave now in the darkness before anyone found out. Raven had supplied his boat with everything he needed. In two hours he could be far out into The Sargasso Sea.

Above The Drift the moon was rising. For a moment he turned and looked behind him. Everywhere in the old ships the fish-oil lamps were winking out one by one.

Chapter Nineteen

WHITE FLOWERS IN A BOWL

After he had stowed the gasoline in his dinghy, he walked back to the cabin of his ship to pick up his compass and the white shirt that Pao had made for him and an armful of other supplies. He hesitated for a moment at the door and then quietly opened it. The room was empty. He entered, closed the door carefully behind him, and lit his lamp.

Pao's note lay undisturbed where he had left it. On his bed there was a depression, and across his pillow lay a long strand of black hair. He wondered how long Pao had lain there, her long hair falling across the pillow. Perhaps she had left only a moment before he came. How, he wondered, would he ever have had the power to leave if he had found her sleeping in his room? Why had he risked everything by returning here one last time? Certainly The Hatchmaker would have given him a compass. He knew the answer without really forming the words in his mind: part of him would always long for The Drift—the corner of his mind that for a few days had persuaded him to forget his whole life for its sake. He stared at the water hyacinths that floated in the brass bowl on his dresser. They drifted in a slow circle around the edge, as if blown by a tiny, soundless wind. White flowers in a bowl. Drifting. And in the moment before he extinguished the lamp and the room went dark, he could feel Pao's touch upon them. Her white fingers were the wind that blew the slow, delicate petals in a circle.

An hour later he lowered the dinghy into the water. He mde a quick check of everything in the boat: motor, twenty-five gallons of gasoline, paddle, eight jugs of water, dried fish and seabread, hook and line, net, compass, two blankets, rubber poncho, rope, two shirts, hat, sweater. Then he pushed free of the old bilander and began to paddle through the weeds toward the open sea. He was alone now. With that one step he had left Pao and Tabor and *The Mary Strattford* behind.

Then it occurred to him that he had never seen The Drift from the water. He wanted now to paddle around it in silence and watch it unfold like a revolving stage. It would be a way of saying good-bye.

Slowly he paddled along the edge of The Outland. The brilliant moonlight in the clear sky illuminated everything. It was like an enormous junkyard, an island of the dead. But after he passed Driftsend it assumed its familiar romantic character. The ships loomed above the light mist that had gathered on the water like broken cathedrals after an earthquake, tilting at insane angles against the moonlit sky.

He paddled westward along The Northside Cliff. Once he tried to raise his sail, but there was no wind anywhere. For a while he stopped paddling. After drifting a few minutes he started the engine.

Suddenly a yellow light appeared in one of the old schooners. And then another. He thought of the time he had started the motor to scare the Outlanders. Then people began to appear at the sloping edge of The Cliff. He heard their wavering voices calling out to him across the water. Tabor waved at him and shouted something. One figure appeared very near *The Mary Strattford*. It was a young girl, but in the moonlight he was not sure if it was Pao or one of the girls from The Madrid. She waved to him just once. She did not move or call out to him. He watched her as she followed the course of his boat, as she followed the widening gulf of water between him and The Drift. And then the shadows of the night closed about her and he could see nothing but the yellow lamps and the outlines of the boats. Soon the individual shapes of boats blurred together into a long curved line near the horizon. Then the moon moved behind a cloud and The Drift disappeared completely. The mist was growing heavy now. He turned away and set his course south by southeast. Perhaps in two or three hours he would be out of the windless center of The Sargasso Sea. Then he would raise his sail and let the wind carry him into the trade lanes.

An hour later the peaceful life on The Drift seemed far behind him. Ahead was the open sea, a sea of uncertainty and perhaps death. He felt an unreasonable longing for all the things he had given up so easily. He remembered The Seafields in the morning sunlight, the netted pool, the hours alone in the dark with Pao, the book he and Tabor had planned to write. Now, if he lived through the coming ordeal, he would return to his old life.

His memory of that old life was slow and disconnected. A few odd recollections, like pieces of driftwood on an empty beach. The stony face of his department chairman. His house in Connecticut. The meetings of the historical society he had attended last year in Philadelphia. Miriam.

In the old world there would be dozens of things to take care of if he ever did get back, and he would face everything alone. Back there he had always been alone. How different things had been with Pao and Tabor on The Drift. Suddenly it did not seem to matter that for

The Hatchmaker, for Raven, and for The Outlanders, The Drift was a Lotus Land of illusions, a failure of the will, a prison where nothing real was possible. His other life had been no less a prison, no less filled with false hope, ghosts, delusions. And how much less beautiful it was. It would have been better, he thought, to give up the absurdity of human aspirations in the civilized world of torpedoes and machine guns, where sane men told lies and madmen told truths, where men without vision nodded to slogans and men with vision were crucified, or worse, ignored, where order was a virtue even when it came out of fear, ignorance, or inertia, and disorder was a heresy, even when inspired by genius.

On The Drift there was love, peace, a chance to live simply and with dignity, a chance to dream one's life away in contemplation. All his life, it seemed, he had been looking for a world to live in. Not a world of bored students and classrooms, not Miriam's world of cocktail parties and country clubs, not his own empty childhood in the streets of Paterson, New Jersey, a childhood lorded over by his pious mother and his stern father, both victims of their Christian guilt and their hatred of the world—not these, but another. A place hidden out of time's way. Something beyond the turn of things, where he could set free the real energy of his mind, whatever that might be. A place where he might let go of all his useless fears and petty ambitions. A place where he could leave behind the curious silence that had followed him through the years.

He rested his hand on the tiller of the outboard motor. It would be easy to turn back. He had come only a little way. But the night was all around him now and a fog was settling on the water. He could not even see the dial of his compass.

He pushed the tiller to the left and the boat began to veer in a wide arc to the right. But how far, he wondered, should he turn? How would he know in this darkness whether he was going back in the right direction? His hand froze on the tiller, and the boat made wide circles in the water. He could not make up his mind. He closed his eyes and wished suddenly that the darkness would swallow him up.

When he awoke he was drifting somewhere in The Sargasso Sea. The sun was rising and the luminous clouds in the east hovered near the horizon. He ate some seabread, drank some water, and raised his sail. For hours he thought of nothing. He listened to the sound of the water and the sound of the wind in his sail. He was moving southeast.

By the fourth day his food and gasoline were gone. On the sixth day he caught a bonito and ate it raw. During the long morning and afternoon hours he thought about Pao and The Drift almost constantly, but by the end of the first week and a half he was numb with hunger and thought of nothing but food. On the tenth day he ran out of water. On the twelfth day he was saved when it rained for three hours. The rain brought him out of his stupor and he collected enough in his eight jugs to last another five days. On the fourteenth day he ran into a school of fish and caught nearly a dozen in his net.

The wind was steady. By day it carried him through the yellow arc of the sun's journey; by night, toward The Pleiades, hovering near the eastern rim of the sky.

On the sixteenth day he slept in the shadow of his sail until noon. He dreamed that his boat had drifted north, back to The Sargasso Sea, and that Pao was waiting for him. Then, with the high sun in his eyes, he awoke. He had a fleeting memory of Pao running away, fading, resolving into something small, distant. White flowers in a bowl of water.

He blinked in the bright glare of the sun and then stared at the horizon. A line of black smoke rose in the west. In ten minutes the smoke had lifted over the outline of a large merchant ship. A half hour later three men in a motor launch towed his dinghy toward the enormous gray hull.

After he had boarded the ship he shook hands with the captain, a portly smiling Dutchman, was treated to a large steak and a glass of orange juice, and then slept for two days.

Chapter Twenty

THE DREAM

The next week he returned to Harrington University. It was like returning to a life he had lived in a previous incarnation. The long carpets of grass, the gravel parking lots, the concrete and glass dormitories, the incredible noise of shouting students and automobiles all seemed to be from a different century, a different age. Suddenly he was a thousand years old.

His return caused, as he had imagined it would, a good deal of confusion and embarrassment. Everyone was terribly surprised. The response of his colleagues in the History Department and of his wife's friends somehow confirmed his own view of himself. He was a stranger here in this polished world of libraries and classrooms.

Dr. Ratcliffe was friendly, as always, but there was the distinct impression that his resurrection from the dead was an inconvenience, a breach of etiquette.

"It's very good to have you back, Peter," he had said that first afternoon in his office. Dr. Ratcliffe had not changed, but Peter saw him as he had never seen him before. The pursed lips, the gray face, and the cautious formal nod were all so characteristic of him, but now they seemed strange, like the gestures of a mannikin.

"Of course you realize that we'll have to put you on leave of absence until next semester since we've already hired Mr. Reston to teach your courses," he was saying. "But please don't hesitate to call on us in the meantime. Anything we can do to help—"

Peter was edging toward the door. "Yes, sir. Thank you very much."

"You must have had quite an adventure, lost all those days on the water."

"Yes, sir. It was quite an adventure." Peter stood in the doorway. He glanced down the long empty hall.

"We must talk about it sometime," said Dr. Ratcliffe. For a brief moment he made a pinched smile that sharpened all the lines in his face. His smile, as always, was sudden and mirthless, a convulsive movement of his cheeks and lips that spoke only of emptiness and old age.

Peter smiled and nodded and closed the door behind him.

That evening there was a party at Miriam's house. The pale, elegantly furnished rooms were filled with dozens of people whose names he at first could not remember. After a few minutes he stepped out onto the stone patio to hear the sounds of the cool October evening. The stars above him were infinite and bright. He remembered the old astral globe in the navigation room of The Hatchmaker's clipper ship. He remembered the arrows of Sagittarius pointing north, between Arcturus and Andromeda, into the empty sinking spaces of that curved eternity. He had meant to give it to Raven as a sort of gesture of friendship. Something he could keep in his own room with all his maps and magazines.

Gradually others drifted out onto the patio. There was an aging tennis player named Basil Queen who had no hair and who read Kipling, and his very slender wife who drank too much and who ate nothing but soft-boiled eggs, except on weekends. There was Tony Berendtson, a young man with soft blond hair who had once worked in his father's oil refineries in New Jersey for six months, who lived with his mother and his astrologic charts in Provincetown and who had seen Swan Lake seven times. There was Harry Ranton, Miriam's new lover, who owned his own real estate business and who drank everything straight. There was Miriam herself, the gay divorcee in her yellow silk dress, who loved men, hated women, despised dogs, cats, and scholars. There was Miriam's younger sister, Beverly, a plain, flat-nosed girl of nineteen with a figure like a surfboard who always talked about The World of Feeling and who would probably never marry. And there was Mary Rhys Beacher, a well-known Boston psychiatrist who at that moment was telling her many disciples, who sat around her like tame geese, about The Renaissance Image of The Dance of Life. Soon Peter was driven back into the living room.

About an hour later Miriam served martinis and bits of tartar beef on squares of rye bread as a prelude to her midnight buffet.

"But why don't you agree, Peter?" Mary Rhys Beacher was saying. "I mean as a historian?"

"Don't I agree to what?" said Peter. He felt very weary.

"That we are all part of The Cosmic Dance, The Infinite I Am, as Coleridge put it." Mary Rhys Beacher smiled at him and pursed her lips as if he had been a naughty child for not listening.

"Perhaps you're right," said Peter. He had the distinct impression that Mary Rhys Beacher was not a person at all, but a very large green frog.

"I'm not sure you really understand," she said.

"You'll have to forgive me," said Peter. "But on The Drift they do a dance with Black Narwhales and fire monsters and bare-breasted maidens. I'm afraid it makes Coleridge look a little pale."

"Wow!" said Tony Berendtson.

Mary Rhys Beacher looked up at him with what seemed to be great concern and interest. "I'm not sure I understand your allusion," she said.

"I'm not sure you do either," said Peter. "But you mustn't feel badly about it, Mrs. Beacher. We all have our limitations."

She stared at him and then at her silent audience.

"Peter, you've had too much to drink," said Miriam. "You're getting silly."

"Yes, that's true," he conceded. "But then we've all had too much to drink. Everyone, that is, except Mrs. Beacher."

"Your little fantasies are very interesting," said Mary Rhys Beacher after a long moment of silence.

"So are yours, Mrs. Beacher. But let me tell you about my fantasies, since they do happen to be true fantasies." And he began to tell her about his days in The Sargasso Sea. One by one people stopped talking and began to listen. Even Harry Ranton, who had been talking to Basil Queen's wife, turned around in his chair and smiled at him. Rather maliciously, Peter thought. Harry had always been especially delighted at the prospect of Peter making a fool of himself.

"Peter, what in the world are you talking about?" said Miriam after he had gone on for several minutes.

"I'm talking about what happened during the two months after my boat sank," he said. "I'm talking about a place called The Drift, where there is no wind and no current, a place where people live on ancient boats and listen to music and eat seaweed and everyone has true fantasies."

"Peter's pulling everyone's leg," said Basil Queen's wife, who was an alcoholic. She stared at him with glazed eyes. "How charming," she added.

"I don't think he's pulling anybody's leg," said Beverly, Miriam's younger sister, from the farthest and darkest corner of the room. It was the first thing she had said to anyone all evening.

"Well Peter," said Harry Ranton, who was still smiling, "I've never expected you to actually make sense, but even I am a little disappointed in that fruit cellar you call your mind. You must have lost it out there in the ocean."

"And a good thing too," said Peter. "It didn't happen a moment too soon. I pity you, Harry, that you never lost yours. But then you've got your mind glued into your head so firmly I don't think anything could ever shake it loose. No, I'm afraid The Drift would have had no effect on you."

"The Drift? That's the name of the place where you went off your rocker?"

"The Drift is all things to all people," said Peter breezily. "To the eye only, it is an island of ships set in an eternal calm. To me it was a city of light and darkness where shadows were everything and the world was well lost. To you, Harry, it would have been just an eyesore. Something irrelevant. A bad piece of real estate. A large collection of plastic ducks floating in the pool of the Taj Mahal."

Tony Berendtson laughed. "Never mind about the plastic ducks," he said. "Tell us more about your adventure."

"He's still pulling your leg," said Basil Queen's wife. Her eyes were still glazed.

"Let's talk about something else," said Harry Ranton. "Peter's little fairy tale doesn't seem to have an ending."

"Don't be a snot, Harry," said Tony Berendtson. "Let Peter finish his story."

"Let me see," said Peter, smiling at Harry Ranton, "where was I?" He tried to pick up the story of The Drift where he had left off, but somehow it would not come out right. It did not matter whether they believed or not, but he found that he simply could not tell the real story to all these strangers. And so Pao became a dream, The Drift itself a spirit city that rose out of the water once in a thousand years to cheer the hearts of shipwrecked sailors. Everyone seemed vastly entertained. Everyone but Harry Ranton and Mary Rhys Beacher, who had gone into another room to play billiards.

Later Miriam served her midnight buffet. Eight silver candlesticks glittered on a long table filled with lobster, ham, corn bread, and a profusion of cheeses, salads, and wines. At one end sat a great samovar filled with Flowery Darjeeling. Miriam made sure that Peter was served first, much to Harry Ranton's annoyance. It was his reward, apparently, for being the raconteur of the evening.

Beverly came rather timidly to his corner of the room while he was eating his lobster roll and salad.

"What did your story mean?" she asked.

"What do you mean, what did it mean?"

"I mean, about all the fantasy things," she said. "You were using it to tell another story. A story about something that really did happen."

Peter smiled. "That's true, Beverly. But I can't tell you the real story. When I first got back I tried to, but no one believed me. I can see now that I'll never be able to tell the real story."

"Maybe someday you'll tell somebody," she said, looking rather unhappy. "I mean, maybe someday you'll trust someone enough to tell the real story."

"Perhaps."

"It's a very sad story, isn't it? With all the ships sinking back after a few days for another thousand years and no one knowing where they went. And all the ghosts who wanted you to stay with them and live at the bottom of the sea."

Peter thought about it for a moment. "Yes," he said finally. "It's a sad story. But I think it would have been a sad story if I had stayed. You see, I don't think I could have been happy there at the bottom of the sea. Not for very long."

"I'm sorry," said Beverly.

"Don't be sorry," he said. "Choosing between The Drift and Connecticut is kind of an absurd position to be in. It's like choosing between your liver and your lungs. Normal people don't make such choices. But then perhaps there are very few normal people. Most of us go around chopping ourselves to pieces, making absurd choices that ought never to have been made. We let some things become so important to us that we miss everything else in life."

He could see that she was trying very hard to understand. Suddenly, before he could think what he was doing, he took her hand and then kissed her on the cheek.

"Perhaps someday I'll tell you," he said.

She looked at him and her lips parted in astonishment. "You mean we could be—friends? I mean, in spite of my sister and everybody?"

Peter pressed her small hand inside his two large ones. "We are friends, Beverly. We're very good friends. And don't be too hard on your sister and her friends. They're probably not such bad people. I never really got to know them, so I'm really no judge."

"But The World of Feeling is something that seems to escape them!" she said, trying very hard to control herself.

Peter laughed in a friendly way. "Yes," he said, "they certainly do. I mean it certainly does."

As Peter was leaving, Harry Ranton clapped him on the shoulder, a little too roughly. It was not a gesture of friendship.

"Well, Peter," he said. "I guess I can admit one defeat. I mean, considering all the other times past and yet to come."

"You don't have to admit anything," said Peter.

Harry Ranton walked away and then stopped for a moment and turned, as if there were something he had forgotten.

"What were you going to say, Harry?"

"I said it all tonight, Professor. I haven't got another thing to say to you. Not for a while."

"I thought perhaps you were going to point out in a rare moment of honesty that this was really a very silly game we played this evening."

"Why silly?" said Harry Ranton.

"It's silly that you should fear me and work against me and sleep with my wife just because I'm a professor with an advanced degree. It's silly that I should fear you because you talk too much and make too much money and know too many people. It's silly that we should treat each other like beastly objects and play these lousy war games year after year at cocktail parties."

Harry Ranton smiled. "Are you trying to be friendly?" he said.

"I'm not sure. But it does occur to me that people who have lived as narrowly and as defensively as we have, will never really get along with anybody and don't really deserve to be happy."

Harry Ranton frowned. "I get around and I do pretty well," he said. "But you've never been anywhere or seen anything. You don't know anything about the real world. That's your main problem, Professor." He looked away, out across the shimmer of Miriam's nightblue swimming pool to the copse of weeping willows beyond. Again it seemed to Peter that he was thinking about something he could not quite bring himself to say.

"I'm not talking about where you've been or what you've seen," said Peter. "I'm talking about how you've been there, about how you look at things."

"That's really food for thought," said Harry Ranton.

"You'll just have to give me time to think about all this." He grinned maliciously.

Together they walked out toward the copse of trees which hid the large oval lot where their cars were parked.

"Don't misunderstand me," said Peter. "I've had an awful time with you and with a lot of other people. It hasn't been easy. I don't really understand what I've been up to for the last twenty years."

"Yes," said Harry Ranton flatly. "That's clear enough."

"But I'm working on it, Harry. I'm coming out of the woods."

Harry Ranton turned to him, and for the first time since their confrontation in the living room he looked directly into Peter's eyes. The sarcastic smile faded from his lips. He looked doubtful for a moment and then stared at his shoe.

"I wish you luck," he said. "Perhaps we should wish each other luck."

The next morning, on a whim, he began packing some shirts and socks and a few books into his old navy bag. He would go on a short trip somewhere. After all, there were still five months to kill before the second semester began at Harrington University. His mind was filled with a restlessness, a quickness that made him think of a dozen things all at once: he would visit the house where he had grown up; he would rent a cottage near the water somewhere in Connecticut and swim every day and read every night until four in the morning; he would write Beverly a long letter; he would give up teaching and go into newspaper work or the diplomatic service; he would travel through Venice and Rome and Greece and The Aegean and write a book about the effect of the sea upon man's imagination and spiritual growth.

At one o'clock he caught a train for Paterson, New

Jersey, and the next day he walked through the streets where he had lived as a boy. He discovered very quickly that no one he knew lived there any more. Very soon he was depressed and lonely. The next day, with the distinct impression that he was wasting his time and money, he took a bus to Newark and from there caught a plane to Miami. In Miami there would at least be lots of people, even if it were off season.

When the large four-engine Constellation left the ground, he suddenly felt very tired. The motors droned in his ears. The air within the pressurized cabin was cool and heavy. A ray of sunlight slanted in from his window and traced a line of warmth on his cheek. His head sank into the soft cushion.

The plane rolled gently with changes in the air currents. Outside he could see that the wind was green and thick. Occasionally pieces of Sargasso Weed floated by, and sometimes a school of yellow fish would glitter and flash in the green light. Slowly the plane began to sink into the deep water.

"We're going to the bottom of the sea," said Pao, who was standing next to him in the bow of the ship. "Fasten your safety belts everyone."

The ancient sails waved and rippled in the currents of green water. The droning of the boat carried them deeper. At the bottom of the sea lay a great forest, alive with voices. The trees spoke to one another. Hundreds of pathways, marked with spired houses of white coral, wound their way in and out among the trees.

Together they traveled north along a river of ice that moved beneath the forest. They listened to the songs of white birds perched like glass ornaments in the labyrinth of branches above them.

The river emptied into a land of ice that rose up in great towers to the surface of the water. He took Pao's hand and together their spirit rose on shadow wings to the surface, where they saw The Great Island of The

North Pole, and beyond that, glittering points of icy starlight a thousand light-years beyond.

"I see now that the stars are made of ice and snow," said Peter. "Seawater frozen forever and thrown up into the sky."

Beyond the stars they followed a great black river as wide as The Milky Way. And beyond the river, white shapes moved in a great city of light that stretched on and on into forever.

Pao put her arms around him and pressed against him as they flew on together through eternity. "Nothing can touch us now," she said. "Nothing can take you away from me."

But suddenly he felt a subtle shift in the universe, and he began to fall through space. From somewhere came the droning of engines. "Fasten your seat belts," said Pao. "We're now arriving in Miami."

He opened his eyes. The world came back to him with a painful, sudden rush. He closed them again, but he was awake now and there was no way back to The Drift. The Drift was a lost romantic century that old men remember as it never was. Or a childhood that in real life he had never known and had always longed for.

There was of course no one to meet him at the airport. For a while he wandered through the terminal, listening to the voices and the mechanical droning of the loudspeakers announcing the arrivals and departures. There was nowhere, really, that he had to go, no appointments or schedules for months and months, not until the second semester began that winter at the university. He would have time to think about all that had happened to him. Perhaps too much time.

His adventure on The Sargasso Sea seemed now like a dream, a bizarre sea-delirium, but he knew that in many ways it had changed him. It had taught him the desire to give in, to drift, to follow the course of experience for its own sake and to open his mind to sensation, to the color and texture and shape of things, and not merely to their uses. And so he had learned to touch with his mind and his feelings instead of with his hands only. He had learned that all things were variations of other things, that life was a series of metaphors, and that the play of the mind expanding in a circle of associations and feelings was perhaps more valuable than the objectives that he had once set for himself.

His childhood, his schoolwork, and his marriage had all turned him away from that kind of insight, and then, for a short while, his adventure on The Drift had turned everything upside down. It had taken a miracle, a world of impossibilities where nothing in his old life was relevant or real, to change him after so many years. It made him think of an enchanted knight lying on a medieval hillside, a knight who found an important truth woven into the allegory of his sleep.

But dreams must end, he thought. There was night for sleep and the stars for meditation, but there was also morning and noon that were not made for sleep, save for those who are content to grow pale, to atrophy in caves of silence where sunlight cannot enter. What was it he had said to Beverly? Something about the absurdity of choosing between The Drift and his old life. Yes, like choosing between night and day. But suddenly it came to him that he had not really chosen between those two forces, the centripetal that drew him inward and the centrifugal that drew him outward into the world of man's progress and failure, for in leaving The Drift he had not really left his dear friends and the timeless, ruined ships where they lived. He was free now in a way that he had never been free before. His life seemed open, full of vague possibilities. Even the next school year appeared as an uncharted territory to him, a territory that he must somehow travel in a different way, not knowing what he would encounter or how he would respond. No, he had not lost The Drift. He would carry it with him always.

Then he thought for a moment of Pao and Tabor,

and his heart filled with pain and loneliness. He thought of the book they had planned to write, a book that would never be written. If only they might have come with him from their world into his. But then he remembered that the figures in dreams cannot live outside their shadowy land. They cannot cross the dark sea that separates the dreams and ideals of the imagination from reality, though he knew he would never lose them, never forget them.

The next day he discovered that the beaches, contrary to his expectations, were nearly deserted by the end of August except for the beachcombers and the police. And so for hours every day he brought his towel and lay on the warm sand, staring out into the sea.

THE QUEEN'S RIVAL
Shannon Clare

LB590TK $1.95
Historical Romance

In Victorian England, nothing was more important than propriety, and the Queen's family set the example. But Alexandra de Grey, separated from the husband who murdered her brother, was drawn by passion into an affair that threatened the stability of the Empire—with the Queen's husband!

POWER OF DARKNESS
Doris Sutcliffe Adams

LB567TK $1.95
Historical Romance

Durande was alone against the forces of evil until Helie returned from the Crusades to stand by her side. Two against the demon horde was still unequal, but the young couple found a love that gave them the strength they needed to prevail.

FORBIDDEN SPLENDOR
Ralph Hayes

LB565TK $1.95
Historical Romance

General Bonaparte's army could defeat the Egyptians, but who would fight his battles with the faithless Josephine? His only ally was Pauline Foures unhappily married to an officer in the French army. Their flirtation grew into a passion so fiery that it could consume an empire yet unborn!

BANNERS OF DESIRE
Lorinda Hagen

LB598RK $2.25
Historical Romance

As an actress, Caroline travelled both sides of the lines in the Civil War, and as a spy she played both sides as well. Finally, she had to decide between her family and duty in the South, and her heart and future in the North!

DAUGHTER OF CONQUEST   LB646 $2.25
Robert E. Mills   **Historical Romance**

Isolated within the French colony in Cairo, Louise Rouland longed for an adventure to relieve her boredom. Martin Braddock, an American engineer, joined Napoleon's expedition to Egypt to have a part in history. When they met they knew their fates were one, but adventure, history, and Napoleon's ambition stood between them!

THIS SPLENDID LAND   LB638 $1.95
Chet Cunningham   **Historical Romance**

The Breckenridge Saga concludes with Jed and Jeannie building their new ranch in Texas into an empire. As the ranch grows, so do the passions of those on it, and Jed's tempestuous affair with the Mexican beauty Teresa leads to an armed showdown, with the whole future at stake!
Setting: Texas Panhandle, 1840's

DESTINY AND DESIRE   LB639 $1.95
Lorinda Hagen   **Historical Romance**

Orphaned Letitia Cooper got a sudden opportunity—to go west and live on her uncle's ranch. Before long, he'd been killed, and someone was out to get control of the Sierra Lorena spread. Two men stood at Letty's side, but one of them wanted to kill her!
Setting: Nevada, 1867

SEND TO: LEISURE BOOKS
P.O. Box 270
Norwalk, Connecticut 06852

Please send me the following titles:

Quantity	Book Number	Price
_____	_____	_____
_____	_____	_____
_____	_____	_____
_____	_____	_____
_____	_____	_____

In the event we are out of stock on any of your selections, please list alternate titles below.

_____	_____	_____
_____	_____	_____
_____	_____	_____
_____	_____	_____

Postage/Handling _____

I enclose..... _____

FOR U.S. ORDERS, add 50¢ for the first book and 10¢ for each additional book to cover cost of postage and handling. Buy five or more copies and we will pay for shipping. Sorry, no C.O.D.'s.

FOR ORDERS SENT OUTSIDE THE U.S.A.
Add $1.00 for the first book and 25¢ for each additional book.
PAY BY foreign draft or money order drawn on a U.S. bank, payable in U.S. ($) dollars.
☐ Please send me a free catalog.

NAME _____
(Please print)

ADDRESS _____

CITY _____ **STATE** _____ **ZIP** _____
Allow Four Weeks for Delivery